Christmas at Grandfather's House

MARK LEEVER

PANTHEON
Hill
PUBLISHING

Library and Archives Canada Cataloguing in Publication

Leever, Mark, 1964-
Christmas at Grandfather's house : a novel in stories / Mark Leever.

ISBN 978-0-9783059-0-1

I. Title.

PS8623.E445C47 2007   C813'.6   C2007-902157-3

The author is grateful to the following for permission to reprint copyrighted material:
Small Town
Words and Music by John Mellencamp
© 1985 EMI FULL KEEL MUSIC
All Rights Reserved / International Copyright Secured

Design: Fortunato Design Inc.
Cover illustration: John Mantha
Author photo: Paul J. Lawrence

Printer: Friesens
Printed in Canada

To my grandmothers and grandfathers.
To Uncle Don and Uncle Harry.
And to my mother.
This book is for you all. Forever.

Contents

FINE THREAD

I t is Christmas Eve and you are at your grandfather's house. Your father stands next to you, his hair greying, his belly bulging more as each year passes, but still, he looks fine for his age. You place an arm across his shoulders and bid him good night. He doesn't hear you. He's sharing a chuckle with one of your relations.

You glance thoughtfully at an open door to your left and you think, *No, wrong; not a good night, a* wonderful *night.*

The year is 1955. Inside one of the spare rooms you've slid into bed, snuggled neatly beneath the blanket. It is not merely a blanket, though. It is a patchwork quilt, this one a cacophony of colour. Your grandfather has lots of these, more than enough to cover each bed in each of his spare rooms. He has lots of those, too, seeing as he's lived alone since your grandmother passed. You barely remember her. You were only five when she left—or was it six? You're not sure. At ten years old, you can't be expected to remember everything, certainly not the sad things. You won't expect that of yourself for many more years, until maturity provides you with an understanding that reflecting on the sad and inevitable things is what allows you to fully appreciate the wonderful things, both past and present.

Your room is dark except for a long, rectangular block of buff-coloured light that stretches across the wood floor, its glow also catching a generous portion of quilt at the bottom of your bed. Your grandmother made this coverlet, as she made all the

others in the house, and beneath it you feel safe and warm. You
pull the fabric snug so that just your head is visible, and the fine
threads that dangle from its fraying edge tickle the soft underside
of your chin.

The light peeks inside your room from beyond the open
door. You always sleep with the door open. You're still too young
to feel at ease in total darkness. There is a strong smell of cedar
and mothballs inside your room. It's a combination that always
piques your senses, but you've grown accustomed to it, visiting
your grandfather as often as you do. A jutting closet wall blocks
your sight line to your bedroom door, and past the door's threshold is a large open space where the dining and living rooms are.
To the left of your room, a short hallway leads to the kitchen and
bathroom.

Tonight your aunts and uncles, your grandfather and parents
are gathered around the dining table. Like you, your two brothers
and cousins have been shipped off to their own spare rooms. You
can't be sure if they're sleeping. The table the adults sit at and
stand near is a half-century-old oaken treasure that is close
enough to your room that no sounds elude your ears. The card
game of choice on this evening, as it has been on so many
Christmas Eves past, is canasta. But the game isn't important. It's
merely a tiny piece of the fabric that bonds everyone, keeps
everything together.

Your grandfather's outdated, wind-up Victrola is happily
streaming out age-old carols by timeless crooners. The music
comforts you, despite the scratchy sibilance that accompanies
the melodies drifting from the speaker.

Unseen figures pass your door, busily, to and fro, their shadows visiting for split seconds inside your room, across the floor, across the patchwork quilt at the bottom of your bed. You wonder if these shadows are checking in on you, to see that you're safe, sleeping.

You hear voices floating toward you through the darkness, clear as day, each one as familiar as your own. Uncle Earl is speaking. He's the older of your father's two brothers.

"As a general rule, Bob," he says in a serious tone, "to receive a weekly paycheque . . ."

You hear the crisp snap of cards, repeatedly, over and over. Someone is riffle shuffling.

". . . most employers *usually* require that you show up for work. At least occasionally, anyhow."

Laughter erupts. Uncle Bob, who is your father's youngest brother, laughs loudest. You'd recognize that loveable chortle anywhere.

"Gee," Bob replies in mock surprise between snorts, "I've never heard anything so queer."

At home you recall your parents periodically talking about Uncle Bob. It seems he's had a long string of bad luck where employment is concerned, his greatest success a two-year stint at a hardware store.

"Just thought I'd make mention of that rather absurd fact," says Earl.

"Thanks, big brother. Now, if I had an alarm clock that was occasionally willing to work, I suspect I *too* could occasionally make it in to work!" For Christmas three years ago, Earl gave Bob an alarm clock.

In the seclusion of your room, you imagine the two of them

sitting opposite one another, wry smiles taped loosely to their faces.

"Oh, you two," a voice says. You know immediately it's Uncle Bob's wife, Violet—Aunt Vi, as you call her. If ever forced to select a favourite aunt, she'd be your choice.

"Alarm clock?" your grandfather bellows.

"Shush," your mother whispers. "The children are sleeping." Your mother's actions have long made you feel her sole job is demonstrating deep concern for you and your siblings, and this comment does nothing to dispel such a belief.

"No alarm clocks in my day," your grandfather continues, lowering his voice marginally. "Your mother was *my* clock." Then his voice drops even more, its cadence changing, now sincere, deliberate. "Your mother was the best thing that ever happened to me." He pauses and you think you hear a sniffle. Is he crying?

The sound of shuffling cards ceases. You hear someone taking a seventy-eight off the Victrola, perhaps to replace it, perhaps merely to get ready for the anticipated nugget of nostalgia your grandfather is surely preparing to unveil.

Anxious silence.

"And her frequent bouts with insomnia were the best thing that ever happened to me, too."

The ancient dining table creaks. Someone must have leaned forward, elbows weighing on oak, eager to get a better listen.

"Most times," your grandfather says, "she'd sit in her rocker through the late hours of night, till the wee hours of morning, making those quilts, each stitch carefully drawn by hand. She took great pride in those quilts, let me tell you. Covered every bed in the house with them. Saved me a pretty penny, never having to buy blankets. Probably could've covered half the beds in Brice County, she made so many of the dang things.

"And when it was time for me to get up in the morning, she'd come into the room, whisper my name, then clunk me over the head with a ball-peen hammer! She took great pride in that, too."

The room explodes with laughter and a spattering of voices fold into one another: "You drive me crazy, Pops!"; "That explains a lot!"; "Always knew you had a thick skull!" Then, considering the mood, you're surprised when everything quickly falls quiet.

"Yep, she was my clock, all right," your grandfather admits. "Time sure ain't the same without her. Just not the same . . ."

Now you're certain you hear sniffling. It's loud; you can almost feel the powerful emotion that propels it.

After a few moments, Bob says, "Earl, you gonna deal those cards someday, or is *that* a job and you're waiting for us to first give *you* a paycheque?"

Explosive laughter again. Although you're not an expert on the depths and subtle nuances of humour, even you suspect the comment doesn't deserve such a resounding response. Clearly your grandfather is unaccustomed to displays of emotional vulnerability and, recognizing this, your relations have instinctively reacted in deference to him, elated for his sake at the deflected attention.

The Victrola resumes playing.

"I think it's time for a cider break," Aunt Peggy chimes. She is Uncle Earl's wife, and whenever you're in her company, she's forever pinching your cheeks and calling you "cutie."

"Now there's the remedy!" your father blurts, his voice crackling with what sounds like contrived vitality.

A few others acknowledge Peggy's suggestion as splendid and you hear the screeching of wood against wood as chairs are pushed back from the table.

"I gotta pee," your grandfather says, always to the point. It's one of the many things you love about him. "And I'll have mine spilling from an extra-large glass, if you don't mind," he adds.

It is common knowledge that your grandfather has often foregone a much-needed late night trip to the toilet in favour of the empty Prince Albert tobacco tin he keeps under his bed. You're as hopeful as you are confident that what he wants "spilling from an extra-large glass" is the cider Aunt Peggy has gone off to prepare.

His slow, heavy footsteps tread past your bedroom door.

Within minutes you smell the rich aroma of cider. You figure it must be warming on the stove. The scent is so powerful, it overwhelms the stinging odour of cedar and mothballs in your room.

You pick up whispers just outside your door. Perching on your elbows, you stare down at the end of your bed. Two shadows lie flat in profile on the patchwork quilt, their mouths moving in turn, their hushed utterances clear to your ears.

"Has Dad not been well?" Uncle Earl asks. As part of the promotion Earl received four years ago, he had to relocate with his wife and children to the west coast. Although they return each Christmas for the traditional get-together, he's not always up to speed on current family news.

"No," confesses your father, his voice still not sounding right. "The doctor said no alcohol, period. It's his heart. He also said if he doesn't comply, there's no telling what might happen."

You see a shadow's head tilt downward and shake from side to side, its black image narrowing and widening repeatedly on the quilt. "I'll tell Peg to warm some apple juice for him and add just a smidgen of cider so the stubborn coot doesn't catch on," Uncle Earl says.

The shadows move off, returning you to solitude. You are left with a feeling of uncertainty. Neither of your parents told you Grandpa was ill. *Don't perfect times, perfect families, go on forever?* you think as your forearms slowly slide down and your head sinks softly to the pillow. Just as slowly, you pull the patchwork quilt up until its fine threads caress the soft underside of your chin. You stare in disbelief at the murky grey ceiling.

Before you have time to decide whether your uncertainty is masking fear or sadness—more whispers. You prop back up on elbows, stare down at the end of your bed. Two shadows again lie in profile on the quilt.

"I'm sorry for the way I've treated you these past few months," Aunt Vi says, her voice so low that it's almost indiscernible.

"It's okay," Uncle Bob whispers just as softly.

"No, it's not. You didn't deserve it. Please forgive me."

"It's okay, darling, really."

Darkness fills a portion of the band of light separating the two shadows. You suspect that they have placed their arms around each other.

"I'll find work soon," Uncle Bob says in a reassuring tone.

The remainder of the band of light narrows to darkness as the two shadows melt into one, framed within a soft yellow glow against the quilt.

"Merry Christmas, Bob."

"Merry Christmas, Violet."

Seconds later, after the shadows' departure, Aunt Peggy announces from the kitchen that the cider is ready.

You slip out from beneath the quilt and, kneeling on the bed, you pull back one edge of the small curtain. Outside, snow teems down. You think it's been an hour since you went to bed, maybe two; you can't be sure. You wonder how much longer the relations will stay up, knowing as you do that Santa prefers working solely in the company of his reindeer.

You hear scurrying feet and more jovial voices—those who had left the dining table must be returning. You hear, too, the distinct, ponderous steps of your grandfather.

Loud.

The Victrola streams out a soothing carol.

Louder.

Cups tinkle cheerily on saucers.

Then, as your grandfather's footsteps come even with your room, you glance at the bottom of the bed just in time to see his wide shadow collapse from the patchwork quilt, accompanied instantly by a terrifying thud.

A dissonance of noise follows. Wood screeching against wood. Breaking glass. Thumping footsteps. A child crying. And voices—some strident, others frenzied.

Your aunts and uncles and parents quickly gather outside your room. One by one their bodies pour an ominous shadow over the quilt's fine fabric until finally, it is drowned in complete darkness.

You blink moist eyes, glimpse a hand as it grasps the doorknob. As it pulls the door to your room shut, you hear the unforgettable sound of *your* father as he pleads desperately for *his* father.

Your father pleading desperately for his father.

Father pleading for father.

Father pleading.

Your arm is still extended across your father's shoulders. Your eyes are still entranced by the open door to your left. The year is 1985. Although you are now forty years old, you remember that Christmas Eve in 1955 as if it were yesterday.

The table you and your wife, father, and brothers and their spouses are gathered around is that same oaken treasure from that long-ago night, only now almost a century old. Your grandfather's Victrola has been replaced by a modern stereophonic marvel and softly streaming from its speakers in sibilant-free sound are those same age-old carols by those same timeless crooners.

You stare into the darkened room beyond the open door— the same room you stayed in thirty years ago. Tonight, your ten-year-old boy lies in there, beneath a patchwork quilt. Not the same quilt that kept you safe and warm. That one, although now in a state of utter disrepair, rests amid mothballs in the darkness of a cedar chest in your own home. Occasionally, when it's quiet and your family is off doing their own thing, you open it and give your grandmother's memory a breath of fresh air. It's the least you can do. It's also all that you have of her, that quilt, and on those days when you're leafing a corner of its fabric in your hand, running a finger along the fine threads that once stitched it all together, you think of her and realize, *It's enough*.

When your grandmother died you were just five years old. At that same age your own boy experienced a similar tragedy when your mother passed away, leaving behind a legacy of love, in addition to numerous patchwork quilts she herself made. Though she never matched your grandmother's prodigious output, she drew each stitch with a family in mind. You wonder now, as your boy lies beneath one of those quilts, if it's pulled snug to his chin, the way you often had it. You wonder, too, if one day his grandmother's life will, in fabric and fine threads, still remain. If it does, you only hope, for him, it too is enough.

But unlike fine threads carefully stitched into fabric, there is a single fine thread that still exists for both you and your boy. You already suffered the misfortune of losing one many years ago, long before maturity provided you with an understanding that it is these single fine threads, fragile and almost imperceptible to the eye, that, in an instant and without warning and from something as seemingly inconsequential as an innocent fall to the floor, can, in hushed silence . . . *disappear*.

An explosion of laughter startles you and steals your attention away from the darkened room. Although you weren't listening closely, you conclude the outburst is the result of your older brother comparing the run of queens he's laid down on the table to a run in your younger brother's stockings. Unflappable as always, your younger brother has vehemently stated that he buys only the highest quality nylons and, quite frankly, they don't run.

Then, before the laughter completely subsides, your father bellows, "Queens? Far as I'm concerned, there was only one queen!"

As the explosive laughter just seconds earlier startled you, your father's words do the same. Not because much of the vitality has long since gone from his voice in this, his seventy-second year, but rather because you think he sounds familiar, almost identical to your grandfather on that wonderful, long-ago night.

Thirty years previous, when that wide shadow collapsed from your grandmother's patchwork quilt before your very eyes, your grandfather did not die. Your aunts and uncles and parents, amid panic and pleas, rushed to his side and helped him to his feet. They had overreacted, but considering their knowledge of his health, it was understandable.

Your grandfather gathered himself, assured everyone the fall was merely clumsiness and, repeatedly admonishing himself for it, rejoined the card game.

Later, as the evening neared its conclusion with you still wide awake, your grandfather raised his extra-large glass filled—unbeknownst to him—with moderately adulterated apple juice and proclaimed this the finest of nights, then wished everyone a very merry Christmas.

A month later, while alone in an examination room awaiting his doctor's arrival, and over a hundred miles away from his nearest son or grandchild, he collapsed again. This time neither his family, nor his doctor, nor any of the fine medical professionals who worked unawares inside the hospital a block away, could save him.

His house, and the rich tapestry of memories contained within it, was bequeathed to his sons. In a touching act of love, your father and Uncle Earl, whose careers were already well established and their successful futures a virtual certainty, devolved the bestowal to their youngest brother, Bob.

The house really wasn't worth much. Although it was large, it was old and drafty, and located in a small town where property values started low and finished even lower. Today the house is just as large, just as drafty, and still not worth much in practical terms. But in the three decades that have since passed, it is far richer for the memories, which for you have appreciated.

Two months following your grandfather's death, your Uncle Bob and Aunt Vi uprooted themselves from their small apartment and moved into the home. Bob had been suffering from an unfortunate string of bad luck after all, as your parents had suspected, because he found a job at a bank a month later. After six months of dedication—arriving for work well before a warning from his alarm clock, and giving far more of himself than his employer asked—he received an unexpected promotion that required him to relocate.

For you, Christmas of 1956 was good, but also disheartening. There were no aunts or uncles, no traditional family gathering for the first time in your life and, worst of all, no grandfather. Uncle Earl was too busy with a new business venture to make the long trek from the west coast, Uncle Bob too stressed with the demands of his fledgling career.

In 1978, at the age of fifty-nine, having ascended to the presidency of the largest bank in Maine, your Uncle Bob died. Aside from your grandfather's funeral, Christmas of 1955 proved to be the last time you ever saw him. Things with Uncle Earl were much the same; you did see him on two occasions during the past thirty years, though never over the holidays. Now retired and living the good life in California, he and Aunt Peggy recently celebrated their fiftieth wedding anniversary.

Thinking back, it would have seemed unimaginable to you in 1955 that you would draw your only real memories of your aunts and uncles and grandfather almost exclusively from that Christmas Eve, as you and a patchwork quilt watched and listened to what would ultimately be the last assemblage of those family members. It was a night of shadows: Uncle Earl's, concerned; Uncle Bob's, forgiving. A night your grandfather stubbornly refused to besmirch with his death. You miss them all and you understand, as maturity eventually taught you, that sometimes even love isn't enough to keep it together.

Six months ago your father, long since retired and already without your mother for almost five years, decided he had no reason left to stay in the city; most of his closest friends had passed on. He contacted Aunt Vi in Maine. Your grandfather's house had been vacant for the better part of three decades. He asked if she'd be willing to sell and, in a fitting act, she gifted it to him—not that he needed charity. After a little work, he moved in three months later and has been living there alone ever since. Tonight, as you stand next to him, it's the first Christmas Eve celebrated here since 1955. Granted, it's now your father's house, but you'll forever think of it as your grandfather's. And, for your boy, it will forever be his grandfather's, too.

"Shush," your wife whispers, responding to your father's outburst. "The children are sleeping."

Like your father's words only seconds previous, her words startle you with their familiarity. Her concern for the youngsters echoes your mother's on that long past night.

Then, after your sister-in-law halts the streaming music and the card game ceases, and when your older brother leans forward and the ancient table creaks, sending a ripple through the anxious silence, you realize that you've been here before. Thirty years ago, lying in that room where your boy now sleeps. Actually, although he was shuffled off to bed over two hours ago, you're certain he's still awake. Listening. Watching.

You stand next to your father, arm still draped across his shoulders, listening and watching, too. And as you do, you think about your grandmother's patchwork quilt at home in a cedar chest, and you realize that a family is much the same—each individual a small yet integral piece of fabric that only combined can make a fully functioning whole.

His voice lowered, your father now says something about never forgetting your mother was a queen and that she rarely let him forget he was merely her loyal subject. Laughter erupts. You've heard it before—not the exact words, not the exact laughter, but the sentiment, the mood. It comes from the same family, just a different generation. The quilt may be different too, but it blankets everyone with the same enduring warmth and safety.

You know what comes next. Your father will say something sincere about your mother. A second passes, maybe two. Then, right on cue, he tells everyone Mother was his beloved queen; his kingdom, not the same without her.

Yes, you've been here before. The fabric of your being is stitched into a wonderful night. Only this time you are older, wiser; wise enough to know perfect times *do* in fact go on forever. Sometimes separated by days, or weeks, or even decades, but they do go on. And they go on because perfect families go on forever. It's only the fabric that wears out and gets replaced over time. The delicate fabric of your family and this wonderful night has been carefully stitched for countless decades by the love of your mother, and your grandmother before her, and many others before her.

Silence fills the room. You suspect, as happened years ago with your grandfather, that your father is overcome with emotion. You give the fleshy part of his shoulder a reassuring squeeze, only now, at his age, there is more bone than flesh. Out of respect, you cannot look at him. You refuse to make him uncomfortable.

You remember that night back on Christmas Eve in 1955, lying in that room as a ten-year-old child with joy, concern, and forgiveness seeping into your soul. But surprisingly, you don't recall hearing expressions of love spoken between any of the adults. Certainly it was shown. You could feel it, oozing from the air, dripping through the darkness. But never spoken. You *are* older now, much wiser after all, maturity having provided you with an understanding of appreciation, the blessed consequence of time and tragedy.

You think of your boy in that room, probably wide-eyed and hanging on every sound. Perhaps tonight—now!—the fabric of the quilt should be altered, torn with words of love, then restitched. Perhaps then this exact quilt will be stronger, able to endure and overcome far more. You'll do it for your boy. You'll do it for your family.

You feel the warmth from your father's shoulder course through your hand. It's a warmth you have felt from him since childhood. You will tell him this. You will tell him, too, that he is fiercely loved. You accept that one day he'll be gone, and that knowledge allows you to appreciate without compromise every sight of him, every word that he speaks, every moment in his company. You will tell him this, too. And you will tell him what he meant to you as a child growing up, what he still means to you. And most of all, you will tell him what he means to this family. This quilt. That he is the single fine thread that holds the fragile fabric of this family together. These are the things you want him to know and the things you must tell him.

Turning your head, you gaze at your father, his face mere inches from yours. He's already looking at you. After searching his face, you're bewildered—in part because his expression is composed, unemotional, the opposite of what you'd expected, but also because you see him with blurred vision. Still, you must tell him.

You draw a deep breath and a loud sniffle charges from your nose. *A sniffle?* You're shocked by its familiarity. Something instantly occurs to you, something you'd never considered: on that night thirty years ago, the sniffles you heard must have been from your father, overcome with emotion as you are now, and not your grandfather, as you'd always assumed. You tremble. You draw a second breath: a second sniffle. Then a third.

Your father places a warm hand over yours, which still rests on his shoulder, gives it a comforting squeeze, and smiles. Not a big smile, but a reserved, pleasant one. At that moment you realize there's no need to tell him.

He already knows.

THE WHARTON ECHO

Wharton is a quaint little town. In summer, on Main Street, the three dozen shops with their enticements of GOOD FOOD, CHEAP GAS BUY THE GALLON, ANYTHING FOR FIVE OR TEN, and an assortment of other lures are abuzz with tourists, swarm after swarm of them, coming and going from cottages on the lake or the bay, staying just long enough to pick up supplies and maybe even a quick bite before leaving.

Most days, the heat boils on the asphalt of Main, sweet and wonderful, stirring a sense of nostalgia in the locals. They stand in small clusters like sentinels, dotting the sidewalks, smoking and sweating and sometimes smiling, feeding each other stories in hushed whispers or relating tales from the distant past with great, boisterous reverence, all the while watching the bees with wary but appreciative eyes.

Off Wharton's only paved artery, most of the dirt roads are lined with towering elms, their arching greenery forming cathedral-like canopies above. Sometimes a group of bees, on their way to or from the nectar on Main, glimpse these splendid vistas and venture up the shaded roads. Once there, they find the solitude and quaintness of the homes hard to resist. The quirky but pleasing blend of Victorian and Georgian and Gothic sets their minds to wandering and wondering, with great romantic notions, if this indeed would be a fine place to live. But as quickly as these thoughts come, they are dispelled as the cars bounce from pothole to pothole. Their occupants realize the town's roads are poorly maintained and, come to think of it, most of the residents seen strolling along the side roads and huddled down along Main are in fact elderly and, if that's not enough, shabbily dressed, so perhaps it isn't the best place to live after all.

Before winter officially arrives, each year snow invariably blankets Wharton with a purity and innocence that lays everything to rest. The bees, long returned to their city hives, no longer buzz around Main, leaving the shop proprietors regretful of the lost business, but thankful for the peace just the same. The locals, feeling the chill deep within their tired bones, take their tales to warmer climes: the library or the town arena or, best of all, Floyd's Smoke Shop on Main Street, which houses six pool tables in back.

In just one of those years on just one of those autumn days when the snow fell well before its time, a little girl, no more than eight, stood in the schoolyard of Wharton Elementary. She was the prettiest girl in town, though no one would dare admit this. Her features were perfectly formed, like those of a china doll, her eyes crystal blue, her hair delicate and golden-blond.

She waited off to the side of a swing for her turn. The three other girls swinging seemed oblivious to her. She had been there the better part of ten minutes, making lines in the snow with the toe of her tiny boot. As her foot put the mouth on a happy face, another girl with thin slits for eyes stepped in front of her.

"I'm next," said the girl with thin slits for eyes.

The girl with the china doll face said nothing. She simply stopped drawing in the snow and stared into the thin slits.

"I'm not s'posed to talk to you," continued the girl. "My mommy says you're the devil and you got cooties."

A girl stopped swinging and slid slowly down from the swing. As the girl with the china doll face moved forward, the girl with thin slits for eyes stuck out her foot, clipping the foot that had drawn the *happy face. The girl with the china doll face fell, her forehead catching a jutting bolt on the leg of the swing set.*

The school bell rang. The other children rushed off, leaving the girl with the china doll face lying on the ground, crying, watching the snow around her turn red.

It was a cold December morning. There was no snow on the ground yet, but the forecasters were calling for some tomorrow—a little here, boatloads up north. Two suitcases sat by the front door of my small bungalow, both Jetliners, one half-filled with Christmas gifts. My stubborn coffeemaker with the frayed electrical cord was making more sporadic gurgling sounds than usual. I had the TV on, but its poor reception was wreaking havoc with my nerves. I had just attempted to break my personal best of fourteen knots tied in the belt of my terry cloth bathrobe (I managed only eleven), when the phone rang. It didn't ring often, but when it did, lately I tended to jump.

"Where are you?" my mother asked.

"Here," I answered, still a bit jumpy, the cold black receiver in my hand growing more and more frigid the longer I held it.

"I know you're *there*. I just want to know why."

I wrestled with the disappointment of only eleven knots in my robe's belt. "I got tied up," I said, sucking in my stomach, considering an attempt at a twelfth.

"Well, hurry. Everybody's here already."

"I'm just walking out the door."

Six years ago, when I walked out a trailer's door on a used car lot, a greasy-haired salesman accompanied me. Seconds later he was referring to a certain Ford Pinto he hated to part with as "subcompact." He sat on its hood, jumped off its roof, and once, while negotiating a price, he attempted to kick a tire but instead kicked me in the shin. Unfortunately it wasn't hard enough to dissuade me because, after he mentioned something about a discount and $200, I took it as compensation for the shin and took the car. Shortly thereafter I began calling my Ford "Nautilus," thanks in large part to its rapidly deteriorating condition. In my opinion it was closer kin to a wallowing submersible than it was to subcompact, and like its namesake, that famous old submarine to the south, it had no business being on land.

So, detecting urgency in my mom's voice, I quickly escaped my bathrobe, dressed, and loaded my Jetliners into Nautilus. Pausing for a deep breath inside the car's cabin, I said, "Up periscope," and turned the key in the ignition. Regrettably, Nautilus's engine rattled to a start. "Can't count on you for anything, can I, old girl?" I asked her as she sputtered from the driveway.

Heading north from Toronto, her joints squeaked a familiar tune across the frozen Ontario landscape. An hour into my three-hour drive I manoeuvred her off Highway 10 and checked into a motel. I had little trouble convincing myself there was work to be done.

After settling in and marking a couple of the fifty or so grade nine English exams that I'd brought along, I found myself staring at the room's badly peeling wallpaper, unable—or perhaps unwilling—to concentrate on an essay answer pertaining to the book *The Red Badge of Courage.*

Instead I thought of my grandfather, a man I am forever

doomed to remember. Not because he was a good man, because he was in fact the best; nor because he was the finest of builders, a man whose great talents, it had always seemed to me, were tragically denied the masses because he'd been born and raised, and lived and died, in a town no bigger than a baby's thumb. I am doomed to remember my grandfather because he loved me with all his heart. And as I drifted off to sleep in that motel room, lulled by a dripping bathroom faucet, I thought of my own birth, and then the day of my last arrival in Wharton, three months ago.

According to my mother, when the nurse walked into the room just an hour after the moment of my birth, cradling me in her arms and beaming with a radiance such that I could have been her own newborn child, my grandfather was there, too. At the sight of me, he sprang to his feet so violently that, had the ceiling been just six inches lower, he would have struck his head and ended up in the mortuary or, at the very least, become a patient of the hospital himself.

As time passed and I grew, I came to understand my mother's propensity for stark exaggeration, though I never for a second doubted his general jubilation. He was, after all, a highly emotional man whose emotionality he equalled in nerves. And so, unaware that he'd escaped a brush with death, he simply stood there, turning his grey tweed flat cap over and over in his hands, his lips quivering, his breathing quick.

"Take it easy, Dad," my mother courageously managed to say, considering she'd just gone through the second most painful experience of her life. The most painful one had come two months earlier when my father, whom she had met only ten months before my birth, told her he was leaving, even though he had nowhere to go, seeing as he was pretty much penniless and living with his parents. He also said it was him, not her; that she was the most beautiful, wonderful, funny, sexy lady he'd ever met. As time passed, though, depending on perhaps the alignment of the stars in conjunction with skipped child support payments, her story changed. My father had supposedly said it wasn't her, but him; that he was a lazy, freeloading, no-good son of a bitch and she deserved better. Whichever reason it was, it is all the same and doesn't much matter now; I am indifferent to both.

My grandmother, a staunch supporter of the Progressive Conservative Party, did not attend my birth. As much as she vehemently opposed my father, she was equally opposed to me. Somewhat conveniently, though, with a few months remaining in my mother's pregnancy, the Liberal Prime Minister Louis Saint-Laurent called an election. This afforded my grandmother a great opportunity, since my own father's name was Louis. Needless to say, for two months she campaigned tirelessly for the leader of the PCs, John Diefenbaker, making her rounds to each house in town not once but twice, mentioning, among other things, that Louis was a good-for-nothing son of a bitch and that she had been encouraging her daughter to eat less, on account of the weight she'd put on recently.

Despite her constant pleas to have my mother sent away, my grandfather refused. She suggested Saskatchewan, of all places, where, coincidentally, not only a twice-removed cousin of our family lived, but her patriarchal leader, Mr. Diefenbaker, also resided. My grandfather remained steadfast in his position, however, being a staunch supporter of no political party in particular but rather a fervent devotee of forgiveness and my mother. He was, after all, the man of the house whose word, it had and would come to appear over the years, was rarely final.

My grandmother embarked with equal vigour on her own personal campaign to send my mother west. With seven weeks remaining until my expected arrival, she informed my grandfather that he would have to shop for his own personal toiletries, such as toothpaste and shaving lotion. With six weeks remaining, washing *his* clothes was now *his* responsibility. At five weeks she decreed that the house would no longer be cleaned. And in the fourth to last week, she launched her final, most serious salvo: my grandfather would have to cook his own meals.

My grandfather remained unbending. The childhood fantasies I came to concoct of my heroic grandfather, foul-smelling, bearded, and twenty pounds lighter, hold to this day. His state of disrepair was confirmed by my mother only to the extent that, perhaps simply the result of his quickened breathing coupled with weeks without toothpaste, she recalled a strangely pungent odour permeating the air when the nurse walked into that hospital room with me, an hour old, in her arms.

Regardless, I was born on June 21, 1957, and with great certainty I can confirm that my grandmother *did* celebrate on that day, though as I said she was not present upon my arrival. She was doubtless at home—not cooking, not cleaning, but rather waiting anxiously by the radio for news of Mr. John Diefenbaker's official swearing-in as Canada's new prime minister, ironically, on the very day of my birth.

The town's sole medico at the time, Dr. Glover, delivered me—not from evil, but from a black womb where only an illegitimate child can be harboured. It was a difficult labour, though from the moment my mother reached the hospital until my wailing chased the echoes of hers, a mere fifteen minutes passed. During this fleeting, yet (according to my mother) eternal amount of time, she deafened the right ear of a kindly nurse with a flurry of vicious, piercing screams and, misunderstanding Dr. Glover's urgings to push, instead kicked, striking the man in the jaw and nearly knocking him unconscious. Witnessing this, a second nurse, who had been dabbing my mother's forehead with a cold compress, screamed so loud and for so long that it shocked me into the world.

I fell full throttle into the outstretched arms of the doctor, who had been kneeling on the delivery room floor, moaning some incoherent prayer to a higher power to let the suffering end. It turned out that Dr. Glover's suffering was just beginning. His jaw badly broken, he was forced to eat his meals through a straw for the next long year, at home in the comfort of a recliner.

I was born during what would become known as the Heat Wave of '57, which arrived a week before me and lasted until I was several days old. This accounted for my mother's only sibling, Ronald, three years her junior and already a skilled hunter at fourteen, roaming not the halls of the hospital with a look of concerned excitement on his face, but rather the outlying fields and backwoods and back roads with a .22 calibre rifle slung over his shoulder, in search of sun-loving groundhogs. Apparently, and again according to my mother since Uncle Ron and I tend to speak only in platitudes, he got none that day. I think that, in some obscure way, he blamed me for his bad luck and has since held a grudge, though I have never asked and he has never said.

As the heat wave petered out, Mother brought me home. Because Ronald was influenced strongly by his mother's political campaigning, fully believing Louis *was* a good-for-nothing son of a bitch and maintaining the delusion that his sister's excessive weight gain was solely the result of overeating, it was no surprise that he bolted for his rifle when he first saw me. My grandmother, who had finally given up her vigorous personal campaign against her husband and was preparing lunch in the kitchen, stood idly by as he swept past her on his way to the gun rack. My grandfather, who was strong as an ox then as well as late in life, almost beat Ronald to it. Instead he picked him up and slammed him against the wall, forcing him to drop the rifle to the floor. In defence of my uncle, I was admittedly an ugly, hairy baby; I have to believe he thought me a groundhog.

Louis Johnson—not Saint-Laurent—who had two months previously bade my mother an unceremonious goodbye, had already hooked up with, as my mother never fails to remind me, one of the "countless tramps" that followed her into the Louis abyss.

"I wouldn't be surprised if you're not an only child after all, but one of a dozen or so half-brothers or -sisters out there," my mother has often said, usually after reminiscing through a photo album and glimpsing the only picture she has of my father. Then she invariably stares off into space and adds, "Somewhere."

Supposedly, around the time Dr. Glover was getting kicked in the jaw and I was falling from the womb and my grandfather sat waiting anxiously by my mother's hospital bed, my father was off with that tramp, losing what little he had at a nearby horse track. His own parents, my other grandparents, were equally oblivious to my arrival, though when my grandmother twice knocked on their door during her political campaigning, unsure if their son had given them the news of his impending father-hood, she'd only bitten her lip before stressing that Louis was a good-for-nothing son of a bitch and that she was encouraging her daughter to eat less. The Johnsons agreed and sympathized, saying that bastard Saint-Laurent was making food too plentiful, and their daughter Erma was having a similar problem.

For several months after my birth, my grandmother meticu-lously scanned the town's paper, *The Wharton Echo*, strolled Main Street daily with an open ear, and found not a trace of news regarding a mysterious arrival at the Johnsons'. Evidently each of her days during those months ended in restful solitude, perched on the end of the bench outside Floyd's Smoke Shop with pen in hand, *The Wharton Echo* in her lap. She became such a fixture there that the frustrated proprietor, Floyd Sullivan Sr., barked one cool fall afternoon while sweeping his stoop, "Do you think you could buy something for once?"

She removed her reading glasses and looked up at him. "I'll have you know, Mr. Sullivan, that I do not smoke, nor do I approve of the filthy habit."

"We don't just sell butts, you know."

"I suspect there would be nothing in your establishment of interest to me."

"You'd be surprised," Floyd said.

"With all due respect, it will be a snowy day in July when I pass through that door of yours."

He stopped sweeping and glared at the paper in her hands. "For Christ's sake, we even sell the goddamn newspaper!"

She folded hers, rose, and faced him directly. "I'd watch what you're saying, Mr. Sullivan. Now, if you'd be so kind, please step aside." He did and she never again sat on that bench.

It turned out my Aunt Erma was simply obese, and when her family left town three years later, moving first to Hanover, then to Goderich, then to who knows where, eventually losing themselves and us in the giant fabric of Ontario, she weighed upward of two hundred pounds. I am convinced my grandparents Johnson remained as oblivious to my existence then as they were on the day of my birth. With their disappearance went the much-needed, though sporadic, financial assistance my father had been providing for us.

With my grandmother still working on lunch in the kitchen, and Uncle Ron sulking in his bedroom, my mother sat in the living room, rocking me gently in her arms.

"Well?" my grandfather said, hovering over us like a nervous but lovable loon. "Have you thought of a name yet?"

Mother beamed. "Yes, Dad, I have. Allow me to introduce Mary Ellen Trammel."

"That's a fine name," he said, balling his hat and dabbing his forehead, "a very fine name."

Unlike my direct arrival in Wharton via the womb, the Trammels arrived in Canada on a liner from England, pulling into Halifax Harbour during the early summer of 1896. My great-grandfather, Joseph, then a sapling of nine, accompanied his parents, Edmond and Eleanor, along with six siblings. They immediately headed west and settled in Toronto.

Edmond, unable to find work as a millwright, learned of a great gold strike in the Yukon. Being a highly religious man and a firm proponent of fate, Edmond proclaimed this to be his calling. His dreams, it seemed, were finally coming true. While a multitude of others shared similar dreams, they were sensible enough to wait until spring. It was late September, after all, and Yukon winters were severe. Edmond knew this, of course, but he was partial to the cold and snow. He headed north, leaving behind his family and enough money to last them a year, with promises to return within that time shouldering a king's ransom in gold.

Since arriving in Toronto, Edmund had befriended an equally partial man, Jim Connell, whose geographical knowledge of Canada far exceeded his. They set off by horse and wagon on the twenty-four-hour trip to North Bay. Once there, Jim announced, they would head west by train to Prince Rupert, then north to Dawson City and their undoubted riches. It turned out, though, that Jim's passion for fortune was tempered only by a penchant for drink. He consumed, conservatively, a dozen bottles of whiskey on the journey north. After numerous delays, from bogging down on muddy roads to broken wheel hubs, they pulled into the small town of Wharton, Ontario, three weeks later, far less passionate, and about a hundred miles west of their intended northern course.

Edmond, always a sober man, after getting his bearings and realizing they were no better off than fish trapped inside a tiny barrel—Wharton is bordered by Lake Huron to the west and north, and Georgian Bay to the east—hunkered down in the town's only tavern with not his one-time friend, but instead his own bottle of whiskey. As fate would have it, a local businessman overheard Edmond's solitary rant detailing his family's deplorable trek across the Atlantic on a rat-infested liner, their long, tiring sojourn to the land of little opportunity, Toronto, and the escapades that led him *here* as opposed to *there* (*there* of course being the Yukon and his dreams), and offered the inebriated Englishman a job.

Again as fate would have it, at that very moment Edmond noticed a miraculous mid-October snowfall beginning and so, with the Yukon in his eyes and each snowflake looking like gleaming golden nuggets, he gratefully accepted the offer. The following morning, sober and a man of his word, he arrived at the businessman's granary for work. Two weeks later he sent for the Trammel clan in Toronto.

The arrival of my grandmother's clan—the Agnews—in Wharton had, I'm sure, little to do with luck, bad or good. My grandmother is a coldly calculating woman and I suspect the same of her forebears, although I don't dwell on her ancestry. Whenever the subject was broached through the years, usually during nostalgic bantering at family get-togethers over the various holidays, she was as reticent in her responses as she was with me while I was growing up.

My grandfather told most of the stories. My first recollections of them and what would become our ritual began when I was six. It went something like this:

No matter where I was or what I was doing, when the second-floor oak stairs creaked, their hollow sounds echoing throughout the house, I scurried to them and sat on the bottom step. I would fidget, trying to count to one hundred, rarely making it to fifty. Then I'd tiptoe up the enclosed stairs, stopping when I could peek over the top step.

The third floor attic office was small and gloomy, so his desk lamp was on. His back was to me, his broad, thick shoulders dominating the wooden swivel chair in which he sat. He stared out the gable window, smoking a cigarette. It was the only place in the house he was permitted to smoke. For a few moments I stood motionless, fascinated by the white, perfectly formed rings floating effortlessly upward from his head, one after another. They looked like miniature halos. I watched as they vanished against the pane of glass, each one seeming to escape soundlessly into the outside world. The room had a heavy odour of smoke and my grandfather's cologne. It had an oddly bitter pungency that reminded me of hay coils, sopping wet after a hard rain.

Finally I hopped onto the top step. He heard me and swivelled around.

"Well," he said, glancing at his watch while blotting out his cigarette, "I see you actually made it to a hundred today!" Then he smiled. His bottom and top teeth slanted inward a bit, but it was a wonderful smile and it made me do the same.

Some days I pulled myself up onto the big brown leather chair opposite his mahogany desk and watched as he pulled out his ledger and chequebook, jotting down figures, writing cheques. He maintained a meticulous account of his business finances. Then he removed the cash box he kept in a bottom desk drawer. I marvelled at the sight of his large, strong hands handling such fragile pieces of paper. He grouped the ones, twos, fives, tens, and twenties in piles. When the piles were small, I noticed him frown. All the while he was talking, telling stories.

Perhaps it was because I had no father that most of them revolved around family, to give me a sense of belonging that I was too young to realize I lacked.

He told me that story often about his grandfather, Edmond, how the Trammels in Wharton began with him. Each time, he made a point of emphasizing how one single event can change the course of a life. It was like a fascination with him, his mantra, this common, recurring theme that I came to expect with each of our little talks. For Edmond it was a "wrong turn" somewhere on his way to the Yukon.

He told me about his own father, Joseph, and the single event that changed the course of his life. Joseph was twenty-two and the last of his six siblings remaining in Wharton. Each of the others had already headed for more prosperous grounds in Toronto. He had been preparing to do the same when Edmond got his arms badly mutilated in a thresher, leading to their eventual amputation three days later.

A kind-hearted man, Joseph couldn't bear to leave his mother alone with the burden of his now disabled father. Though he wasn't an officially trained millwright, he had assisted the elder Trammel occasionally in both the repair and design of machinery for the various mills dotting the landscape of Wharton, rebuilding several Wicks Upright Boilers for the paper mill in particular, and servicing the mechanical ills of Wharton Wood, the town's furniture factory. So Joseph assumed Edmond's position, with the town happily accepting him in the role (it was the least they could do, all things considered), where he remained until his death in 1943.

I always sensed a genuine fondness when my grandfather

spoke of his father. He bubbled with enthusiasm. Sometimes he almost giggled, as if he was a boy again, with his father sitting opposite him. But it was only young little me in the brown leather chair.

Like Edmond, Joseph dreamt of the Yukon. There was a story about him that my grandfather and I role-played, and it always made us laugh.

My grandfather would stand, ceasing his jotting and writing and grouping and counting for a moment. His plaid shirt would flare out like the feathers of a peacock as his chest rose. He would give me a stern look. He wasn't overly tall, my grandfather, but he seemed like a giant to me then, with me just a speck of a girl in that brown leather chair, my shoulders not quite reaching its armrests.

"Percy," he said, pretending to be his father, Joseph.

Wide-eyed with wonder, and now an incarnation of my grandfather's real-life brother Percy, I would look almost straight up at him.

"You get yourself packed," he continued, "because you're coming to the Yukon with me, where our gold awaits!"

I nodded.

He whispered, "You're supposed to say no."

I shook my head "no."

"What's this I hear?" he bellowed, and then he pointed a finger at me. "How about *you*, Barbara?"

His sister Barbara—me again!—shook her head "no."

"And can I assume the same of you, George?"

I shook my head "no."

My grandfather shook his head in a mousy sort of "you made

a mistake" way. Then he nodded in a short and quick "you're supposed to say yes" way.

I nodded "yes."

He shook his head no, yes, no, and I did the same, and together we would break out in a fit of dizzying laughter.

I was always a little puzzled by those exchanges. Never did he include himself, James, in the silly Yukon bantering, but only his three siblings. Had he noticed some inherent flaw in my character that made me unworthy to play the role of him, albeit for brief seconds? It made me wonder. And as time passed, the more we bantered, the more I wondered.

Other days, after I'd hopped onto the top stair and my grandfather had spun around and blotted out his cigarette, he would ask me to come close and he'd lift me up and I'd lay back in his lap. Together we'd stare out the window, over the elms at the top of the driveway, across the blameless blue water of Lake Huron, and into the endless horizon. Everything moved in slow motion for me there, resting warm and safe in his lap, my head nestled in the crook of his bristly neck, as if Time were a great, languorous god.

"It's a big, beautiful world," he told me, the two of us looking out into it, "but my world is here."

And my world is here too, I thought, since Wharton was the only place I'd ever known.

I remember one late fall afternoon when I was eight. The sky was grey and low, and the setting sun was shooting the occasional shaft of light through breaks in the shifting clouds. As usual, my grandfather's desk lamp was on. When he said what he often said, "But my world is here," my eyes suddenly refocused and I saw our reflections in the windowpane. It was then that I noticed he wasn't looking outside at all. His eyes were downcast. He was looking at me.

It was there in my grandfather's attic office, on a Saturday four days before my tenth birthday, that my life changed.

He was detailing the single event that led him onto the path his life had taken. I'd heard the story many times before. I was in my usual spot in the brown leather chair opposite him, though by now my shoulders rose above its armrests. I was also restless, our little ritual having started to wear a bit thin on me.

"*The Wharton Echo* billed it as 'The Hurricane From Hell,'" my grandfather was saying of the disaster that struck in 1934, battering the hundred-year-old log and wood plank structures that dominated Wharton at the time. I felt the urge to yawn, but managed to suppress it.

Apparently, while most structures survived the storm, suffering only minor damage (blown out six-over-six sash windows being the prevalent problem), more than a dozen were devastated. Most of these were family dwellings, but some were businesses, including Kane's General Store (which would later become an IGA) and Floyd's Smoke Shop on Main Street.

"My dad told me, 'James, you'd better get yourself down there right this minute and help them rebuild our town!'" he continued, wrapping his hand into a fist around his pen and slamming it against the desk for emphasis. Pausing, he smiled. The windowpane rattled behind him. I yawned.

Lacking enough capable volunteers and tradesmen to assist

him, Angus Black, the town's skilled joiner, glazier, bricklayer, carpenter, plasterer, and stonemason all rolled into one, immediately put him to work. He was only nineteen at the time and as yet undecided about his future.

"So I watched closely, listened intently, and did as I was told." He was looking down, jotting figures in his ledger as he spoke. He glanced at me. "There's something to be learned in that, Mary."

"I know, Grandpa." I yawned, jotting no figures myself, but instead fiddling with a pen.

Angus, who was sixty and whose own children had left Wharton in search of prosperity, watched closely, too. It didn't take long for him to notice James's natural talent. The young man learned to skillfully frame windows and doors, and to do it with a swiftness that had taken Angus himself years to master, and all this after only a few weeks.

"Yep, I sure impressed old Angus," he said with a chuckle. Then he finished with his jotting and put his ledger away. He swivelled his chair around, his back now facing me. I found it curious that he didn't pull out his cash box.

"He pleaded with me to be his apprentice. Imagine that. The great Wharton builder, Angus Black, pleading with *me* . . ." His voice was dreamlike in its quality as he stared out the window. "He was a good man, that Angus. Taught me everything I know . . ."

With my grandfather still talking, I slipped from my chair and tiptoed away, the stairs barely creaking under my light step.

I grabbed a bag of seed and went into the yard to refill the various birdfeeders. The sun was high, and burning like a branding iron. I wore baby blue shorts, a blue striped T-shirt, and white sneakers. By the time I'd refilled my third birdfeeder, I also wore a thick coat of guilt. How could I treat my grandfather as I'd just done, if not in my thoughts, then by my actions, sneaking away without so much as a word? Instantly, I dropped the bag of seed and ran inside.

I dashed up the second-floor stairs, only to arrive at the top and find the attic office empty—my grandfather was gone.

I sat down in his wooden chair. How could I have been so callous, so cruel? Swivelling around so I faced the window, I gathered in the brilliant, yellow-streaked sunshine and wondered what he had been looking at outside.

I quickly scanned the gloomy room to make sure I was alone. Hesitated. Withdrew a cigarette from the pack on his desk. Held it awkwardly in my fingers. Put it clumsily between my lips, only to have it fall twice to the floor. Turned on the desk lamp.

"So," I said through the side of my mouth in a deep, slurred voice to imaginary me in the brown leather chair, "did I ever tell you the story of my brothers and sister and how they all left Wharton for—what's that? No, silly girl, not the Yukon. Toronto. They all left Wharton for the city!" I didn't like my tone of voice. Actually, I hated it. It was almost as if I was mocking my grandfather for the stories he told. Nevertheless, for reasons I cannot explain, I continued talking.

I removed the cash box from the bottom drawer. Broke off a match from the matchbook he kept tucked under a corner of his desk blotter. I didn't light it. I did not light it.

I lit it.

Raised it an inch from the cigarette that dangled between my lips.

Still talking, I opened the cash box with my free hand. My eyes nearly fell from their sockets. Inside, the cash box glowed a brilliant golden-orange from the stack of fifties on top. I'd never seen a fifty-dollar bill before. Something about it was so utterly beautiful, so utterly entrancing that I fell silent, feeling I'd grasped in that instant the lure of the Yukon that my grandfather so often spoke about. A sense of awe gripped me. I sat frozen, staring at the fifties.

The burning match singed the tip of my finger and thumb and I let out a muffled scream and dropped the match. The cigarette followed it to the floor. I forgot about both.

I grabbed a fifty. Turned it over in my hands. Studied its back. Ran my scorched thumb over the picture of the rocky shoreline. Thought I could actually *feel* the rocky shoreline . . .

The stairs creaked.

I glanced up, heart racing. The threshold was still empty. I quietly lifted the cash box and placed it carefully inside its drawer.

I was standing beside the desk when my grandmother appeared seconds later.

"Oh," she said, gripping the oak handrail as she took the last few steps. "I thought your grandfather was up here." Though she was only in her early fifties, her face was flushed and she seemed winded from the climb up the steep stairs.

I was having my own trouble breathing. "No," I squeaked.

A part of me wanted her to call me out, to question the smell of sulphur that, to my mind at least, still hung heavy in the air. I wanted her to stroll around the desk and notice the cigarette, which, I realized, was lying on the floor beneath my grandfather's desk, probably right next to the charred match. At least then I could explain myself, tell her that I was not a bad girl. That I had no intention of actually lighting the cigarette. That I was a child simply playing a child's game. That I'd accept whatever punishment she saw fit, and be done with it.

And an even bigger part of me wanted her to insist I open my clenched fist. To ask where I'd gotten that fifty-dollar bill, so I could tell her it wasn't as it seemed. And she could refuse to listen and punish me for stealing from my grandfather and be done with it.

I wanted to be done with it.

"Well, child, it's almost dinnertime. You should start thinking about getting washed up," was all she said.

I was barely able to nod, but I did, and then charged down the stairs.

Outside, I grabbed the bag of seed I'd left and raced to the bottom of the yard. There, beneath a tall pine whose bottom branches began about five feet above the ground, I sat and rested my back against its wide trunk, invisible to the house and my deception.

I unfolded the bill, held it across my cupped palms, stared blankly at its back. Pictured were rocks, a shoreline, crashing waves, rippling water, and a pink-tinged sky spotted with clouds. When I looked at the pictured horizon—I mean, really looked *into* it, stolen as it was from a mere image and trapped on this tiny piece of paper—I saw the same endless horizon my grandfather and I so often looked upon from his attic office window, and so I buried my face in my hands, knowing that whatever I did now, I could never go back.

It rained for me then, a storm of raging tears that forever stained the landscape of my life.

The girl with the china doll face sat on a plain wooden chair in the corner of the principal's office at Wharton Elementary. She was so tiny, she looked like Goldilocks dwarfed by Papa Bear's chair. Her little hand held a white cloth against her forehead, though beneath it the bleeding had stopped.

When a dark-haired man rushed into the room, the principal greeted him immediately and calmly detailed the accident, while the dark-haired man politely listened.

"She's going to be just fine," finished the principal, smiling. Both men looked down at the tiny girl.

After thanking the principal, the dark-haired man knelt beside the girl. "Here, sweetheart," he said, gently taking the cloth away and studying the gash. "You're going to have to be more careful." His voice was soft and soothing.

The girl looked up and stared sullenly at the principal with her big blue eyes. She shook her head.

"No? Yes, sweetheart. You must be more careful."

Still staring at the principal, she shook her head again. Then her eyes filled like great pools of blue and when she blinked, tears streamed down her cheeks. She lunged forward and, throwing her arms around the dark-haired man who knelt before her, began sobbing in his warm embrace.

Of course, not everyone leaves Wharton. Some, like my great-grandfather, Joseph, and my grandfather, spent their entire lives in the little nook. Others, like my grandfather's grandfather,

Edmond, while mistaking his misfortune for incredible good fortune, came and actually stayed.

I guess if any one thing can be credited with encouraging even the slightest population surge over the years, it would have to be summer. Summers are intoxicating here, invigorating and charming, and when one is walking along Main Street on a warm July afternoon, it is easy to be fooled. There are dozens of shops, and outside them the sidewalks echo with endless footfalls. Most of these are the tourists, the "just passing through" gang down from Manitoulin Island heading to the city, or heading to and from places unknown. And they are the "in from the cottage for supplies" crowd, probably the largest of the groups. They bustle about with great jubilation, giving the town an aura of vibrancy and leaving each of these visitors with a swelling of the soul, a wonderful sense that here, life is thriving.

Intermingling with these visitors are the spectators, the townspeople, a fragmentary spattering of mostly elderly folks there to conduct what little they require of business, but mainly to watch and see it all, their town, their home, a stark and much-needed luminous reminder that indeed all is well. Passing them on the street, any traveller would be hard-pressed not to receive a welcoming "Howdy," or "Fine day, isn't it?" or at the very least, a warm smile.

Personally, I never understood why everyone seemed so happy here. There is little to do in Wharton, which lacks the barest of essentials to pass the time; there is neither a cinema nor a bowling alley with even a single lane.

Once the thrill of Main Street has passed and all that is to be gotten has in fact been gotten, you veer from it, venturing down quiet streets lined with homes, most of them built by my grandfather. There you find men tinkering under hoods of rusty old trucks, and women on their knees, tending gardens of unspeakable beauty that have reached that state through the fact that the tenders have unspeakable amounts of free time. Others can be found trimming hedges, cutting lawns, or relaxing on sturdy wrap-around porches, sipping cool beverages and reading the newspaper. All of them, upon noticing you, momentarily stop what they're doing, wave, and smile that warm Main Street smile, grateful for another excuse to pass the time productively.

Those who are fooled long enough to uproot their families from the city and move here quickly realize there are no jobs. The businesses on Main Street are family businesses, and if you're not family (which you never are), then you have no business working here. So after a year, maybe two, with their tails between their legs, the uprooted families return with great resentment to the places from whence they came.

The ones that manage to stick are usually retired and, not in need of work, able to amalgamate seamlessly into the town's creaking rhythms off Main Street.

My mother was not family. Having decided not to finish high school following my birth, she was forced to get a job in a neighbouring town. It was a bad job, which led to other jobs in other neighbouring towns, each one a little farther away but not quite as bad as the last.

On weekdays during my mother's years of drifting from one bad job to the next, my grandmother tended me, and in a manner quite unlike those who tended gardens in Wharton. She was impatient, grudging of her time, a harsh disciplinarian, and quick to cut me off like a bud from a stem, teaching me to speak only when spoken to, eat only when told to, and that she, and only she, was right in all matters.

When I was seven my mother found still another job, this one as a cashier at Woolworth in the small city of Owens. It was a good job as jobs go up here, but the way I see it now, it was the start of the end for me in Wharton. Owens was a full hour's drive south, and it left my mother with the perception that the farther away she went, the better things got. It was a fair assessment, and with it came the news of my end in Wharton during the winter of my tenth year—though, admittedly, it had a bit to do with me. It happened on December first, a day not unlike today, with snow heaving itself upon our sleepy little town.

My grandfather was in front of the house, performing what had become another of our "rituals." The first day of each December saw the start of the Christmas season at the Trammel house. He had brought out the ladder and the decorations, and was struggling with a strand of uncooperative lights. He wore a black toque that left half of his ears exposed, his large floppy lobes puffy and apple-red in the crisp afternoon air. His cream-coloured coat had brown reindeers frolicking motionless over its fabric. They were actually moose, but in my mind I always pretended they were reindeer.

Snow already lay on the ground and along the topmost branches of the two large elms at the head of the driveway, and the branches of the numerous spruce trees bordering the drive drooped under the weight of snow. My grandmother stood staring out the front window, bundled in a warm sweater, sipping from a mug of hot tea. Uncle Ron had left to find his fortune in Toronto a number of years earlier.

Although it was a Friday, having been reminded the night before of the day that lay ahead, I'd sauntered home from school with far less enthusiasm than normal. I stood nearby wearing a red, knee-length coat, its fur-rimmed hood pulled tight around my head. Usually I'd be doing my best to help, which meant holding onto a bottom rung of the hulking forty-foot ladder that stretched up to the house's gable, watching, and standing as near to my grandfather as I could. But there was awkwardness between us now, a fissure that had started a few days before my tenth birthday.

He'd never mentioned that missing fifty-dollar bill during the past five months, yet I knew he was aware of it. He had to be. After all, the money in that cash box was crucial to his business's viability, used for minor disbursements, and also to top up his bank balance when necessary to pay bricklayers and other tradesmen who framed and formed the homes that he took great pride in building. Nevertheless, the week following my crushing indiscretion had been an interminable hell for me at home, as I tried to avoid *him* as much as I could, finding every excuse to gravitate more toward my grandmother.

"Want help baking those cookies, Grandma?" I asked one day. "I've got a rip in my skirt, Grandma." (I'd torn it on purpose.) "Can you teach me how to sew?" I asked on another.

It must have comforted him at first to see this, my grandmother and me finally getting closer, two females at last starting to bond. Perhaps he perceived it as a coming-of-age thing. But it was terror that pushed me into the cold shadows of my grandmother, sheer terror that he might sense just from being in my presence that his little granddaughter was imperfect, corrupted, and nothing short of a criminal. It never for an instant occurred to me back then that he might think me simply human, my mistake forgivable. Much like he hadn't batted an eye when my mother informed him of *her* "little" mistake when she was seventeen. Yes, Dr. Glover delivered me, but as I said, not from evil.

On the following Saturday, just three days after my tenth birthday, I had walked along Main Street, racked with fear and an aloneness that was so profound, it felt like an open, festering wound on my heart. Having no place to turn, I went into Chester's Five & Dime in search of penny candy.

When Mrs. Chester handed me the little brown bag and asked for thirty cents in payment, I searched inside my vinyl Little Orphan Annie purse for the fifty-dollar bill. Then I felt around inside my shorts pockets. Mrs. Chester frowned, all the while thrumming her fingers impatiently against the glass candy counter. I removed my white sneakers and checked thoroughly inside each of them. Finally I stared up at her with an expression of complete dismay.

She forced a smile and said, "Well, it *was* just your birthday, Mary. Why don't you take the candy and run along." As I was racing out the door, I heard her call, "And you be sure to share that candy with your grandmother and say hello to her for me!"

Frantically I retraced my steps, finding only a shoehorn, two bottle caps, a wooden nickel, and what at first looked like a silver dollar buried in a patch of weeds that had sprouted up between a break in the stone sidewalk. (Wharton had terrible, ailing sidewalks, and with every manner of weed and grass growing from between their sloping and separating stones, they were more apt to be mowed than swept.) It turned out what I'd thought was a silver dollar was merely the silver backing of a button. When I flipped it over, it read PEARSON FOR PRIME MINISTER. From school I knew Lester Pearson's term as Canada's current prime minister was coming to a close. I also knew he was a Liberal and, as with my father Louis and the former prime minister Louis St. Laurent, his name would be taboo around my house in general, and around my Conservative-loving grandmother in particular, so I left the button but kept the shoehorn, wooden nickel, and bottle caps.

In the frigid cold on December first of my tenth year, I stood a heartbreaking ten feet from my grandfather. He was calling across that ten-foot chasm, making small talk, asking me about school, what I wanted for Christmas. I was studying the patterns the toes and soles of my boots were leaving in the snow when my mother's car raced down the driveway. He dropped the lights, took two giant leaps, and swept me up as she slid to a stop just a foot from the base of the ladder.

My mother practically jumped from her car. "I got it!" she yelled, snatching me from my grandfather's arms and dancing me around in a snowy circle. "I . . . got . . . it," she sang in piercing vibrato, "I . . . got . . . it. I . . . got . . . it."

"Got what?" my grandfather asked, unsmiling, finding it difficult to share his daughter's exuberance when, just seconds earlier, she'd almost run us over. He picked up the strand of lights that lay half buried in snow near his feet.

She stopped whirling and took a few seconds to catch her breath. "A job! And a great one!"

"Well, good for you," he replied, now smiling, sounding genuinely happy. "Where? The new IGA on Main?"

"No, Dad, I said a *great* job. Secretarial. In London."

"Oh. England's a long way off," he said, trying to act casual and make a joke of it. He'd resumed working on the tangle of lights and was jerking on the cord that connected everything.

"*No,* Dad. Ontario."

He started jerking harder on the cord. I sensed my grandfather knew the London of Ontario was a long way off, too.

"And I start on the eleventh."

"Of January?"

"December! Less than two weeks! Much . . . to . . . do," she sang some more, spinning me about. "Much . . . to . . . do."

"Where will you and Mary live?" he asked, shifting his weight back and forth from one leg to the other. The strand of lights had somehow bunched itself into a massive ball against his chest. His hands were buried somewhere inside that ball, tugging and twisting, battling the lights like a man would wrestle a bear. He had a real problem on his hands.

"I've already been looking into some furnished apartments," she said, dropping to one knee and taking me by the shoulders. "But only if it's okay with Mary. What do you say, Mary? Do you want to go?"

My grandfather instantly ceased the fight and stood motionless, looking down at me with his gentle hazel eyes.

And there it was. Up to me. The question—*the* question— that seemed to hang frozen in the cold December air for an interminably long time. With me standing right next to my grandfather and his ladder, I told her, "Okay."

As my mother went back to her car, dancing like a circus bear, he managed a smile and quietly said, "The move will be good for you. You'll make lots of new friends." I knew by his voice that his heart had broken.

I couldn't even nod; couldn't even look at him, for that matter. Mom returned carrying her purse.

"I'm happy for you, Carol," he said, letting the lights and the tangled cord that held them all together fall into the snow again. Turning, he mumbled something about needing pliers.

I glanced toward the house. My grandmother, who had left the window, now stood hugging herself in the open doorway. As my grandfather passed her, he slowly slipped off his black toque and disappeared, consumed by the house he'd built for his family.

The tangled lights sat there for three days. And for each of those three days it snowed. And for each of those snowing three days my mother flitted about the house on a cloud, organizing this and organizing that, her jubilation blunting her to the profound sadness that I, even as a ten-year-old child, knew my grandfather felt.

During the morning of that third day—a Sunday—Dr. Glover appeared unexpectedly at our door. He is a tall man, Dr. Glover, about six-foot five, with a puggish nose at the centre of a near-perfectly round face. His eyes are just as round, though small and copper-tinted, very much resembling a pair of pennies. At the time, his chestnut-brown hair had turned mostly grey, badly thinning in front, with a bald spot the size of a saucer on top. He also had the makings of a modest paunch bulging his white button-down shirt, on which the bottom of his checkered necktie rested comfortably.

Though he had always been the lone doctor in town, the consensus was, the broken jaw he'd received during my botched delivery had subsequently skewed his judgment—a jaw, it was secretly suggested, that remained misaligned even after it had healed. It was a question of his competence as much as a response to the population explosion (Wharton had grown by one hundred souls since Dr. Glover began his career twenty-five years earlier), that prompted the town to keep on the doctor filling in for him during his year-long recuperation.

My grandfather did not share the town's opinion. The fact that Dr. Glover managed to maintain his "post" and "catch" me after receiving a severe blow to the jaw at the foot of my mother was an act of unerring valour, far greater than anything my grandfather had witnessed in the six months he'd been on active duty with the RAF during World War II. No, Dr. Glover was a hero, and when his house mysteriously burned to a cinder two years after my birth (his wife and two teenage children, thankfully, escaping the blazing inferno unharmed), my grandfather arrived with a work crew the very next day, to begin the cleanup of charred remains and discuss designs for a new dwelling. It turned out the Glovers favoured a structure similar to what they'd had: a modest Victorian with three bedrooms and only a trifling of minor improvements.

With a second medico now servicing the ills of Wharton, Dr. Glover saw this as an opportunity to take his first official vacation. So, packing no bags, having lost virtually everything in the fire, the family got in their Buick, waved goodbye, and headed for sunny California. Upon their return six weeks later, they drove their Buick not once, but three times past the lot where their former house had stood. They were, after all, weary from the long drive, and minds can play tricks. Only when my grandfather emerged from the nearly completed home with a level and hammer in hand did the Glovers stop and inch their way slowly from the car. ("In fact," my grandfather told me years later with a chuckle, "they inched their way so slowly from the car, they looked like a bunch of confused snails!")

Mrs. Glover, awestruck at the sight of her family's new three-story, Victorian-style mansion that she would later find out contained not three but six bedrooms, a library, an unheard-of main floor laundry, and a kitchen twice the size of her last, began weeping uncontrollably before collapsing into her husband's arms.

Typical of grand Victorian homes, the house had double front doors, very ornate, each door containing twenty-four small, stained glass panes that connected to form a large rectangle, and inside each rectangle, an indigo oval ran vertical with a large crimson poinsettia at its centre. It was Mrs. Glover's favourite flower, and when my grandfather saw her reaction to that in particular, he relaxed and leaned against the doorframe in rakish relief. Half smiling, he pushed up the brim of his cap with the tip of his level, satisfied that his act of benevolence was fitting retribution for what he saw as Dr. Glover's supreme act of heroism.

After welcoming Dr. Glover in on that snowy Sunday, my grandfather led him to the kitchen table. My mother, having spent the previous day flitting long into the night, was sleeping late. While my grandmother and I made coffee, prepared a plate of assorted cookies, and got the creamer, sugar bowl, and serving tray ready, I listened as Dr. Glover told my grandfather of a rumour floating around town that he wasn't feeling well.

On the contrary, my grandfather retorted, he felt fine. In fact, it was Dr. Glover and that jaw of his, now almost ten years healed, that my grandfather was worried about. Then my grandfather laughed. Dr. Glover assured him his jaw felt as fine as my grandfather did, and as proof he'd eat the whole damn plate of cookies that we were preparing. Before the cookies reached the table, though, they were drifting down the hall, the taller Dr. Glover with his arm across my grandfather's broad shoulders, each with an unlit cigarette in hand.

"Jim," I heard the doctor saying as they faded farther from the kitchen, "you're positive there's nothing wrong?"

Five minutes later, Dr. Glover left. I'm not sure what else was said, if anything. Perhaps they simply sat opposite one another in my grandfather's attic office, smoking, not needing to speak the unspoken of two men, both born and raised in the town, both losing their children to the lure of the city.

Whatever was exchanged between them, it seemed to have worked. By noon my grandfather was outside, digging up the mess of lights now buried deep in snow.

"You get out there and help him, child," my grandmother insisted as we stood side by side at the front window, watching him resume the battle.

Reluctantly, I did as I was told.

Outside, I bit my lower lip before saying, "Mommy says we're going to be visiting you and Grandma a lot." He was forty feet away, at the top of the ladder, attaching lights to the peak of the gable. For all it mattered he could have been in London, Ontario *or* England, or—the way it struck me, with all the misty white snow falling— heaven, with him so far away in the clouds he didn't hear.

I repeated myself, this time screaming.

His head jerked violently to the side and he looked down, and when he did the ladder roared a chilling metal clang and shifted what must have been two feet to the left. My heart leaped in my throat. Every inch of me hung on for dear life.

All I remember is, he smiled from way up there, from that place where heaven joined earth, not seeming the least bit unsettled, as if shifting, shaking ladders were a common occurrence to him. "You better, sweetheart," he called down to me once the ladder steadied itself. "You better."

Of course, that was eighteen years past. And as abruptly as the ladder stopped shaking back then, in my mind it started again three months ago, when my mother phoned.

"He's taken a bad turn," she said. A long pause followed. At last she blurted, "He's barely hanging on."

Naturally it wasn't entirely my fault. I *had* screamed, the ladder *had* shook, but it was my mother who drove. We officially left Wharton in her Ford five days later, on a Friday, returning two weeks after that for Christmas. The following year we visited at Easter, spent what was an uncomfortable week for me in Wharton during July, and came again for Thanksgiving and Christmas. The next year we skipped Easter and summer, and the year after that we skipped Thanksgiving.

By the time I was fifteen I was finding every excuse imaginable to avoid Wharton, spending more and more time with the new friends my grandfather had been right about me making in London. I even went so far as to join the swim team, devoting much of my summers and weekends during school months to swim meets. It was a real stretch, considering, in my earlier years of swimming the cool blue waters of Lake Huron, I'd barely mastered the dog paddle. My mother told my grandparents it was teenage angst. I think my grandfather knew otherwise. At least that's the way it appeared one Christmas when I called.

"Merry Christmas, Grandpa," I said from my dorm room. I was nineteen and attending York University in Toronto; I no longer needed my friends or the swim team to avoid Wharton.

"Merry Christmas, Mary."

We made small talk for a bit before an awkward yet familiar silence lingered over the phone.

"Do you know where I am?" he finally said. "I'm looking out my office window."

I imagined him leaning back in his chair, cigarette in hand, blowing perfect halos of white into the pane of glass.

He continued: "Do you remember the little talks we used to have in here?"

Remember them? How could I forget? For a time I loved them more than anything I'd ever loved in my life, but I didn't want to go there right now. "Yes," I reluctantly admitted.

"You know what I see?"

Our beautiful horizon, I thought, but didn't say it.

"I see you teaching here in Wharton, once you get your degree. Have you ever considered that?"

"There aren't any jobs, Grandpa," I quickly replied, "and if there were, they wouldn't pay like they do here in Toronto."

Then he said the first of two things that made me believe he knew, and it terrified me and, at the same time, angered me, because he didn't challenge the coward that I was and throw it directly into the air like a bird with a broken wing, forcing me to mend it so we again could fly.

"Well, money's not everything," he said.

His words clicked inside me as if he'd cocked the hammer on one of his old rifles. I couldn't speak.

"Whatever I did that's keeping you away," he added, "can we put it behind us?"

And there it was. Like a shotgun blast, the words sounded in my ear, dredging up the memories of that day when I'd pretended to be an adult, cigarette between lips, lighting a match. And that fifty-dollar bill. That damned fifty-dollar bill.

In his considerate, compassionate way, he was at that moment accepting blame for something he had no part in, giving me an opportunity to save face. He was giving me an "out." I was too afraid to take it.

"You did nothing, Grandpa," I somehow managed to say, fighting back the tears. "I've just been really busy with my studies." Then I wished him another merry Christmas and ended the call.

Unlike *that* call, when all I did afterward was bury my face in a pillow, the call from my mother three months ago sent me into Nautilus and made me drive north in a record two hours, shaking the whole way. And the whole way, screaming at myself, still angry after eighteen years for taking that cursed fifty-dollar bill and losing it, but mostly angry for losing my grandfather and Wharton, and all because I was ashamed and terrified to admit the truth about myself. And even worse, to admit the truth to my grandfather, because I was terrified he'd be disappointed in the person I'd become.

But he was hanging on, my mother had said. Barely, but hanging on. I held out a tiny glimmer of hope when I burst through the front door to my grandfather's house. Maybe it was all a dream, a nightmare, a vicious joke—this life I had led up to now a thing of fiction, a great concoction from one of the clever writers I had studied in English Lit class.

I found my grandmother standing over the stove, awaiting the kettle, my mother at the kitchen table with tissues in hand, her eyes puffy and red.

When I quietly opened his bedroom door, he was staring straight up at the ceiling. His head was deep in a pillow, his neck disappearing beneath a thick quilt. It looked like a magician's illusion, the quilt hardly bulging where his body should have been. As I leaned over him, it was all I could do to keep myself from collapsing. This was not my grandfather. This man's face was sunken, a mere shell, his eyes lifeless and hollow, his lips dry and white. I tried my best to smile. I don't know if I did. Tears filled my eyes.

He strained to say something. I couldn't hear. I moved closer.

"Stay . . . a while," he said in a hoarse whisper.

I nodded but couldn't speak. A few sparse strands of white hair hung down his forehead and I gently combed them aside with my fingers. Then I slid a hand beneath the quilt and took his hand in mine. He managed a slight squeeze.

"I still remember," he continued, stopping to swallow a difficult mouthful of air, "the day you were born."

It was then that I noticed a tiny spark of life glint in his eyes as he looked directly into my eyes, and a slight smile shaped his lips. My grandfather. My wonderful grandfather. The way I remembered him.

At that moment I began shaking uncontrollably, as tears washed over me in a great flood of hope, and before I could utter a single word from the litany of words that had gone too long unsaid, there, in the town of our births, inside the house he built with his very hands, he closed his eyes and died.

Today is December 24, 1985. My grandfather is already three months gone and I find myself still shaking, silently screaming, barely hanging on inside my car. The motel with the badly peeling wallpaper is now several hours behind me, and a day behind that, my TV with the poor reception, my fickle coffeemaker with the frayed electrical cord, and a bungalow holding the remnants of a still-knotted bathrobe belt.

The forecasters were right—boatloads of snow, on the ground and still falling. I hear Nautilus's wheels crunching over the snow-packed road. It is almost six on Christmas Eve, already dark. Headlights flash in the rearview mirror. A car angles out and zips past, honking. *Merry Christmas,* I think, *to you and yours.*

What's left of mine wait fifty yards ahead, inside my grandfather's house. Mom. Grandma. Uncle Ron and the flavour of the month (the last I heard, it was Diane, his fourth wife) and his three kids (unless, of course, he and Diane have added to the brood).

Though the elms at the top of the driveway were lost to Dutch elm disease in the '70s, I can't see the house for the tall spruces. I don't want to see the house for the spruces. I don't want to see the house that I suspect will be unadorned with the

Christmastime splendour that it had become accustomed to over the years. I understand he is gone, but there will be a sense of finality to such a sight, one I feel ill prepared to handle. I brake and ease Nautilus off to the side, twenty yards shy of the driveway. After a few deep breaths and a slight gathering of sorts, I gun Nautilus's troubled engine. Her wheels spin helplessly before she gets a grip and lurches forward.

And there, while barrelling down the long, curving driveway of my childhood, I breathe a sigh of relief. The house is fully lit, alternating reds and greens running along the eave of the wide front porch and running up the gable, although some bulbs, I notice, are burned out near its peak. A huge wreath has been added, framing the gable window, which I think is a nice touch. He would have liked that.

Everywhere is snow—falling, in the trees, on the ground, billowing over the porch awning like cake icing. When I notice four mounds of the white stuff fast approaching, it occurs to me I'm still barrelling. I brake hard and Nautilus slides into the back of one mound, which I quickly discover, as the snow drops off, is a large silver car. Fortunately the collision made little noise, perhaps thanks to a muffling cushion of white and Nautilus's fragile front end. I put Nautilus in reverse and as she backs away, her headlights illuminate a fine chrome bumper now bent into a V-shaped frown. Apparently the four mounds are four cars, parked in two rows of two.

As I'm parking in the other row, racked by a familiar sense of guilt, my mother opens the house's front door. Her hair is black and naturally straight, but she has it curled and tidy today, no doubt her Christmas 'do; a nice change. Up until last summer, she'd had a beehive style for almost fifteen years. She is wearing a red minidress with padded shoulders.

For a mom of forty-five, she still looks good, and is reasonably trim. She is also a romantic, forever clinging to the hope that Mr. Right is just around the corner. The only problem is, as she often laments, which corner? And, the scariest part for her, is she even in the right town, city, or country? Which probably explains why she travels so often—Florida, Bermuda, Europe, and three years ago, an African adventure. She'd called me direct from a tiny village in Uganda to tell me about a nice man she had just met named Unathi. Later, when she arrived back in London (Ontario, not England), she said he wasn't exactly her type after all and left it at that.

She has an apron tied around her waist, dishtowel in her hands, and as I struggle to the door with my two Jetliners, I notice she's also wearing a frown similar in size to the large bumper I just dented. "Well," she snips, removing her apron and flipping it over her shoulder with the dishtowel, "only a day and a half late, I see."

I choose a flimsy defence. "Have you looked outside and seen the snow?" When she ignores this, I grab at another straw. "Not to mention the shape my car's in these days."

"That's it, blame Nautilus," she says, grabbing a Jetliner and dragging it inside.

The succulent aroma of ham glazes the air, with an undercurrent of scalloped potatoes that strikes me like a soft, welcoming fist. An instrumental version of "The First Noel" is playing softly in the background.

"I'm not talking to you," she adds, refusing to look outside for any length of time to confirm the weather or the condition of my car that, I noticed when passing, now has a smiling V-shaped dent on her front bumper.

"Merry Christmas, Mom," I say.

I try to give her a hug, but she avoids me with a timely turn, manoeuvring the Jetliner to the side. "I've been worried sick," she says. "I must have called your place a hundred times."

"I—"

"I don't understand you, Mary." She practically throws the other bag to the side. It's the one partway filled with gifts and it makes a rattling noise. "Give me your coat."

I do. Footfalls pad quickly along the hallway as I'm down on one knee, unzipping a boot. Uncle Ron's six-year-old appears. He stops abruptly, almost nose to nose with me. He has shaggy blond hair, pale skin spotted with freckles, and a runny nose.

"You're a lost because?" he says, sniffling, then wipes his nose on the sleeve of his white dress shirt, leaving a thin, dark line of moisture.

"Hello, Chas," I say, trying my best to smile.

"My name's Declan."

Mom rolls her eyes and shakes her head. "Chas is Ron's *middle* child, Mary."

"Oh. Well, thanks for asking, Declan. But I didn't get lost. The weather was bad."

"I weren't asking. Daddy said you're a lost because, that's all."

Despite the bad grammar, I now get the point. "No. That's 'cause,' Declan, not 'because.'" I stand and tousle my cousin's hair. "Your daddy meant that I'm a lost cause."

"Yeah, that's it," he says, and then kicks me hard in the shin.

Mom rolls her eyes and shakes her head again. "See, you've even upset him," she observes, before following the speedy little Declan down the hallway. As I hobble behind, she calls back, "And don't forget, I'm not talking to you."

At the end of the hallway I stop where it opens up to the living room on the left. The angle gives me a clear view of the Christmas tree in the far corner. It's a Douglas fir, crammed with ornaments of every shape and colour. At its peak is an angel, and flowing down its length from that angel are several red ribbons with silver trim, which gives the tree a "wrapped" appearance, much like the many presents beneath it. On top of the wood-panelled TV next to the tree is a nativity scene, and strung along the ceiling's edges are waves of red and white streamers.

Straight ahead is the staircase to the second floor. Around the corner at the top of these stairs is the enclosed staircase leading to my grandfather's attic office. It has been many years since I've been up there. During the four days I stayed here three months ago, it was all I could do to get by those stairs and make it to my old bedroom. I would walk past with my eyes tightly closed, trying to shut out the image of little me sitting there on the bottom step counting to a hundred. It is a painful memory.

They are all painful memories, those that revolve around him, because of their briefness, made scarce as the result of my cowardice and, when you get right down to it, selfishness. I could have had so much more; *we* could have had so much more. The memory of that phone conversation from my dorm room when I was nineteen is especially painful. I see him sitting up there alone, looking into our horizon, knowing the truth about his granddaughter yet hoping beyond hope that I'd return to teach in Wharton. But worst of all is the knowledge that he only had two years remaining after officially retiring in 1983. Two years to see the world, perhaps even the Yukon of his ancestors' dreams. Two years to finally get out of Wharton. Two years to await my return. Two years of knowing I never would. Two years.

I slump against the wall. Though the country charm of my childhood is still evident everywhere—mirrors framed in pine, burnished copper, lace curtains, the dulled-steel watering cans and old washboards and hand-carved wood duck decoys sitting on ancient pine crates with the burned stampings of long-deceased companies—I feel a cold emptiness surrounding me. There is no longer any reason to be here. It was a mistake coming, and in many ways another betrayal of my grandfather—he leaves and I return! I also sense a hostility brewing that I want no part in. Things started off badly with Mom and Declan and can only get worse.

To the right of the staircase is the dining room and it's abuzz with voices, mostly my mother's. Through the wall I hear her saying something about me finally arriving, then a hand takes me by the arm from behind.

"Merry Christmas, child."

I turn and instantly tears fill my eyes. "Grandma," I say. I want to hug her, embrace her so fiercely the past will wash away. But I am feeling small, eight years old instead of twenty-eight, and this is my grandmother, I must remind myself. In all the time she cared for me while Mom worked, I don't recall a single hug exchanged between us. Warmth, I learned early on, was a foreign commodity with her, strictly forbidden.

She is short and thin like me, my grandmother, with pale

skin, but her eyes are set wide apart and large. Behind her horn-rimmed cat's-eye glasses, I notice, her benign growth has grown further, now drooping from the outer edge of her right eyelid. Her hair is white, with the odd splash of grey hiding beneath the loose curls.

"Merry Christmas," I reply, wiping my eyes.

She would never verbally acknowledge tears, but she has an almost sympathetic expression on her face.

"Declan," I add, reaching down to rub my leg. "He kicked me in the shin."

"Ah. He's a little monster, that one. You can't take your eyes off him for a second." You can hear the age in her voice, but it remains strong. She pulls a tissue from the sleeve of her dress and hands it to me. "Come," she says, walking around me toward the dining room. "We're about to start dinner."

At the dining table, my mother is still talking. "You could've at least called to let us know you'd be late," she says, setting a heaping plate of ham down in the centre of the table before seating herself between Uncle Ron and Declan, who is nearest me to my right.

I am at the head of the table, a place traditionally reserved for my grandfather. I have no right being in this chair, but Grandma instructed me to sit here. She is directly opposite me at the other end. Behind her are two large, twelve-over-twelve sash windows that offer a stunning view of Georgian Bay. I used to watch my grandfather sitting here, mechanically chewing his food while staring distractedly out those windows. There is nothing visible now in the Christmas Eve darkness, except flurries of snowflakes falling helplessly against the panes.

"Yeah, why didn't you call?" snickers a boy who I know for sure is ten-year-old Chas.

His brother, Patterson, at sixteen the oldest of Uncle Ron's kids, is snickering too. They are both to my left, wearing white dress shirts with snazzy ties like Declan. They are looking across the table at their father, who, it appears, is trying his best to contain a smile.

"Stop that," whispers Diane, who is sandwiched between them. Chas grimaces. Her hidden hands must have either poked or pinched her stepson beneath the table. Diane is a real catch compared to Wilma before her, and before *her*, Cynthia and Hyacinth. She is all legs, with flowing blond hair, and the lashes of her emerald green eyes are so stunningly long, they keep most women like my mother envious and at a distance.

Grandma gets everyone's attention by striking a wineglass several times with her fork. "Since this is our first Christmas without your father—" she speaks slowly, glancing at Mom and Uncle Ron "—and grandfather—" she glances around at the younger crowd, me included "—it would be nice if someone said a few words before we eat."

Uncle Ron pushes his chair back and is standing before I can blink. Three months earlier when the question of a eulogy came up, he did much the same thing, appointing himself. Then, it turned out his was short and not too sweet, speaking about his dad in terms of "loyal" and "tireless worker" and "reliable," as if he were describing a favourite piece of machinery he'd just lost. He never once mentioned what he was like as a father, though I doubt he really knew.

When he was eighteen and finished with high school, Ron

literally bolted for Toronto. After several ambitious ventures that failed (one was importing ice from the Arctic, figuring they had so much of the stuff he could get it for pennies), he hooked up with a renegade phone technician who believed the "brains" of a phone could be modified slightly to form the "brains" of a computer. At the time, computer technology was advancing rapidly, with the mass market of personal home computers in the foreseeable future.

Following three years of disasters, they eventually developed Bellco Brain (apparently the phone technician was sentimental and a former employee of Bell Canada). Luckily for them, a wealthy Taiwanese businessman had designs on the lucrative North American market and, in an effort to keep Bellco Brain away from his main rival, IBM, bought the upstart company. As Uncle Ron is never shy to admit, the all-cash deal netted him three million dollars. And he hasn't worked since, now spending most of his days golfing, fishing, and occasionally, as he'd done on the day of my birth, hunting for groundhogs.

Uncle Ron raises his empty wineglass and looks up at the ceiling. He is taller than my grandfather was, and just as ruggedly built, with short-cropped, rust-coloured hair that leans more toward red than brown and is parted to one side. His face is still spotted with the freckles of his youth and his big, bushy moustache curls around and down past the corners of his mouth. "Here's to you, Dad," he says, thrusting his glass skyward—short and anything but sweet.

He settles into his chair again, and immediately plates are lifted. The food—ham, scalloped potatoes, and the sundry sides— moves like a locomotive around the table. Drinks are poured. The adults get a nice red. I favour what the kids are having.

"Still on the wagon, Mary?" Patterson asks, snickering as I pour myself a glass of milk. He has managed to corral a glass of wine in addition to his milk.

"I just can't get over you arriving a day and a half late," Mom says almost perfunctorily, spooning a helping of potatoes onto her plate.

"Get over it," advises her brother.

"I can't. She said she was leaving yesterday, and I was getting a busy signal on her phone earlier today."

A busy signal? "Mom, I did leave yesterday. But the weather—"

"The weather? Huh!"

"Oh, would you just get over it," Uncle Ron repeats before stuffing a healthy forkful of green beans and potatoes into his mouth. Some of the creamy broth paints itself onto the bristles of his moustache. He calmly wipes it away with a napkin speckled with miniature Christmas trees.

"I will not get over it!"

"Yeah, you can't get over anything, can you?" he says, concentrating on loading his fork again.

"What's that supposed to mean?"

"It means get over it."

For years, Mom and Uncle Ron have been at odds with each other. Part of the reason is that he has money and she doesn't. But the big reason, I believe, is that Ron has never been short on mates while Mom is bitter because she can't find one.

"Why don't *you* get over it and stop embarrassing this family with divorce after divorce after divorce!"

Diane, directly across from my mother, is clearly having a

difficult time finding somewhere to comfortably rest her gaze. She decides staring at the large serving plate of ham in the middle of the table is best.

"I would," explains Uncle Ron, pausing for a sip of wine, "if you hadn't set such a bad example by embarrassing this family with an illegitimate child."

Mom freezes, as if she's been shot in midstride. "Is that what you think?"

His words shoot me, too, because the truth is, he's partially right—I'm the embarrassment, not my mother.

My grandmother, who strictly forbids loud talk at the table, is casually cutting up a slice of ham on her plate. Diane has decided her nervous gaze is more comfortable resting on the half-empty casserole dish of scalloped potatoes.

"No, that's what *everyone* thinks," says Ron.

Declan kicks me under the table. "I don't like you," he whispers, his eyes narrowed.

"Just look at her life and how you've influenced her," continues Ron. He leans back in his chair with wineglass in hand and lets out a satisfied sigh. "Any beaus lining up to wed you, Mary?"

Patterson, across the table from his dad, bursts into laughter, and Chas and Declan quickly follow.

"That's not fair," says Mom, glaring fixedly at her brother. "I've had lots of proposals over the years, but I'm waiting for the right man."

Ron ignores this. "And how about work, Mary? Got a halfway decent job yet?"

I want to tell him that yes, I do in fact have a good full-time teaching job, and have for almost two years. But my heart is lodged painfully in my throat and I know tears would accompany even a single word.

"I've got a good job," Mom snaps.

Grandma finally jumps in, her voice surprisingly untroubled by her children's dispute. She stares straight ahead as if she and I were the only two in the room. "Did you know Mrs. Samuelson is retiring at the end of the school year? They'll need a replacement in the English department at Wharton High in September."

Ron isn't finished. "And how's Nautilus doing, Mary?" Nautilus's reputation precedes her.

"Oh, yeah!" Patterson screeches, wielding his knife excitedly in front of him and pointing it mostly in my direction. "I got my licence this year! Did you see the cool black Caddy in the driveway that Dad bought me?"

"I want a Caddy," says Chas.

Declan kicks me in the shin again.

"When you're old enough, son." Uncle Ron looks at Mom with a smug expression. "At least *I* provide for *my* kids."

I had been on the verge of tears, but an inner resolve grips me. "Shut up," I say.

Uncle Ron's head wheels around in a blur of red. "I beg your pardon?"

"You heard me, you arrogant, selfish son of a bitch. You should be ashamed of yourself."

Chas, Declan, and Patterson stare at me in disbelief. Diane is wide-eyed, staring across the table at her husband, who looks like he's going to leap over Declan and strangle me. Now it is my mom who wears the smug expression.

"And you should be ashamed of yourself, too, Mom," I continue, getting up from my chair. "It's not always about you. Your dad died barely three months ago, and you two are oblivious to that fact, selfishly bickering over your petty disputes. It's shameful. And believe me, I have every right to say that because I'm no better. I know all about shame. I've lived with it for too many years. My answer was to ignore it and hope it would go away. But it never does. Even now. It was *shame* that destroyed me—" I look sternly into Uncle Ron's eyes "—and not your sister. Do you understand? She had nothing to do with my failures. It was entirely my fault.

"But if there's one thing Grandpa's death has taught me, it's this: you can't move forward until you first move back, as impossible as that may seem sometimes. But I'm moving back now, a little at a time. Whose silver car is that outside?"

The room is so quiet you could hear a fine thread drop.

I ask again.

Patterson squeaks, "That's Dad's Cadillac."

"Well, Uncle Ron, in answer to your question, Nautilus is doing fine. So splendid, in fact, that she just put a big dent in your bumper."

"For Christ's sake! That's a brand new car!"

"Consider yourself lucky, as always," I say, stepping back from the table. "If she'd known it was yours, she would have hit it twice."

I am sitting on the bottom stair and this time I make it to one hundred. I have left behind an eerie silence on the main floor. When my tentative footfalls reach the third step, I hear my grandfather's voice.

"Can I tell you a story about dreams?" he says. His voice sounds the same as it did twenty years ago as it echoes inside my mind.

"Yes, Grandpa," I whisper, almost silently.

The stairs continue creaking.

"Well, come on up, sweetheart, and sit yourself down."

"I'm coming, Grandpa."

When I reach the top stair, his voice falls silent. His attic office is dark, except for traces of silvery light trickling in from the curtain-free gable window. The desk lamp with its rounded shade forms a silhouette against the window and for a second I think it is him. My hands feel their way through the darkness and find the leather chair. The leather is smooth and hard and cold to my touch. My fingers locate the lamp and turn it on.

The room is as I remember, though there is no pack of cigarettes on his desk, which is not surprising. Neither is there a book of matches tucked neatly under a corner of his desk blotter. The green rotary telephone is where it always was, and so is his pen and pencil holder—a mug with the words *Home Hardware* printed in red on its white ceramic surface. His wooden swivel chair is facing away from me, toward the window.

My mind is astir with thoughts and memories as I move slowly around his desk, my finger tracing an outline along its outer edge. I feel his presence in this room, his cologne and smoke still hanging like the scent of hay coils in the air, only fainter now.

I lower myself into his chair. And as I begin to cry, the stairs begin to creak.

I am standing beside the desk when my grandmother makes

it to the top stair. Her face appears noticeably flushed even in the lamp's modest glow. She's carrying a brown paper bag.

She pauses for a moment to catch her breath. When I take a step forward, she raises a palm to halt me, and then moves forward herself. "Are you crying, child?" she asks.

"A little."

"Declan?"

"No. Grandpa," I say, wiping my eyes.

She takes hold of the desk and uses its weight to support her own, lowering herself slowly into the brown leather chair, letting go before she's actually seated. The chair lets out a soft *whoosh* of air. She starts smoothing out the rumpled paper bag in her lap, as if she's petting a cat, watching me closely from behind her horn-rimmed glasses.

And I am frozen in time, ten years old instead of twenty-eight. Standing next to the desk. Fist clenched, holding a fifty-dollar bill. I could seat myself in my grandfather's chair and forget the whole thing about first moving back before moving forward, or charge downstairs and make the same mistake again. That would be easy. The echoes in Wharton are everywhere, after all. Of creaking stairs, and people's footfalls endlessly coming and going. And mistakes. Those cursed mistakes. The echoes in Wharton are everywhere.

I clench my fist tighter. Anxiety flutters inside my chest. But there is a surprising calm at my centre, a calm that knows I now have the courage to admit the truth—and with it the unspoken fact that most of my life has been a tragic lie. "I—" I stop suddenly. Even with the person I cared most about gone, the person whose trust I violated, the truth is still hard.

I have my grandmother's full attention. Her hands have stilled and are folded atop the bag in her lap. She's waiting, it seems, with bated breath.

"I owe you an apology," I blurt, still delaying what must be said.

"*For . . . ?*"

"Downstairs. I called Uncle Ron a—you know." My face flinches at the memory of me actually calling my uncle a son of a bitch, saying it in front of the family, and the worst part, in front of his young children.

"Well, I guess that would make me a bitch!" I notice what looks like a tiny, lopsided grin playing on her lips.

"I'm sorry. I didn't mean it like that when I said it."

"No one need ever apologize for telling the truth, child. And besides, it certainly would appear I've been quite a bitch over the years."

"No, Grandma," I say, and turn away, not unable to look at her, but instead wishing simply to pull my grandfather and his warmth closer to the beat of my unclenching heart. Giant snowflakes are swirling outside the gable window. I picture him on his ladder there, smiling his warm, wonderful smile, happily affixing lights to the gable's peak in the bitter cold.

"I want to tell you something . . . something that happened a long time ago." I glance briefly back at my grandmother.

"Oh?" she says.

"I stole fifty dollars from Grandpa," I confess, the words falling from my tongue like a sad refrain, and sounding pitifully trivial, doing no justice to the lifetime of anguish they caused. My fist opens, the ancient truth vanishing into air. But the burden remains on my chest. I blink and a tear trickles down my cheek.

"Fifty dollars? Nonsense."

"I did, and he knew," I say, my voice cracking on this, the hardest part of the truth. He *knew*. And all I needed was the courage to admit the truth to him so we could have gotten on with our lives; freely together and freely apart, as grandfather and granddaughter, and with it the closeness of mutual love and admiration that relationship naturally brings. The truth, when laid too long to rest and hidden deep within the folds of life, can be a terrible, insidious thing.

I continue staring out the window, trying desperately to glean a comforting piece of my grandfather's beautiful horizon. But the Christmas Eve air is dark and snowy, and with the added reflective discord caused by the glowing desk lamp, not a single shred is visible.

"No, child. None of his money ever went unaccounted."

"Why won't you believe me?"

"Because it's not true."

My head jerks around. My grandmother is sitting stoically in the brown leather chair, looking up at me as if I'd given her mundane news about the weather. For a moment I am overwhelmed with a feeling of great relief. Perhaps I only imagined that horrible day, here in his office. Perhaps it had been a dream. I can think of no instance, after all, when my grandmother has been wrong about anything. She is just that sort of lady.

But then I remember walking along Main Street and falling into Chester's Five & Dime and the look on Mrs. Chester's face when I couldn't find the fifty. That was certainly no dream.

"Yes, Grandma, it is true," I say, a tone of resignation in my voice. I turn back to the black, shapeless horizon.

After a long moment of silence, my grandmother says, "Do you know what's out there? Besides snow, of course!" She smiles. Her smile seems cold and awkward, yet it's oddly comforting.

I shrug, this time relieved by a fresh inquisition.

"You have no idea, do you? Did you ever wonder why each house on this side of the street faces north with the exception of ours?"

"I thought it was because of the driveway," I reply without too much thought. The fact is, I had never given it much thought. I knew my grandfather built this house shortly after he and my grandmother were married, and, eventually, built pretty much every house on this road, but why he made it slightly askew compared to the others was anybody's guess. That it was positioned to meet the driveway flush, which is long and winding and shaped like a partially formed *C*, had always seemed as likely a reason as any.

My grandmother lets out a muffled laugh. She is so out of practice, it could easily be mistaken as suppressing a cough, which a part of me suspects it might actually be.

At the same time, downstairs someone must have cranked up the record player's volume, because an instrumental version of "Away in the Manger" trickles up the staircase and into the room. It gives me a great sense of deliverance, as if Grandma's laughter combined with the music is a symbolic, collective sigh of all those in the house, signalling things are right with everyone again, that life will go on, that forgiveness has been granted and normalcy has returned. It is all anyone can hope for.

"Oh, child," she says, sitting up abruptly, her eyes sharp and wide and looking steadily at me, as though she just remembered something extremely important. "You teach English. Correct?"

"Grand—"

"Just answer me. Do you teach English?" Her voice is as focused as her eyes.

"Yes."

"Well, then, let me teach you something that *I've* been well schooled in." She slowly removes what looks like a folded newspaper from the brown paper bag in her lap and leans forward, placing it carefully in the centre of my grandfather's mahogany desk. "Not your typical Christmas present, but merry Christmas just the same," she says.

"Grandma, I don't need—"

"Hush, child," she interrupts again, her voice now low and harsh and much the way I remember from childhood. "You'd better sit down and prepare yourself for a long-overdue lesson."

"A lesson?" My own voice is quiet and still sounding foreign to me.

"Yes," she says. "A lesson in history."

The sun had risen above the horizon, its warm yellow rays turning the fine autumn snow into puddles of slush. The girl with the china doll face stood alone at the point farthest from the only swing set in the schoolyard of Wharton Elementary. She had a bandage on her forehead and felt embarrassed by this. As the toe of her tiny boot made a sad face in the slush, the girl with thin slits for eyes, along with her mother, approached. They stopped about

ten feet away, the mother eventually coaxing her daughter forward.

"I'm sorry," said the girl with thin slits for eyes. She reached inside the bag she carried and handed the girl with the china doll face an apple. Then she gave her a box of Crayola crayons before looking back at her mother, who urged her on with a hand gesture. Then the girl with thin slits for eyes offered the girl with the china doll face a tin of homemade chocolate chip cookies, a packet of colourful ribbons for her golden-blond hair, and some pink sunglasses for her crystal blue eyes. The arms of the girl with the china doll face were so full, it was amazing nothing fell to the wet ground.

"Can I be your friend?" continued the girl with thin slits for eyes.

As the girl with the china doll face nodded, the woman moved up beside her daughter. "Are you all right?" she asked.

Again the girl with the china doll face nodded.

The woman withdrew a bright red ribbon from the packet in the girl's arms. And as she went behind the girl with the china doll face and began gathering up her hair, she said, "You're such a pretty girl."

At that moment the girl with the china doll face glanced down and saw her sad face had disappeared in the slush.

"Do you remember Joan Compton?" my grandmother asks. "The girl whose eyes always seemed half closed?"

I have seated myself in Grandpa's swivel chair and lightly run a finger through the long bangs of my blond hair and along the imperceptible scar across my forehead.

"I see you remember." Grandma has settled back in the brown leather chair and looks relaxed again. "Go ahead," she says, glancing at the newspaper on the desk. "It's yours now. I should have given you that years ago but, alas, I've made a great many mistakes myself." She closes her eyes and draws a deep breath through her nose. Her face morphs into a melancholy cringe: the smoke, I know, and not the cologne.

I unfold the newspaper. It is a yellowed copy of *The Wharton Echo*. Published weekly since 1900, around the same time the Trammels arrived in Wharton, this copy is dated Friday, June 21, 1957—the day of my birth. It looks to be about thirty pages thick. The headline is a tragic one, but before I have a chance to read anything else or speak even a single word, Grandma says sombrely, "Turn to page twelve."

The paper is fragile, like tissue paper in my fingers. With the exception of the front page, handwriting in black ink that I recognize as my grandmother's neat script is cluttered tightly down each margin and column. There is so much of it that each page—combined with the paper's published, though somewhat faded print—appears mostly black.

After I stop flipping pages, she says with equally dry sombreness, "Top right corner, I believe."

I rotate the paper slightly so I can get a better view of the handwriting, which is slanted upward in the narrow margin. My eyes grow wide as I read what is written. With my heart beating wildly, I ask, "When did you write this?"

"Oh, I don't know, exactly. The day you were born. The day after. Or maybe when you were five years old. It really doesn't matter. What matters is that every manner of sin is present in big cities as well as small towns. People will be people, regardless. But the difference is, small towns like to talk. And when

Wharton talked, I listened—and wrote! Everyone talks about everyone else, and yet nobody believes they themselves are being talked about! It really is quite humorous when you think about it." She chuckles lightly to herself, and this time it *does* sound like a laugh.

I feel a shiver race down my spine. "Why did you write this?"

"Why did I write that? Isn't it obvious? If I hadn't, do you actually think Joan would have apologized for hurting you? Do you think Joan would have become your friend? Her mother made her. I'd called her the same day Joan tripped you in the schoolyard and demanded it . . . or else I'd tell the whole town the truth about what her husband had done. It made no difference that his indiscretion occurred years before. She was terrified I'd expose him publicly, even though probably most around town already knew."

"No, Grandma, *why* did you write this?"

"Why?" she says, looking past me, out the gable window. "Why?" she repeats somewhat peevishly, then looks back and fixes her gaze on mine. "Because I know how hard it is, growing up in a small town as an illegitimate child."

Instantly I feel the wind knocked from me, and that wind is now blustering me down a steep cliff. I can hardly breathe. We shared something in common, my grandmother and I. We shared a deep, common bond all these years and she never mentioned a single word of it, or a single word about a difficult childhood. Certainly mine wasn't overly difficult here in Wharton. Sure, there were incidents, but those incidents always led to quick apologies, eventual friendships, and, come to think of it, gifts. And now I knew why.

My eyes start feverishly skimming more handwriting on the page. Most names are familiar, like Peter Compton's—Joan's father—and some indiscretions just as chilling.

"You see, I know from experience how cruel children can be." Her head drops and she begins absently fiddling with a corner of the paper bag in her lap. "And I know how equally cruel adults can be."

Her face grows grim as she continues with the history lesson. Apparently her own mother, Helena Agnew, was only fifteen when she naively fell in love with a drifter who walked into the small farming town of Langford, Saskatchewan, almost as quickly as he walked out. With Helena's parents lacking the financial means, or a willing family member at a distant locale to receive her, she stayed in Langford and had her baby, Claire. After years of torment and ridicule, with Claire suffering both verbal abuse from adults and physical abuse at the hands of children, Helena could watch no more. Having earned some money, she took eight-year-old Claire and left for Fleshley, the town just south of Wharton, to stay with a distant cousin. They were introduced to the new community as sisters. It was in Fleshley that Claire's life finally took a dramatic turn for the better, her illegitimacy long lost but in her mind never forgotten.

Though the desk lamp's glow is dim, I now see my grandmother in a new light. She is no longer the cold, uncaring second mother of my childhood, but a woman whose tortured inner child has kept those who loved her from getting close. That thought alone is heartbreaking enough; in some ways, it makes my own pain seem insignificant.

I motion with the newspaper, raising it slightly above the

desk. "You did this for me?" I ask, my words barely audible, trying to imagine the unspeakable horrors my grandmother faced in Langford, and the life-altering traumas she most certainly suffered.

"Don't be silly, child," she replies, a trace of that good old Grandma harshness returning to her voice. It's a tone I now understand and hold no bitterness toward. "I did it for him."

"Him?"

"James. Your grandfather."

The mere mention of his name reminds me of why we're here, what I did, and I feel my eyes welling with emotion. I raise the newspaper farther so she can't see my face.

"When he refused to send your mother away to my relatives in Saskatchewan, I realized then it would break his heart if you ever left Wharton. I knew I had to protect your childhood so there would be no reason for you to leave." She sighs. "So, on the day you were born, I went uptown and bought that day's copy of *The Wharton Echo* for you. I figured it would be my little gift of posterity—"

"But Mom told me you stayed home. To listen for Diefenbaker's swearing-in on the radio," I say impulsively, sounding like a little girl.

Laughter bursts through the newspaper between us and momentarily drowns out "Silent Night," which has replaced "Away in the Manger" and, for me, has begun weaving a tapestry of inner-reflection inside the room.

"Oh, child. Your mother had no idea what I was doing the day you were born. I made it clear I disapproved, but Diefenbaker?"

"John Diefenbaker. The Conservative."

"Given my history, is it any surprise I'm a Liberal? And given your mother's ability to embellish, is it any surprise she is *not?*" My grandmother laughs again, this time in a more reserved fashion.

"No," I say. "I guess not."

"Now, where was I? Oh, yes. It was then, after I'd bought the newspaper, that something peculiar happened. I was on Main Street and someone—I forget who—came up to me and told me one of the most despicable tales I'd ever heard about a resident in town. After we parted company, and so I wouldn't forget, I jotted it down in the margin of the paper. Then somebody else approached me, who confided another tale. By the time I'd arrived home, I had started amassing quite a collection of 'dirt' in the newspaper. And so I continued, making a point to stroll Main Street whenever I could. Every time I heard something— a rumour, a fact—it didn't matter, in the newspaper it went. The day you left Wharton was the day I stopped writing . . ." Her voice trails off.

My arms are starting to tire, holding up the newspaper, so I lean forward and rest my elbows on the desk. I have thoroughly read each notation on the two pages before me, and though a few indiscretions could be considered truly criminal, the majority are minor, unearthing an unethical character in some while revealing immorality in others. I doubt city folk would care about having such things exposed to their general public, but in a small town appearances are everything, and keeping things hushed is of supreme importance; I can understand the leverage my grandmother had over Wharton and, in essence, the control over my childhood, ensuring it would be a reasonably happy one here.

"Turn to page six, child, near the bottom," she instructs once more, her voice again sombre.

I flip three pages and this is what I see: *Mary Trammel stole fifty dollars from James Trammel (June 17, 1967).*

I stare at the words in disbelief while remaining hidden behind the newspaper. "You knew," I say.

"I knew. And you should be ashamed of yourself."

Before I have a chance to explain myself, that indeed I am ashamed and have been for over eighteen years, that I loved my grandfather dearly, that I would have done anything for him, that I'm a weak person and not a bad one, she tells me to turn to page four, middle column around centre.

There is a disagreeable heaviness tugging at the pit of my stomach as my now shaking hand fumbles with another page. Her script is even smaller here, so I twist the paper to gain illumination from the desk lamp. The angle exposes my grandmother, who is staring placidly in my direction as I read what is written: *Claire Trammel stole fifty dollars from Mary Trammel (June 20, 1967).*

"But—" I can hardly think straight. "Did . . . did he know what I'd done?"

She shakes her head. "No. I returned the money to his cash box."

Suddenly I feel like I'm standing inside a skyscraper and the building has just been razed. Every lie I told, every excuse I made to avoid my grandfather, all stemming from my one transgression and my failure to confront it, are the walls, and they are crashing down on me, obliterating me, leaving my soul in a heap of ruins from which I may never recover. And all because they were constructed for a reason that never existed. *He didn't know!*

When I am finally able to see through my tears, Grandma is standing beside the desk, her arms held out to me. I drop the newspaper and for the first time in my life I fall into her embrace.

"I'm so sorry, Grandma," I say, my chest heaving on every word as I cling to her. "Please believe me. It was a terrible mistake."

"I know, child." Her hands are warm and they tenderly stroke my back. "You can't be too hard on yourself. You were very young when it happened."

"But I grew up to understand what I did and still did nothing."

"It's horrible, the inexplicable things we do to the ones we love. What you did to your grandfather was bad. But . . ." She pauses, pulls back, and hands me a tissue. "What I did to you was far worse."

She looks away, toward the gable window, and I am instantly stunned. *The inexplicable things we do to the ones we love*, she said, and *What I did to you was far worse*. Which would mean—

She quickly looks back and says, "One day he asked if I'd taken fifty dollars from his cash box. Immediately I remembered that look on your face a couple days earlier when I came into his office, not to mention that smell of burning matches—"

"One match," I say, choking out the words.

She flashes me a look of disdain, as if this fact is profoundly irrelevant, which I know it is. She resumes: "So I knew you had been up to something. I searched your room, located the money in your purse, and stole it back. I returned it to his cash box and told him I'd found it under his desk."

I am still crying. "Can you hug me again?" I ask. She smiles, and her smile is as warm as I remember my grandfather's being. It makes me wonder how she could have kept it so well hidden throughout my childhood. She takes me in her arms.

After several minutes of mutual silence as we hold one another, we again seat ourselves in our respective chairs, she in the brown leather, me in the wooden swivel. The newspaper is splayed open on the desk, and once more we face each other. "Silent Night" has been replaced by "God Rest Ye Merry Gentlemen," which rambles like a joyous anthem inside the room. Children's voices can now be heard, a little raucous, and close, probably originating from the second floor.

"You see, child, you never stole anything from him. It was *I* who did the stealing. As the days, weeks, and months passed, I witnessed a terrible separation growing between you two. Yet at the same time—" She stops and drops her gaze. I can see whatever it is she's about to say is very difficult. "I felt *us* growing closer," she continues. "So, selfishly, I said nothing. Do you understand? *I* said nothing. By not confronting you immediately and getting it out in the open, by letting it foolishly linger, in effect, I stole his granddaughter from him."

"No," I say, feeling genuinely sorry for her.

"Yes, I'm afraid so. It was never my intention, but my selfishness harmed both you and your grandfather. Please forgive me."

Pity has replaced my tears. "There's nothing to forgive," I say. "It was my fault."

"No."

"Yes."

She lifts her gaze and stares tiredly at me. "Let's not argue."

After a few moments, she abruptly sits up again. This time it's with even more energy than earlier and it does no justice to her seventy-one years. "Do something for me, child. If not for me, for your grandfather. Make things right."

"Right? What are you talking about?"

"Take that job at Wharton High. Move back." She has shifted so far forward in the brown leather chair that her behind must be hanging from its edge, though I can't see that for the desk.

"There's no guarantee I would get the job, even if I applied."

"Ah," she quickly replies, arching her eyebrows wickedly and raising a finger high in the air while glancing down at *The Wharton Echo*. "Millie Brown does the hiring. I think she can be . . . *persuaded.*" My grandmother is beaming now, and it really is a wonderful smile.

"Grandma! I'm no longer a child!"

Just then the phone rings, sounding tinnier than I remember, and I jump. On the second ring I snatch it up and hand it to my grandmother, relieved by the interruption and her intimation of skulduggery—a practice, I suspect, at which she has become quite proficient.

"Hello," she says, then, seconds later, covers the receiver and lowers it into her lap. Smiling, she asks, "Do you have a beau you're not telling us about?"

A beau? My face scrunches in confusion.

"Well, there's a handsome gentleman on the phone asking to speak with Mary Trammel."

"How do you know he's handsome?" I ask playfully.

"I'm good with voices," she says. "Like yours. When you were a baby and you first started speaking, I knew you'd turn into a beautiful woman one day."

I roll my eyes and shake my head. She continues smiling. I take the phone from her. "Hello," I say. "Yes . . . Yes . . . That's okay . . . Well, that's something . . . I understand . . . Thanks for calling . . . Merry Christmas."

I quietly hang up the phone and stare blankly at my grandmother. Then I break out in hysterical laughter. I am laughing so hard, tears start spouting from my eyes, and the most joyful pain begins tightening around my abdomen. It is a pain reminiscent of the giggling fits I had with friends when I was a child. Ironically, it reminds me most of one I had with Joan Compton about a year after she tripped me, and I find myself missing her, missing my childhood, and yes, missing Wharton most of all.

I grab a pen from the Home Hardware mug on the desk. I spot an available space on the opened pages of *The Wharton Echo* and somehow manage to steady my hand enough to write. When I finish, I turn the paper toward my grandmother, who has gotten to her feet, a look of concern streaked across her face.

She leans awkwardly over the desk, adjusts her glasses, and reads what I have written: *Mary Ellen Trammel burned her own house down (unintentionally, it should be noted!) by way of a faulty coffeemaker (Dec. 24, 1985).*

"My God!" Grandma shrieks, looking at me in complete shock.

"Yes. It's true," I say, nodding eagerly and still laughing in maniacal fashion. "That would explain the busy signal Mom got when she called my place this morning!"

"Phone out of service?"

"Either that or the fire melted it off the hook!" I reply, the absurdity of my comment sinking in and getting me laughing even harder. "And I didn't even have house insurance!" I add, buckling at the waist, the pain is so gloriously bad.

"Child!"

"Nope."

"Did you have a mortgage?"

I catch myself and with great effort turn my laughter into low, humming moans. "Yeah," I admit, breathless, the word vaulting itself into the rafters at such a high pitch one would think I'd sucked helium from a thousand balloons. Then I squeal, "Two of them! A first and a second! Isn't it wonderful?" and break into hysterics again.

My grandmother's hands cover her forehead, grief blankets her face. "Was anything saved?"

"Strangely enough, just the TV, which was still playing when they got the fire out!" I'm laughing so hard now, the convulsions pull me forward. The swivel chair slides out from under me, and my rear thumps on the floor. The shock of the fall straightens me up. I peer over the desk and it arouses in me a sober realization. *And maybe me,* I think, but I don't say this.

My grandmother falls back in the brown leather chair, exasperated, and lets out a quivering gasp.

A minute later, once we've had time to catch our breaths and briefly contemplate our previous admissions and our own personal admonitions, I get up off the floor, fold the newspaper, and hug it tightly to my chest. "Thank you so much, Grandma," I say, and as I lower myself into the swivel chair, I hear the creaking stairs echo inside the room.

Seconds later, Declan's head appears above the top step. He walks gingerly into the room, carefully carrying a piece of pie on a plate, stopping next to me. "Sorry for kicking you lots," he says through pouting lips.

His nose is still running, so I produce a clean tissue and wipe it dry. "That's okay," I reply, flexing my leg and smiling. "See, it still works."

Declan doesn't smile. He places the plate on the desk in front of me. "Daddy says you should have some punkle pie."

I glance at my grandmother, who had been looking more perplexed than I, but now seems to be struggling to restrain a laugh. I hold back my own laughter.

"That's a fine piece of pumpkin pie," I tell little Declan. Then to my grandmother, "Anything in here about Uncle Ron I should know about?" I ask, setting the newspaper on the desk. Declan's offering strums a familiar chord, reminding me of Joan Compton and several others whose verbal and physical assaults on me led to their bestowal of gifts.

We both smile and she shakes her head.

"I guess I should apologize to him," I suggest, recalling what I said to Uncle Ron just a half-hour earlier at the dinner table, not to mention the dent in his bumper.

"Why? You spoke the truth. And besides, he had it coming," she points out.

"Well, I should at least compliment him on the wonderful job he did with the Christmas decorations."

"The tree? *I* decorated the tree, child."

"No. Outside. The lights and that new wreath—"

"Huh! That wasn't Ron's work. The wreath was a gift from Dr. Glover in memory of your grandfather and he hung it himself, in addition to the lights."

"Dr. Glover?" I say, eyes wide. "He climbed up Grandpa's forty-foot ladder? Why, he must be—"

"Old!" my grandmother cries, and we laugh.

Declan has moved over to the gable window. His nose pressed against the glass, he asks, "Where's Grandpa?"

My grandmother and I look at each other, the levity instantly drained from our faces. I swivel around and pull Declan into my lap. He settles back and nestles his head in my neck directly beneath my chin.

Where's Grandpa? Declan asked. I could lie to him, tell him he'll be home shortly and hope he'll eventually lose his grandfather's memory. Or I could tell him the truth. I could tell him about a little girl who, for many years, stood at the bottom of a ladder that was so tall she thought it went on forever. And from the bottom of that ladder she watched a dear man who loved the family of his past and present with all his heart. And when she watched him at the top of that ladder, high in the clouds and above all others, she believed he was in heaven, the place he is now, and most certainly the place he will always be.

"Sweetie," I say, feeling Declan's perfect childhood innocence course through my body while trying to glimpse the horizon but seeing only my cousin's beautiful little reflection in the gable window, "let me tell you a story . . ."

Mary Trammel ended up telling Declan many stories. And while she did, her grandmother, Claire, sat and listened quietly. It was an education as much for her as it was for Declan. She had heard the stories before but, like most things, time had stolen some of the finer details.

After finishing, Mary turned to her grandmother and asked if the ladder was still kept beneath the backyard deck and where the replacement Christmas bulbs could be found. Then Mary, holding little Declan's hand, left the attic office.

Now, fifteen minutes later, the house is deathly quiet. Claire sits and stares at her reflection in the gable window. *Old woman,* she thinks, *you don't deserve to be happy.* And perhaps she isn't. It is such a fleeting emotion, after all, and really just a state of mind. But her mind is saying she is because she can't stop smiling. She sees it in the window. No matter how hard she tries, she can't wipe the happiness away. She reaches behind her and pulls the chain on the desk lamp. Instantly the room is draped in darkness, her smile vanishing from the window. In fact her whole image disappears. But inside, the happiness remains. She can feel it, like a child at Christmas, like her grandchildren on Christmas morning.

Outside, beyond the window, things are as they should be: snow falling, and a warm Christmas chill clamping down on Wharton. But farther out, there is more. She never did get around to telling her granddaughter why her husband built his house facing northwest. Perhaps that, too, is as it should be. Nor why, conversely, the back of his house faces southeast. That southeast is where Toronto lies—in many ways a foreign land, yet it was as real to him as Wharton. That most of his family left for there, dreaming of a prosperous future, and from his seat at the dining table downstairs he felt closer to them and, in his own way, could watch over their safety and happiness.

Claire hears the soft murmur of voices and she steps up to the window. Below, trudging through the deep snow, she sees Mary, bundled up and carrying one end of the ladder. Declan follows in her footsteps. Then Carol, Mary's mother, appears, holding the ladder at its centre. Then, following, is Ron. Carrying the ladder, all three are working together as a family on Christmas Eve. They move parallel and away from the house, in the direction of north-west. They could be aboard a train, Mary its conductor, heading off toward the glistening rails of Lake Huron and beyond. Claire hopes they are simply making a wide berth around the parked cars in the driveway before turning back.

Claire decides she will tell her granddaughter why the house faces northwest. If she remembers. If Mary comes back.

SNOWFLAKE

Thomas Mullen has never seen them so big, not in his twelve years on God's green earth, not ever. Well, he knows there is a chance he has, maybe sometime in his first few years, but after the age of five, no, his memory is certain—nothing like this. He would remember.

Kneeling on his bed in front of the window, he watches thick snow pour like milk from the sky, the drops so big, Thomas is giddy with joy just watching them. So delightfully big, in fact, they seem more like silver dollars, spreading their riches across the land.

"*Awe*-some," Thomas whispers.

He presses face to glass and looks up. Dozens of icicles hang from the fringe of a frozen eave: an army of icy warriors, standing at attention with their sharp-tipped sabres, ready to pounce on any unwelcome invader.

In the deepening darkness, the streetlights finally come to life. The milk turns to buttery cream; the icy warriors sparkle like wondrous diamonds. Across the way, past the billows of sleeping white, a red and yellow arc suddenly ignites and flares out through the snowy air—from Mrs. Meriweather's house, Thomas thinks. Then two houses down, blue and green fire up at Mr. Jones's, if he's not mistaken. At another house—the Hamptons'?—gold and more red. Then another house, and another, until there's an inferno of colour, a symphony of sights, blasting out, meagre sparks turned to raging flame.

Then a sound. Music. Barely discernible at first, but definitely music. The window has started to fog with Thomas's breath. He uses an arm and wipes the chilled pane clean. A group of adults, adorned in full-length coats, prim hats, and warm gloves, stand before an open door, down the road a ways. Great puffs of smoke burst forth from their mouths. Yellow light burns inside the house, transforming the rectangle of the open doorway into a brilliant fireplace, its veranda a warm hearth. And yes, they sing into the fire . . .

"*Peace on earth, and mercy mild, God and sinners reconciled, joyful all ye nations rise, join the triumph of the skies . . .*"

Thomas nods. The triumph of the skies. The triumph of the skies.

A magical time to be alive.

December twenty-fourth, 1985.

Christmas, finally arrived.

An exhaled breath and the front screen door clicks shut. A heavy thump, thump, thump.

"God-*damn*," a voice cries out, each syllable floating up to Thomas's room. The voice is Papa's—his grandfather, but to Thomas and his siblings, always Papa.

The screen door again. Inhaling, then exhaling. Tired. Old. Seconds later, inhaling, exhaling, thump, thump, thump . . . "God-bloody-*damn!*"

Thomas leaves the window.

Downstairs, Papa is huffing, his wizened face pale, strained, his ramshackle hair powder-grey and sticking up at odd, pointed angles. He sags into the doorframe between the front hall and kitchen, a pond becoming a lake beneath his big, floppy boats for galoshes.

"What say you?" Papa asks, acknowledging Thomas on the bottom stair. The boy shrugs.

Then, in as big a whoosh as could be expected of an old man, the screen door inhales, and he is gone.

That morning, while most still slept beneath furrowed blankets, snug on soft mattresses set safely within warm homes, Thomas, along with his younger brother and sister, his mother, and with his father, Harold, behind the wheel, sped from the city. Dawn was just breaking. As the sun crept like a spider crafting its web, sending out spindles of golden light across the horizon, the landscape gradually changed. Congested cement and steel became spacious clapboard and eventually vast, open fields of browns, yellows, and greens and contented cows and frolicking horses, their breath chill in the morning air. There was no snow.

Several hours later, as the gates to his grandfather's town hove into sight, their car—driven glittering new off the lot less than a month earlier—sputtered, let out a great cough and a shock of black smoke, then died.

At noon, with the car towed to the local garage, the troop of five finally made it to Grandfather's house. The old man kissed his daughter, gave a firm, appreciative handshake to his son-in-law, and bathed in the love from his adoring grandchildren.

Above the din of giggles and laughter and pure joy, Harold, referring to the sole thorn that had pricked their journey, said, "They don't make them like they used to."

The old man froze in the process of closing the door. "I . . . I think I see one," he murmured.

The screen door inhales and the old man is back, his black coat speckled white. The screen door sighs. Thump. Thump. Thump. And the thumping strays into the kitchen. A soft, puckered *pop*. Thomas stretches out from the banister to get a better view.

"God—" the old man cries, but catches himself, conscious of his grandson. He shuts the freezer door and deflates against the doorframe. His coat is a glistening jet-black now, his hands stuffed deep inside its pockets. His boats list in the lake that is fast becoming an ocean.

"Papa, are you all right?" The boy steps down from the bottom stair.

"Just old, Tiger." To the old man, Thomas is always Tiger, for no reason other than nicknames are terms of endearment. Though there are certain ferocious connotations inherent in the moniker and Thomas is anything but, being slow of foot, slight of build, and shy of the contemptuous pride shown by most who succeed in sport, "Tiger" is never spoken with even the slightest of ironical intents. The old man simply loves the boy.

"You're not old."

"Wore out, then."

"Tired."

"Okay, tired." He puts the boy's mind at ease with a porcelain smile, then looks outside through the screen door, which is now garnering some much-needed rest. After a few moments, he says, "Tiger, I need your help. But first, come with me."

Swept along on the gentle stream of his grandfather's wake, Thomas sails close to the old man during their descent to the cellar. It is dark and dank, smells of mildew, and the solitary bulb at the bottom of the stairs throws little light to diminish the gloom.

Over in the far corner near a boarded-up window, the old man carefully shucks a mountainous tarpaulin that peaks near seven feet at its centre. The plastic flutters free from the mountaintop, and a gigantic hoard of . . . of . . . *things* remains. There are kitchen appliances, pans, power tools, gardening tools, anything and everything imaginable. There is even a small bathroom vanity sticking out from a corner of the massive pile. And there are toys, too. So many toys, Thomas's eyes can't keep track of them all.

The old man dips a palm into the detrital stew and scoops out a pair of needle-nose pliers, no longer very pointy, with one prong missing. He hands it to Thomas. Then he removes a toaster minus a cord, a pot minus a handle. He gives these to Thomas. He reaches in again and this time withdraws a doll without limbs.

"This I know was your mother's," the old man says, a trace of a smile forming at the thought of his daughter in youth. He hands the doll to Thomas, whose own intact arms are now quite full.

The old man vanishes behind the shrinking mountain and emerges holding a perfectly fine-looking jewelry box. "And this, your grandma's, I think."

"I don't understand," Thomas says.

"Look. *Look!*"

Thomas glances down, the dim lighting making it difficult

for him to clearly comprehend the missing cord and handle. The missing limbs and broken pliers are obvious, though.

"Don't you see? Nothing, and I mean *nothing*, lasts forever," the old man says, while unhooking the latch of the jewelry box. He lifts the lid. Inside, the box appears as functional as its outside appears pristine. "And some things that could and should last longer, oftentimes don't." The old man chuckles, and the boy takes in the sweet warmth of his peppermint breath. "Probably the colour of this—" he raises the lemon-yellow jewelry box "—fell out of your grandma's fancy." He sets it atop the rising hill in Thomas's arms. "It happens to everyone at one time or another. It's human nature. You certainly can't fault your grandma for that. She was such a lovely, lovely lady and, oh, how she loved *you* . . ." The old man's voice drifts off into a darkness that, to him, glows like radiant light sent from heaven.

Thomas's grandmother passed away when he was five. "I wish I could remember her."

"Funny of you to say," replies the old man, "since Christmas *is* a time for wishing." He pauses for five seconds, ten, then brushes past Thomas and dissolves into the blackness at the opposite end of the cellar. While passing, he clips Thomas's arm, and the boy's precarious hill comes crashing down.

When the clatter dies, a warm voice rides out of nowhere along a cold blue steel rail, heading straight for Thomas. "All those who believe in Santa Claus . . . climb aboard."

Across the street, inside the house whose exterior burns red and yellow, a bleak grey renders the warm air cold. The well-stoked fire in the main floor sitting room does little to remedy the chill. Dr. Glover, a town physician for fifty-three years, stands next to John Meriweather in the second-floor hallway.

Downstairs in the kitchen, John's wife, Libby, keeps their two young daughters busy, first making popcorn streamers, and now on the Christmas cookie production line. The buttery scent of shortbread fills the house and collides with the swelling moans that roam through the bedroom door beside the two huddling men.

Dr. Glover whispers, "I'm sorry, John. There is nothing more I can do."

The moans ebb and resolve themselves into a quiet whimper: "Frederick . . ."

The two men listen.

"Frederick, Frederick, *Frederick* . . ."

Then the moaning begins again.

"She's been like this all day—moaning for a spell, then calling for Dad; moaning, then calling for Dad," says John.

"Your father's death last year was hard on her. I've never seen anyone take a loss so hard."

John thinks about this for a moment. "She loved him."

Dr. Glover gives the other's shoulder a comforting squeeze. "Prepare your family for the worst, son. I'll have the vicar say a prayer at Mass tonight."

"Thank you, sir."

The doctor turns, black bag in hand, and totters off down the wanly lighted hallway. The strip wood flooring creaks beneath his feet. John watches him leave. When the man nears the top of the stairs at the end of the hall, he sways even more unsteadily, his girth wide, shoulders narrow, and bald crown wreathed in a fringe of white hair. For an instant John imagines the doctor at the end of a very long lane in a bowling alley and, thinking of the constant sadness that must strike a man during a long medical career, he wonders, *What keeps the pin from falling?*

The heavy rain of white continues and deepens the ocean of snow. Drifts and banks, like islands, quiver and rise up out of the great sea, one after another after another. The cement sidewalks and roads, the yellowy-green lawns and boulevards that breathed the clear, crisp air less than a half-day past, are now forgotten relics beneath the glorious tides. Occasionally a passing car reminds us of what used to be, splashing aside a tiny trickle of the flood in two long, slippery lines, revealing the ocean's chalky grey floor, telling us it isn't just a memory, a dream; it was real— is real, still alive.

Knee-deep in this ocean, Cyrus Sims, thirteen, clambers up the tallest of those islands. Like a general, he surveys the rolling battlefield. To the rear, two privates make a similar ascent.

In the silence of dusk, they hear a door close, followed by the slow crunch of snow beneath heavy footsteps. The soldiers retreat to peer over the island's crest. When they sight the enemy through the clouded air, they send forth a volley of three round, snowy bombs that shine silver in the streetlights. The first bomb lands wide of the mark, crashing into metal. The second and third find their target, one detonating against a hand, the other exploding off a face like fireworks.

Dr. Glover is stunned and momentarily blinded. He rocks

back on his heels, snatches at his car door. His black bag plummets into the white ocean. He wipes the icy debris from his eyes. "You!" he shouts, shaking a fist in the air. "You—you—" one last, stern shake "—kids!"

Hunched behind the island, the confederates cover their mouths and giggle. When an engine starts, General Sims takes a peek. "Fat old pig going . . . going . . . *gone!*" he says. "Oink, oink!"

And the trio break out in hysterical laughter, grabbing at their bellies in joyful agony.

Like a newly kindled fire, the flame of light begins with a flicker, then abruptly erupts in a blast of coal-hot white. Thomas partially shields his eyes, it's so bright, and then steps over the ruins of another time—a doll, a toaster—drawn toward the flame.

In the cellar's remote, northernmost corner, beyond the oil furnace and water heater, the old man holds the top of an enormous, snow-white chest freezer open. Plumes of smoke swirl from its frigid interior. A chaise lounge rests nearby.

"Well?" says the old man, gesturing with his head toward the battered lounger, its red fabric torn in spots and badly worn in others. In the radiant northern light, it looks oddly reminiscent of a sleigh. "You climbing aboard?"

Thomas's mouth begins to open, but he's denied the chance to speak.

"I know it's hard to believe in *him*," continues the old man. He bends and his upper body vanishes, devoured by the freezer's icy north. His voice comes out muffled now, as if spoken from a distant land. "With hundreds of Santas at hundreds of malls, who do they think they're fooling?" The old man's head pops up and he looks at Thomas. "You weren't fooled, were you, Tiger?" Then he immediately drops down and is devoured again.

"Naw, I figured that out when I was ten."

Crisp clinking sounds emanate from within the freezer, as if a king's ransom in gold bars is being stacked, slowly, methodically.

"Ten, eh? I think I became a nonbeliever around that age, too," the muffled voice replies, "but I don't rightly remember." His head pops up once more, wrinkled cheeks rosy, a childlike twinkle in his ancient eyes. "Although . . ."

Moving with the swiftness of a man half his age, the old man dives in yet again. The clinking sounds quicken.

"Al*though?*" the boy prompts, curiosity moving him closer. A long arm flies up and out of the freezer and gently guides Thomas to the side until his legs contact the lounger. "Although *what*, Papa?"

The clinking sounds end, replaced by fiery groans from the furnace. The old man straightens, empty-handed. "*Although*," he says, "you do remember what I just said, don't you? Of course you do. Nothing lasts forever. Nothing. Even states of disbelief must end. I can still remember the very instant when this old man here, your old, old Papa—" he pauses, smiles, and says in a whisper "—became a believer again."

Thomas climbs aboard.

It happened on Thomas's mother's third birthday, the old man explains. But before he explains how and why and what and where and every detail a precocious twelve-year-old boy would want to know, he does something else: he pulls two miniature candy canes from his pocket, hands one to the boy, and asks him to eat, which he happily does.

The old man eats the other and, just finished, he says, "Time for that Christmas wish, Tiger."

With Thomas stretched out on the lounger, head elevated, his grandfather works quickly. He dips in and out of the freezer that still burns white, still blows smoke from its great mouth. He seats himself on the edge of the lounger. He opens a sterling silver pillbox. The number 77 is taped to its top. He holds up a pea-sized object, solid as a pearl and pure white, and studies it for a split second in the light.

"Don't chew this," he says.

Thomas's eyes are wide in anticipation and he nods several times.

"Now, close your eyes and open up."

The old man draws a deep breath, and then carefully places the snowflake on Thomas's tongue.

"So *cool* . . ."

"Shhhh, mouth closed," says the old man. "And keep those eyes closed, Tiger; keep watching."

Inside his mind, Thomas sees a Christmas tree so utterly huge it towers over him. A carnival of lights dances around its branches, like playful fireflies, a carousel of reds and yellows, greens and blues. And from those branches a waterfall of tinsel pours, each long, flowing drop shimmering in the tree's starlight. Ornaments, big and small, float like delicious gumdrops in a candy store, so real Thomas reaches out for one in the chilly cellar air.

The old man whispers, "You're there. You're seeing."

Thomas nods and lowers his arm. His eyes remain closed.

He moves slowly around the tree. He can feel his footfalls trembling gently through his limbs, the soft carpet spider-tickling his feet. Hey, wait! The beige carpet. The lilac wallpaper. The tiled fireplace. Papa's living room! He can see it, sense it, even from down here in the bowels of the house.

Excited, he takes an intense suck on the melting snowflake. It tastes like nothing more than cold, fresh water, but oh, what flavour for the senses!

A flame of dazzling orange and yellow burns in the fireplace. Thomas feels its pull.

A voice rings out. "No you don't, sweetie," it says, and he is swept off his feet from behind. He is spun around and quickly swallowed in an embrace. "That fireplace is no place for little boys," says the voice.

"It's Grandma, Papa! I see Grandma!" Thomas shrieks, and his eyes pop open. He knows it was her because his grandfather has pictures of her scattered about the house, only in his mind she wasn't a static image; she was moving, talking, very much alive.

"Ha-ha!" the old man cries, smacking his leg with his hand. He still sits at the edge of the lounger, but now leans raptly forward. "Eyes closed, Tiger. Eyes closed."

Thomas closes his eyes again and finds he is looking directly into the eyes of his grandmother. She gives him a kiss on his forehead and Thomas can feel the softness of her lips, the warmth and tenderness of her touch.

"Now, don't you be giving your Nana a scare like that again, okay Tiger?" she says, her words blowing inside Thomas's mind like a soothing summer breeze.

"I used to call her Nana," says Thomas, keeping his eyes closed. "And she called me Tiger, just like you, Papa."

"Ha-ha! I forgot about that, but you're right, you're right."

"Her voice is so . . . whispery."

"Yes."

"Her hair's up in a bun."

"That's right. That's right. Always in a bun."

"And . . . wait . . . there *you* are, Papa, just walking into the room . . ."

"Yes. Yes. Naturally I was there, too."

"Holy cow!"

"What? What is it, Tiger?" The old man leans farther forward, so far his upper body is almost horizontal, the side of his face just inches from his grandson's.

"Your hair. It's different."

"Black. It used to be black."

"I see a little black, but no, it's . . . it's . . ."

"It's what, Tiger, *what?*" the old man screeches.

"Holy cow. It's neatly combed."

"Huh?"

"I've never seen it look so good!"

The old man sits up abruptly and gives his hair a couple of grooming pats, out of sight of his grandson, whose eyes stay shut.

"And, I . . . I smell something. I can taste it at the back of my throat. It's like . . . like . . ."

"Lavender! Ha-ha!" The old man smacks his leg again, his hair already forgotten. "Your grandma always smelled of lavender—lavender scented shampoo, perfume, hand cream, she used them all. Ha-ha!"

Not realizing his bottom has been slowly inching away from Thomas with each animated movement, he smacks his leg again and this time slips off the lounger, his rear thumping against the hard cellar floor.

Startled, Thomas's eyes open. And, like his grandmother, the snowflake has melted away.

Thomas helps his grandfather to his feet, but before the two go back upstairs, the old man tells the boy a remarkable tale.

He starts by reminding Thomas that, though nothing lasts forever, what's in here (he taps the side of his head with a finger) comes as close to forever as any of us will get. What we witness during our lives, every last detail, is etched inside our minds by the lenses of our eyes. Our minds, like granite film, permanently record every sight and sound, taste and touch. The problem is remembering those experiences, those memories, while we're still here. That's the greatest challenge.

"And as you age, it gets even harder, not to mention those blurred experiences from early childhood, regardless of how old you are," says the old man. "Tiger, you just savoured a tiny fragment of what you witnessed, experienced, on Christmas Day, 1977—with a little help, of course, from a snowflake! Caught that one Christmas Eve, 1977, when you were four."

Thomas listens intently, eyes wide, occasionally nodding, occasionally saying "uh-huh" or "wow." On this bit of news he says, "*Wow . . .*"

The two of them stand in front of the hulking chest freezer, its vast mouth still bellowing out great swells of icy smoke.

When his daughter was born on December 11, 1946, he was

ecstatic. In addition to a beautiful wife, he now had a beautiful baby girl. He wanted to do something special, to mark the moment. So, almost two weeks later on Christmas Eve, while standing on his porch watching the snow fall, and still feeling about as good as any man could feel, it occurred to him: catch a snowflake! Catch a snowflake and keep a piece of this wonderful time forever.

"Finally caught one on maybe my tenth try. The little critters are tough to catch!" he confides, laughing, the twinkle returning to his eyes.

Years passed. The tiny snowflake sat neatly tucked away in a pillbox, forgotten. One day, on his daughter's third birthday, Thomas's grandmother happened upon it and asked what *this* was doing at the back of her kitchen freezer. He told her and she let out a shriek of laughter. When she opened the metal box for him, he realized how silly he must have sounded. The snowflake now looked like a pill, solid as an Aspirin.

"I took to the basement with it, quite perplexed, thinking maybe your grandma was playing a trick on me. Cringing, not knowing what to make of it, I closed my eyes and touched it to my tongue and *bam!* An image of your mother as an infant passed before me. I licked it again and the same thing happened. I put it in my mouth and, for a couple of incredible minutes, I relived a few moments of Christmas Day, 1946, exactly as I experienced it three years earlier. I was actually there again!"

Thomas is in awe. He stares into the chest freezer while his grandfather speaks. On the right are an assortment of meats— veal cutlets, sirloin steaks, pork chops—and dozens of ice blocks, the size of gold bars, all neatly stacked together. On the left, seven sterling silver pillboxes, one labelled *55*, two labelled *83*, and four *84*.

After that wonderful day he tried everything, catching snowflakes in each of the coldest months, even during late snowfalls in March, keeping them frozen for years. And he learned something: snowflakes grow, getting larger the longer they stay frozen.

The old man sees Thomas staring at the pillboxes. He reaches in and retrieves the one marked *55*. He opens it and shows his grandson a snowflake the size of a grape. The boy's eyes nearly fall from his head.

"These are my last remaining snowflakes. This one, I caught in 1955." The old man closes the pillbox and quickly returns it to the company of its icy comrades. "Believe it or not, a few years ago I had over a hundred snowflakes growing in here. I was a snowflake farmer, a regular snowflake connoisseur! That one there?" He pretends to pick at something between his teeth with a finger. "A bit overdone, I'd say. That one? Needed a touch more salt." He releases a chuckle.

"But whenever I found myself missing your grandmother, I would come here, lie down on my sleigh, and fly back to see her." The old man smiles. "From a hundred snowflakes to seven. Guess you could say I missed her a lot. It's sad, but—" he speaks so softly now, Thomas can hardly hear him "—I can no longer summon her image inside my mind. Can you believe that? I lived with her for almost forty years, and I don't even remember what her voice sounded like. She's there, inside me, but without the help of a snowflake, I can't find her anymore. And because she passed on in 1978, my '55 snowflake will be my last chance to ever truly see her again.

"Your mother would have been nine in 1955, Tiger, and your grandmother young and beautiful. No, I'm saving that one for the rainiest day in the history of my world." He manages a grim laugh.

Then, without skipping a beat, he tells Thomas something else he learned, the most important thing: the magic only works when they're caught on Christmas Eve!

"I know it sounds crazy, especially coming from an old man, but it's as if—" He pauses and his eyes scan the cellar, as if searching for the right words. At last he takes Thomas by the shoulders and looks the boy straight in the eyes. "It's as if each magic snowflake is a present from Santa Claus. How else can you explain it, Tiger? Christmas Eve is the night, after all, when he supposedly takes flight. It just makes sense that he *is* real, *alive*, putting those magical remembrances of each year's Christmas Day into each year's Christmas Eve snow. It makes sense—the snowflake is his greatest gift of all."

Thomas, who had been nodding and saying "uh-huh" and "wow" during much of the tale, now ponders his grandfather's final summation for a minute, and then departs from the usual and says, "Papa, I believe."

Upstairs, the old man holds the screen door open for Thomas. The boy darts past him, chilled pillbox in hand, and then darts back. His shoulder catches the doorframe as he turns into the kitchen. It spins him around, jarring the pillbox loose, and it hits the floor with a hollow, tinny sound. The snowflake melts in seconds.

On his second try, his feet fly out from beneath him and he crashes to the floor. He groans as he watches the pillbox slide across the slick linoleum, coming to rest at the base of the fridge.

By his fifth painful, equally unsuccessful attempt, he is ready to quit.

"You can do it," says the old man, his voice encouraging but firm.

"I can't. I'm not fast enough."

"Nonsense. You're far faster than I ever was." The old man grimaces as if, at this very moment, a sharp pain is shooting through him. He bends and slowly rubs a leg with his hand. "I wouldn't ask for your help," he says, pausing to let out a wincing sigh, "if I didn't think you could do it."

Thomas gives his grandfather the five-times-failed pillbox, which had begun to warm, and retrieves a freshly chilled one from the freezer. Immediately he bursts outside. He returns just as determined and, without incident, slams the freezer shut.

The screen door softly exhales in the silence. The old man peeks anxiously around the doorframe before joining the boy.

Thomas, hands stuffed inside his jeans pockets, looks at his grandfather. "Can . . . can you check?"

The old man opens the freezer and his arms disappear inside. Seconds later he looks at his grandson and smiles.

"*Yes!*" Thomas exclaims, pumping a fist in the air.

"And she's a beauty," says the old man. "She'll probably be the size of a golf ball in a couple of years."

"Yes, yes, yes," Thomas exclaims some more, while pumping even more fists in the air.

After exchanging high fives, which young Thomas briefly teaches his grandfather before they perform the jubilant rite, the old man resumes his position by the screen door.

An hour and six snowflakes later, the two of them, arms clasped, dance round and round in the kitchen, waltzing lightly through the ocean of water beneath their feet, both wishing the moment would last forever. Trying to hold onto it for as long as possible, they boisterously sing an anthem, its words the only answer they know to thwart the perils of time: *"Catch a falling snowflake, put it in your pillbox, save it for a rainy day . . . Catch a falling snowflake, put it in your pillbox, never let it fade away . . ."*

They sing. And sing. And sing . . . until finally the screen door inhales. And with the sound of voices, their moment is gone.

"Tiger. Not a word of this to your mother," the old man whispers.

A shriek!

Thomas and his grandfather peek around the doorframe.

Thomas's mother stands in the front hall, hands on hips, scowling. She studies the river that flows into the kitchen. "What in God's name is all this?" Thomas's siblings, Brian, six, and Caroline, four, peer out from behind her legs.

"Now, Rose, 'tis but a wee bit of water," says the old man in a badly done Irish brogue. He and Thomas look at each other and break into hysterics.

Rose folds her arms across her chest. "Do you two see me laughing?"

The old man's face falls. "No."

At the request of his mother, Thomas races outside to help his father bring in the tree, freshly cut, its belly big as a boat's hull, its branches full to its high top, like a grand sail.

After a jolly "Ho! Ho! Ho!" and "Merry Christmas," Harold,

hefting the base of the tree, guides it into the living room, thanks his father-in-law for the use of his car, then says, "She's a clunker, but she sure runs like a top."

"She always has, son," replies the old man. "She always has."

With Thomas holding the unsecured tree steady in the tree-stand, his father stands back and meticulously surveys his subject. Like a builder constructing the most magnificent palace for a royal family, he considers his sole responsibility both its appearance and its structural integrity. He tells Thomas to turn, turn, turn, looking for the best side, and tilt, tilt, tilt, to get the structure plumb. The two youngest Mullen apprentices, each with a box of Snoopy ornaments in hand, stand next to the royal builder, impatiently watching the repeated turning and tilting, anxious to get busy themselves.

Out of the family's earshot, Rose says, "Did you have a talk with Thomas, like you said you would?" She is on her knees in the kitchen, drying the floor with dishtowels, while her father happily mops. He whistles "Jingle Bells" as he works.

He stops the sprightly melody to say, "The boy's fine," then continues again.

"He's not, Dad. He has no friends. His teacher says he's withdrawing, barely speaking, and never participating in class anymore. That's a big change for him, and I'm starting to see it at home, too."

Her father ceases the melody again, and with it the mopping. "When I was young, do you know what they called that? They called it growing up. Nowadays they analyze every little thing.

Got terms for everything. You're a little down? *Well*, you *must* be manic-depressive! Oh, what's this, your fingers feel tired? Gee, you've got carpal-watchamacallit! And talk about political correctness. You know what I heard in town the other day?"

Knowing she can never stop her father once he gets going, Rose shakes her head and resigns herself to, "Not so loud, Dad."

He lowers his voice. "Teachers are now telling kids that Santa Claus isn't real, but his spirit's alive. Can you believe that? His *spirit's* alive. Telling them otherwise would be a lie, they say. It sickens me! *He's* the one keeping everyone's spirit alive and they kill him and nobody does a damn thing about it! I just don't get it. Why couldn't things be the way they used to be? It was pretty damn good back then, let me tell you. And let me tell you something else about—" He stops himself.

"About?"

"Nothing." The old man resumes mopping.

"That's all well and good, but it doesn't change the fact that something's going on with Thomas."

"The boy is fine."

"Please, Dad, he thinks the world of you. Please talk to him. He won't tell us anything."

To appease his daughter's stubborn constitution and her uneasy mind, he says, "Okay, we talked. We talked a lot. And let me tell you something, the boy in there—" he points the mop handle toward the living room "—he's all right. In fact, he's far more than all right. Take my word for it."

Rose doesn't take his word. She asks that they continue the discussion after the holidays and resumes swiping the dishtowels over the floor.

The old man begins whistling a spirited rendition of "Santa Claus Is Coming to Town." He glances at the freezer door of the fridge and thinks about the tasty treats within that he'll one day relocate to the cellar. Not the ice cream and Popsicles and frozen pies—those can stay—but what's neatly hidden behind those treats: six snowflakes, the sweetest treats of all, each resting comfortably inside its own silver box, waiting to absorb the delicious flavours of Christmas Day, and promising to keep those flavours fresh and piquant until savoured in a year, or five, or twenty, refreshing the palate with a reminder that every tomorrow will never be, each today never was, and the wondrous magic of Christmas is the closest any of us will ever get to forever.

No, the old man is certain, his grandson is so much more than all right.

He crouches down between Brian and Caroline, surprisingly nimble for such an old man, and wraps an arm around each of their tiny shoulders. He takes a deep breath. The strong, sour smell of pine fills his lungs. "*Ahhh*," he sighs. "Doesn't that smell good?"

"Stinky," says Caroline.

Though they rarely agree on anything, Brian concurs.

"Oh, come now, little ones. You'll hurt Santa's feelings."

Rose bursts into the living room after sliding a batch of sweet dough into the oven. "And you'll hurt my feelings if you say the same about my chocolate chip cookies," she says.

"Cookies! Yay!" the two little ones cheer.

Thomas is struggling with a string of badly tangled lights.

Harold enters the room, having just put on a record. The soothing voice of Bing Crosby follows him in. A royal builder again, he stops ten feet from the green monument and thoughtfully studies it.

"A fine tree, Harold. A fine tree!" says the old man.

Everyone gets busy. The dazzling coloured lights are carefully stitched into the fabric of the tree. The delicate streamers are wrapped like fancy shawls. The ornaments are evenly spaced and precisely placed—sparkling buttons on a glittering suit of golden green!

While they work, the banter is lively and light, until Rose speaks. "They said a prayer for Mrs. Meriweather at Mass tonight, Dad."

After she and Harold and the two youngest children picked up the tree, they attended Mass, a Christmas Eve tradition Rose rarely missed, one started by her mother during childhood. Her father, on the other hand, had little use for church, regardless of the occasion.

She continues: "Dr. Glover stood up and told the congregation that he's never seen anyone miss somebody so much. He said she's dying of a broken heart and probably won't make it through the night. It's so sad."

The old man slowly shakes his head as he places an ornament at the tip of a high branch. "She's a fine lady. And Fred? Never met a finer man." He stares off into space, remembering, trying to remember.

"They were. I recall one time . . ." Rose tells a vague tale of when she fell from a bicycle, or wagon, or while skipping rope, and received a bloody gash over her right eye. Mrs. Meriweather, who'd been watering her flowers or sitting on the porch sipping lemonade at the time, saw this and screamed. She rushed over, cradled Rose in her arms, sat down on the sidewalk and, while rocking back and forth, soothed her with comforting words. "I've still got the scar to prove it," Rose says, pointing to a spot near her right eyebrow. "But what I remember most is how loved she made me feel."

Thomas, his hands rich with wads of silver tinsel, has been standing silent and motionless behind the tree for some time. Finally, with the banter once again lively and light, he gestures to his grandfather. "Papa," he whispers, "can I talk to you for a second?"

And the two of them, like conspirators in the night, sneak away undetected, save for a mother who smiles as her watchful eyes see them disappear through the cellar door.

"Papa! Papa!" Thomas exclaims. They are drowned in darkness beside the chest freezer.

"What is it, Tiger?"

"You heard what Mom said. About Mrs. Meriweather."

"Yes, she hasn't been well for—"

"About her broken heart! And missing Mr. Meriweather!" Thomas's voice is a race car, its engine low, but its speed at full throttle and racing blindly into the darkness. "And about what you said earlier. About falling out of people's fancy. Maybe Mrs. Meriweather has fallen out of life's fancy, like Grandma's jewelry box. Maybe she could and should last longer! Maybe it's not her time!" The last sentence comes out as a wheeze, as Thomas runs almost completely out of breath. His engine sputtering, he coughs.

"What are you saying?"

There is silence. Blackness. Coldness. Dampness. Mildew trying to creep into the bones. Then . . .

A radiant light smashes everything. It bursts forth—loud and glorious to the ears, clear and sweet to the eyes, warm and invigorating to the soul—as Thomas raises the top of the chest freezer until it is fully open.

"Let's give her a snowflake!"

"A . . . One of my snowflakes?"

"Maybe if she sees Mr. Meriweather again, that will help."

The old man looks down at the seven remaining pillboxes.

"We can give her one of your '84s," Thomas says.

"No. Fred passed in February of '84. He wasn't around for Christmas that year."

"Then we'll give her an '83."

The old man considers this for a moment. "Yes, we—no!" he shouts.

Thomas jerks his head up, startled.

"Fred was very ill during Christmas that year. I . . . I can't make that mistake again." After a moment he admits, "Your Papa was a fool."

He tells Thomas about his own father, how he could be a pretty nasty, bitter man at times. "But your mother had such fond memories of her grandfather—the few she had. He died when she was nine. So when she was thirteen or fourteen, I confided to her the snowflake phenomenon as I did with you today—" he flashes an uneasy smile "—and then gave her one to bring her eighth Christmas back to life." The old man shakes his head. "I only meant well."

"What happened?"

"He was sick that year, and that worsened his mean-spiritedness. Turns out he was especially nasty to her on that Christmas Day. Your mother was in tears, saying I ruined her grandfather's memory. She said she didn't need to know how he really was, just how wonderful she perceived him to be. Whether her perception was correct or not, it was the *truth* to her. She said she never wanted to see another snowflake for as long as she lived."

Thomas stands beside his grandfather in sombre silence.

"I guess some remembrances are better left unseen," the old man finishes, clearly shaken by his own remembrance of the incident.

After a moment Thomas says, "Let's give Mrs. Meriweather the '55."

"NO! NO!" The old man screams so loud, it shakes dust loose from the floor joists above.

A creak. Footsteps. A voice.

The old man scurries to the stairs and grabs the handrail for support. His daughter, already halfway down the stairs, continues to the second step from the bottom. "Is everything okay down here?" she asks, looking around cautiously.

"Fine, just fine," he says, and nods in the direction of the furnace. "Tiger and I are just . . . *talking*," he adds with a wink.

She smiles and places a hand on his. "Thanks, Dad."

And it strikes him—a remembrance, full flavour for the senses. The warmth of his daughter's hand; the way the light catches her face just so; the sound of her voice. And that soothing smell and taste—a delight on the tongue—that sweet, sweet thing called . . . lavender!

Softly, the old man says, "Rose, you remind me so much of your mother."

She looks into his eyes. "You never told me that before."

"I never saw it before, but I do now, Rose."

"Thanks for that, too, Dad."

She gives his hand a squeeze and, as if it were connected to some intricate system of irrigation, a tear pulses from his eye. He wipes it away.

After a moment, she says, "I never liked it down here. It's so cold."

"Odd," the old man replies, "I always find it the warmest place in the house."

He watches Rose ascend the stairs. Then he returns to Thomas. "Let's give her the '55. She needs it more than I do."

Out of necessity, Thomas is charged with the responsibility. But before he moves, the old man mentions one tiny, yet infinitely important detail about the Christmas Eve snowflake. "They melt fast, Tiger, *fast*. An ice cube might turn to a puddle in an hour. A similarly sized snowflake? Maybe twenty minutes, and with not a single drop left behind. They're truly magical, Tiger. Poof—they're gone!"

The old man leans into the chest freezer and opens the pillbox marked 55. His grandson leans in too, and together they stare at the snowflake that's the size of a grape.

"This one here? I'd give it ten minutes."

Without considering the sea of white or biting cold that lies between the two homes (though, to the boy's advantage, the snow has ceased falling) and the inappropriateness of Thomas's

T-shirt and slippers, they consider only the briefness of time—the snowflake's, Mrs. Meriweather's—and so, when the old man closes the pillbox, *poof!* Thomas is gone.

Thomas reaches the bottom stair in two seconds flat but stops suddenly, catching the handrail. "Papa! What about the candy canes? Doesn't she need to eat one first?"

"No!" the old man cries. "For the love of Christmas, *goooooo!*"

And Thomas takes the stairs three at a time.

"I just like their flavour," the old man mumbles to no one but himself.

Past the cellar door he races, the pillbox bulging in his front right pocket. His footfalls thump down the hallway, through the living room and the Christmas warmth of pine- and cookie-scented air, past the jovial voice of his father, the laughter of lights on the tree, and the laughter of his siblings, their faces glowing, anticipating what tomorrow will bring.

Three paces from the front door, his mother steps out from an archway and brings Thomas to an abrupt halt by snatching his arm. "Where do you think you're off to, young man?"

"Let me go!" Thomas pleads, yanking at his imprisoned arm without success.

Before she can respond with or without favour, a voice rises calmly from the cellar doorway. "Let him go, Rose," the old man says. "It's time to let him go. Take my word for it. He'll be all right."

This time Rose *does* take her father's word for it, but not before telling the boy to bundle up. Thomas jumps into his boots, jerks on his coat and, leaving it unbuttoned and bellying out like a parachute, he bounds outside with only twenty seconds forever lost.

Finally clueing in to the commotion, Harold takes his eyes off the tree. "Would you like a drive, son?" he hollers.

The screen door replies with a gasp.

Fortunately the distance is short. Thomas tackles the mountainous white peaks in his path flawlessly, ascending and descending without a stumble or fall.

In response to his persistent raps, John Meriweather opens the front door. A pleasant voice calls out from behind, "Who is it, John?"

"It's Rose's boy, Tommie," he says.

His wife, Libby, appears. "Oh, well, merry Christmas, Tommie."

"Merry Christmas, ma'am," Thomas says, nodding to her, then to John. "Merry Christmas, Mr. Meriweather." He retrieves the pillbox from his pocket. "We—I—my grandfather . . ." Unlike his adept handling of the white mountains, Thomas stumbles on his words. "He wants your mother to have this."

John takes the sterling silver pillbox and opens it. "What is it?"

Realizing how ridiculous he will sound explaining everything, and with little time to provide such an explanation, he stumbles further before saying, "It will help her."

John turns his head and calls over his shoulder, "Dr. Glover!"

Seconds later, the doctor is by John's side.

"Tommie Mullen brought this medication for Mother."

Dr. Glover dons his spectacles, studies Thomas briefly, and then holds up the snowflake to the house light. It is now noticeably smaller than a grape. "Looks like . . ." Dr. Glover mutters, scrutinizing it with squinted eyes. "Looks like . . ."

Before he can divulge what exactly he thinks it is, a snowy bomb explodes off the front window of the Meriweather house, the sound made all the more loud and frightful by its unexpected arrival. Then a second bomb strikes the window, followed by a third.

The doctor pushes past Thomas onto the porch. "I know that's you, Cyrus Sims!" he shouts, shaking the fist-encased snowflake in the cold air. "You had better believe your parents will hear of this!"

He returns the snowflake to the pillbox. "I'll not be giving this to my patient," he says, handing it back to Thomas.

"I'm sorry," adds Libby, and she and Dr. Glover fade like embers into the house.

"Thanks for thinking of her," says John.

"But Mr. Meriwea—"

"I'm sorry, Tommie, doctor's orders. Wish everyone a merry Christmas for us, won't you?"

Thomas nods and then drops his head. "Yes, sir."

And the door quietly closes.

The snowflake is now a touch bigger than a marble.

He turns to leave amid more bombs. One in particular peaks so high, Thomas imagines it's a shining silver star atop a giant tree, awaiting Christmas Day to witness and precisely remember what each of us will one day forget: the subtle touches, the loving words, those little kindnesses mired by time. He wonders how many snowflakes it took to make such a glorious star. As he ponders this, lacking the will to move, it falls toward him in a twinkling and strikes his leg.

In the terrible cold, with chilling giggles floating across the white tides, Thomas scoops the near-intact pack of snow from his pant leg. He studies it closely, feeling its coolness in the warmth of his left hand. A thousand—no!—a million snowflakes! Crying for help. Wanting to help. Wanting to give back a million soon-to-be Christmas Days. And in his right hand, a single Christmas Day from 1955. Crying for help. In need of help. And he, Thomas Mullen, wanting desperately to help, but feeling about as alone and far away from forever as he's ever felt.

Without realizing, he begins to cry. Through the tears he sees a million soon-to-be Christmas Days not slowly melting away in his hand, not slipping through his fingers, but magically, miraculously, refusing to die . . .

This time Thomas's attack on the door is ferocious.

When John Meriweather answers, Libby and Dr. Glover are with him.

"Can . . . I use . . . your bathroom?" Thomas sputters between sobs. Tears pour down his cheeks. A thick pack of snow adheres to the left side of his face, which he shields with a hand. A light dusting of snow covers most of his body. He is quite a sight.

"Damn that bloody Cyrus Sims," mutters Dr. Glover.

"Oh, you poor thing. Of course, dear," Libby answers. "Top of the stairs to your right."

"But please be quiet. Mother's resting," adds John.

Thomas jumps out of his boots. In passing, he hands the pillbox to Dr. Glover, who made a point of asking for it. He hears it open and then click shut as he reaches the stairs.

Outside, beyond a towering island of white, a young private breaks rank and smacks one of his confederates in the back of the head.

"Ow! What'd I do?" asks General Sims, grimacing and rubbing his head. "It barely touched him."

In the bathroom, Thomas is composed. He kneels and slides the snow from his face into the cast iron tub. With a prodding finger, he rummages through the icy pile and finds the '55 snowflake, now the size of a marble. He forms a snowy nest in his left hand and places the magic gem at the centre of this mini-freezer.

He opens the bathroom door a hair. The hallway light is negligible. Faint moans come from a distant room. Without wasting another second, he rushes out.

Dr. Glover, who at that same instant had exited an adjoining room, turns in surprise. His large, round frame lunges awkwardly as Thomas blows past, a hand glancing off the boy's shoulder just enough to knock the big man off balance. He sways for a moment, lets out a long, wailing sigh, and falls with a raucous crash to the floor.

In the bedroom, Thomas crouches at Mrs. Meriweather's bedside. Her face is withered and drawn, fringed by matted grey hair. A plump white pillow cradles her head like a soft, snowy palm, while a drift of lustrous white fabric covers her body. She is ghostly pale.

"Mrs. Meriweather?" he whispers.

More moans.

Lively footsteps and John Meriweather's voice waft in from beyond the bedroom door.

"Mrs. Meriweather?"

Closed eyes.

"Please, Mrs. Meriweather, please, can you hear me?"

No response.

Thomas glances over his shoulder and sees the doorknob turning.

When John enters the bedroom, his mother is sitting up, her face radiant in the glow of the bedside lamp. She is smiling.

"Oh, Frederick, I'd forgotten how handsome you were," she says. Her voice carries with it the timbre and cadence and force of someone in the prime of a happy life.

"Mother!" John says, rushing to her side. He quickly kneels and takes her hand.

Mrs. Meriweather opens her eyes. Thomas, now standing, says, "Please keep your eyes closed, Mrs. Meriweather."

Nodding, she does as she's told and gives her son's hand a

firm squeeze. "And there you are, John, my beautiful little boy." Then she laughs, so loudly and joyfully that John begins uncontrollably laughing and crying at the same time. Between sniffles, he chortles with glee!

"Mr. Meriweather, make sure her eyes stay shut until it wears off," Thomas whispers.

John wipes his nose with a forearm. Unable to suppress his laughter or tears, he's only able to nod an acknowledgement. Then, managing perhaps the shakiest two syllables that will forever be spoken, he looks up at Thomas and says with the greatest of humility and gratitude: "Thank you."

Dr. Glover, shaken but unhurt by his fall, stands near the door holding the pillbox. Its silver casing contains only a tiny puddle. Thomas approaches, then stops when the man's free hand rises and adopts the traditional beggar's pose.

"Merry Christmas, sir," Thomas says with a smile, and dumps what had once acted as a heavenly mini-freezer and is now a pile of slushy snow into the doctor's open hand.

The doctor lets out a ghastly squeal, and the boy is gone.

Outside, after leaping from the porch with joyful abandon, Thomas frolics through each drift as if it were the last he'd ever experience. "Thanks, Cyrus Sims," he yells during his dash through the beautiful Christmas Eve snow. "Thanks a lot!"

Behind a towering island, General Sims smacks a subordinate officer in the head. "See? He's thanking me."

"But be mindful of what you're throwing away, Cyrus Sims," Thomas cautions. "You may need it one day."

The offended officer smacks the general back. "See? He . . . he says you might need it one day."

And the two wrestle each other to the ground and scuffle in the snow.

"Guys! Guys!" the private not involved in the infighting says. "We got another one."

In the distance a tall, thick person waddles down some porch steps and heads toward a car.

While the two little ones, Brian and Caroline, undergo the necessary preparations before visiting the world of dreamy Santa slumber—their bodies scrubbed, teeth brushed, and a bedtime story that tonight, of all nights, will surely involve reindeer and elves and jolly old St. Nick—the old man is downstairs, by his lonesome, pacing nervously back and forth.

When he hears the screen door inhale, he exhales at the sight of his grandson. "Well?" he says. "Well? Well?"

Thomas frowns.

"What?" the old man screeches. "The snowflake—where is it?"

Not wanting to torture his grandfather any longer, he displays a dizzying smile. "Ah, Papa, you shoulda seen her," he says, and races into his grandfather's arms.

"Ha-ha!" the old man cries.

And together they hug in warm silence for a minute, maybe two, and, if you're inclined to believe in miracles, maybe, just maybe . . . forever.

They separate and walk around the house, moving from room to room, arm in arm, both too excited to be still as Thomas tells his remarkable tale. Whenever a parent or daughter or son-in-law enters a room they occupy, they simply move on to another, leaving the invader ignorant of what exactly is so thrilling, but shaking a head and sometimes laughing along, swept up in the spirit of the moment.

A couple of hours later, the scent of chocolate chip cookies long-since forgotten and Bing Crosby nothing more than a distant memory, the house is quiet. Rose says, "Thomas, I think you'd better get to bed. It's getting late and Santa comes *pretty early*, you know."

"He does, Mom," Thomas says, "he really does." And within five minutes he is snuggled beneath warm blankets.

"*Pretty early?*" says Harold, taking his wife by the arm.

"Well, we *are* getting older, honey, and we do seem to be going to bed earlier with each passing year."

And the two of them laugh, happy, in love, embracing each other and the time that is now.

And from the kitchen the old man listens, happy, in love, wondering if that's the way it used to be.

At fifteen past the eleventh evening hour, the old man is not in bed. He sits at the kitchen table, alone but not lonely. The tree is amply stocked with the dreams of a child, the house silent. He holds a picture of his beloved wife in his hands.

He studies her for a minute: the flow of her hair, the glow of her smile, the pools of blue that are her eyes. He notes every last detail, right down to the gentle rise at the tip of her nose. Then he turns her around. He stares at the stark white paper backing for a minute. Then he begins again with every last detail. He does this repeatedly until finally he smiles, shakes his head, and springs from his chair.

Outside, snow is pouring from the sky again, thicker, richer, creamier, looking much tastier than earlier in the day. Heart racing, the old man goes to the bottom of the stairs and listens intently for a moment. He returns to the kitchen, dons his galoshes, and removes an empty pillbox from the freezer. In one calm, effortless motion, the screen door inhales, exhales, and a seventh snowflake rests comfortably inside the freezer, awaiting Christmas Day.

He makes two clucking sounds, like a cricket's chirrup, pumps a fist three-times-lucky in the air, then whispers with a smile, "Nothing broken yet, old man."

He looks up and winks in the direction of Thomas's room.

Up the darkened stairway, down the darkened hall, past the darkened doors where two little ones dream of Santa and two Santas dream of them, a darkened door squeaks in the electric quiet of Christmas.

The old man shuffles silently across the bedroom floor, bringing with him the familiar scent of peppermint and pine. "Tiger?" he whispers.

"Papa?"

The old man draws open the bedside curtain. "It's started again."

And Thomas is already kneeling on the bed, staring out at the wondrous spectacle.

"We have thirty minutes before midnight," the old man says. "There's time for a few more."

Thomas doesn't respond. His face is knotted, twisted.

"What's wrong, Tiger?"

"I—I've been thinking."

"About?"

"Grandma."

"What about Grandma?"

Thomas hesitates. "She really loved me, didn't she?"

"I told you she did."

"I've been thinking about something else, too."

"Oh?"

"Can you tell me some nice things?"

The old man, perplexed for a moment, shags the boy's hair with a playful hand. Then he chuckles far too loudly for such a still night. "Tiger," he says, "you know I love you very much, don't you?"

"No!"

"No? Well—"

"No, Papa, don't tell me that. Not now."

"Not now?"

"Tell me tomorrow. And do lots of silly things tomorrow. Make funny faces. Tell silly jokes. Put a lampshade on your head, and a red bow on your forehead, like you did a few years ago. And not just for me; for Brian and Caroline. Let them climb all over you and laugh themselves silly. Tell them how much you love them. Show them they never fell out of your fancy, because they're so young, you know, and I just . . . I just . . ."

"You want them to remember me?"

Thomas nods. "I just wanna make sure there's reminders in our six snowflakes of what a great Papa we had—have!"

"Seven."

"Huh?"

The old man chuckles again and with a wink, he reassures the boy he'll be around for a while—heck, perhaps even longer than a while; perhaps even forever.

In the silvery night, they kneel shoulder to shoulder and stare out at the countless falling snowflakes, each precious gem carrying with it a simple but true promise of Christmas. As they watch, a large snowflake floats toward them, big enough to hold remembrances for a thousand lifetimes, and lands softly on the window.

"*Awe*-some," the old man whispers.

Then, magically, it disappears.

SEASONS' GREETING

"I don't believe it," Betsy said, dabbing away the final tear with a tissue.

"Sweetheart—"

"No. It can't be."

"But, sweetheart, look." Abner Wright brought out the calendar again and set it on the kitchen table before his wife. Pressing a finger to the page, he said, "*Tuesday*—"

"We should be in church. If what you said before is true, I want to go to church and ask God."

"We've already missed Mass," said Abner, referring to the first of two special holiday Masses their church traditionally held each year—one at six, the other at midnight.

"I don't care. I want to go," Betsy demanded.

Abner's eyes moved to the six-over-six sash window. Outside, an endless wall of snow shifted uneasily in the biting wind, trembling downward from the vast sky above. His old Chrysler in the driveway, bare and blue just a few hours previous, was now completely buried beneath a hill of the purest white. "But, sweetheart," he said, "look at all the snow."

"Sand."

"Winter snow."

"Summer sand!" she insisted, glaring at Abner. "Sand and the dunes of summer!" Then, her tone changing: "Aren't they just . . . *grand* . . ."

Her voice drifted off into the icy night. Abner took her

momentary lapse as an opportunity to continue, sliding his finger across the calendar's page. *"December . . ."*

Betsy yawned, now apparently indifferent to the snow and her demand that they attend church.

Again his finger slid. *"Twenty-four."*

Betsy shook her head. "No, no, no, no, no!"

"Sweetheart, I—"

"I don't believe it."

"But I've just shown you."

"You could be lying."

"Do you think I would do that?"

Betsy leaned forward and scrutinized the calendar on the table. Abner gazed at the top of her hair, which was white and matted flat like a bonnet; further down, the sides curled and silvery grey.

Finally she said, "A cheap calendar trick."

"I'm sorry, sweetheart, I didn't hear you so well." Abner fiddled with the hearing aid in his left ear and then turned his head so it faced her.

"A cheap calendar trick," she repeated. This time *she* pressed a finger to the page and looked up at her husband. "It's 1985?"

"Yes."

"Rubbish."

"December twenty-fourth."

"More rubbish."

Abner stepped slowly away from the table and left the room. A minute later he returned carrying a huge assortment of Christmas cards, which he placed beside the calendar on the table. The top dozen or so cards slid off the six-inch stack, revealing a fantastic array of colourful Santas and wide-eyed children and reindeers and snow.

"From our friends around town," he said, watching his wife stare dubiously at the cards.

Betsy leaned forward again. She began picking the cards up one by one, scrutinizing the front of each before setting it back on the table. She studied them far more closely than she had the calendar. Once finished, she said, "From last year, or the year before that, no doubt."

"Swee—"

"If it's Christmas Eve, then where are my grandchildren, Pip and Little Will?"

"You can't call her that anymore," said Abner, taking the calendar and moving around the kitchen table to hang it back on the wall above the breadbox. "You have to call her Patricia now, sweetheart. If I'm not mistaken, she started resenting being called Pip when she was fifteen."

"I'll call her as I choose."

"She has two children of her own now, and she's living in Florida. And Little Will isn't so little anymore. He'd be about thirty-three, and a big movie producer down in California. Do you remember that film we watched last week, starring—oh, what was his name?"

"Prove it! I want to see Pip and Little Will all grown up!"

"As you wish."

Abner stepped away from the table again and exited the room. A few minutes later he reappeared, this time with a large box full of photographs. His fingers began roaming through the black and white past until finally he brought one back to the present.

"My, my, would you look at that," he said, framing the photo before his face and the moment inside his mind. "We gave Little Will that wagon that first Christmas."

In the photo, a young boy, barefoot, bare-chested, and no more than five, sat smiling for the camera aboard a Radio Flyer wagon. A girl around eight stood holding the wagon's handle, staring off into space, a distracted expression on her face.

He handed Betsy the picture. As often happened when he visited the past, he lost himself and so resumed roaming through the forest of his middle life, no longer a man of eighty-three, but a man in his fifties, each brittle piece of paper a leaf having fallen from an ancient tree. And when each dead leaf was raked and lifted from the forest's floor, it sparked to life, blazing bronze and gold and fiery orange inside his mind, before he passed it to Betsy, where it became a seemingly charred ember in her fingers.

"No," she said after studying the ninth photo given to her. Each picture had been of Pip, or Little Will, or both, but always in childhood. "Grown up."

"Yes, yes," he said, remembering what he had been seeking in the first place. He scanned a dozen more pictures until finally, after looking anxiously at his wife, he withdrew one and presented it to her. "There," he said. "Little Will, all grown up." He watched Betsy closely.

"Lies."

"Sweetheart—"

"I see it in the eyes."

"The eyes?"

"You're not fooling anyone. That's you!"

"Oh? Let me see that." Abner took back the photo of himself and pretended to study it. "No," he said, his voice a low, shaky drawl, "I think you're mistaken. This is Little Will, not so lit—"

"Just tell me when they'll be here."

He looked at the clock above the icebox, then glanced nervously at his wristwatch. Given to him over ten years ago as a commemorative gift by Wharton Wood, the town's furniture factory, it had proven as reliable to him as his fifty years of service had been to them. "Soon, sweetheart; they will be here soon."

"And my daughter and son-in-law?"

Abner stared off into space, where time had no meaning. Fifteen seconds passed. Twenty. Twenty-five. Until almost thirty years had passed in the mere blink of an eye, before Betsy, still holding nine photographs, said, "Take your lies!" and threw them at him.

Fragments of the past swirled around his face in a blur before landing softly on the floor. He heard not the gentle click of rustling leaves in an autumn breeze, but the pitter-patter of tiny feet on linoleum. He shifted uneasily in his chair.

Betsy, who'd sat poised and upright at the table for most of their talk and her defiant throw just seconds earlier, slouched suddenly. At the same time her eyes, which had been sparkling with a stubborn vitality, became sullen and worn. "I just can't feel it," she said, her head slumping forward. "I just can't feel Christmas . . ."

Back in the present again, Abner took her hands in his. "Can you feel *me?*" he asked.

She nodded and began weeping quietly.

"There, there, sweetheart, it's all right." He guided her out of her chair. "Let's go into the parlour where it's more comfortable."

She walked ahead while he gathered the Christmas cards from the table. Standing opposite the kitchen counter, he opened a few and read all that was written inside—generic season's greetings inked by an obscure printer, and nothing more. He let them fall into the wastebasket. They made him feel nothing like Christmas, either.

In the parlour, the tasselled light switches shivered in the ghostlike breeze that haunted the drafty house. Fragile webs of spidery doilies adorned the cedar coffee table and its two matching tables at each end of the long sofa. On the sofa were pillows, tasselfringed and soft, and in one corner of the room a single, tasseldraped floor lamp simmered orange. Above, floating beneath the sky-blue ceiling, a cloudy chandelier loomed low and grey.

Below that very chandelier, wrapped tight inside a thick wool sweater, Betsy sat huddled in a well-cushioned wing chair. A carousel of red and yellow and blue lights danced in the dim air and shimmered gold in her luminous green eyes as Abner entered the parlour and stood next to the fireplace. His body was bent at an awkward angle—a brittle twig clad in grey gabardine sweater and black wool pants. He ignored the two red stockings that hung from the mantel, one labelled *Little Will*, the other labelled *Pip*, and instead poked around in the fire until finally the flickering flame rose, crackling high and bright.

He let himself fall into the hickory chair, made with his own hands so long ago he could barely remember, and instantly shadows came to life. He watched them move silently across the floor. Tall and thin. Short and stout. Old and young. He breathed them in and with them, the sweet perfume of hickory and cedar and burning pine.

And how, by God, had it come to this? A lifetime lived in this town, a lifetime laboured. Countless friends come, and yes, many gone. But there were still lots around. Take Jim Bremner as an example, living up on the hill in that old Georgian. Went to grade school with him. Same went for Archie Moore and Phil Exeter. And then there were the younger fellows, friends made near the end at Wharton Wood, like Kenny Stricker and Ben Cotter and Albert Roxton. And that said nothing of Betsy's friends, who numbered even more than his. You'd think one would visit on Christmas Eve. Just one. That would be nice, especially with him in such a fix. Just a quick visit. Nothing too long or elaborate, just long enough to see how things were.

And worse than that, not even a single phone call from any of them! Hell, not even a single Christmas card! And that said nothing of his grandson, Little Will, not so little anymore and down in sunny California. Not so much as a whisper from him. And what about Pip—Patricia? Living in Florida. Thousands of miles away. Might as well be a million miles away! And why? What reason? To live constantly in summer. To never taste a snowflake on the tongue. To never feel the glorious December winds on the skin. To never see the trees, their branches bent and deliriously weary with ice and snow. Or to look across a field, blinded by wave upon wave of entrancing white, and see those trees, looking like old men, weary but content. It invigorated the soul, even for this old man after eighty-three years! No, to never know winter was to never truly know Christmas. Summer was just . . . summer.

Oh, Pip! Little Will! Why live down *there*? So far away. And of all places, in *summer*. Dreary summer. Stifling summer. And after what happened during *that* summer so, so long ago . . .

Seated only a half-dozen feet from the fireplace, with the flame licking higher and higher up the flue, Abner could feel the heat of summer slowly shaping and reshaping his face, first from solid steel, then to pink alabaster, and then to pale silica. As it was about to turn him into a quivering hot lava of bubbling tears, he heard a shriek. Betsy.

"No!" she said. "No, no, no!"

Abner couldn't take the anguish in her voice, but the heat was worse, so he first got up and moved to the sofa. He reached over the wing of Betsy's chair and gently took her hand.

"Why must you fool me like this?" she said, staring at the Christmas tree.

It was a small, unspectacular artificial tree, maybe four feet tall. Betsy herself had bought it almost twenty years ago, and since then it had served them well. On it were several strings of poorly spaced lights flashing red, yellow, and blue, and three clumps of silver tinsel hung thick from three branches near the bottom. Numerous ornaments were spaced in equally lumpy clusters, one grouping here, another there, and the gold star at the top leaned helplessly to one side. The tree looked as if it had been decorated without hope or care.

"I'm not fooling you, sweetheart. It *is* Christmas."

"No doubt *empty* boxes."

Five boxes of varying sizes lay beneath the tree. They were wrapped in various coloured papers, the folds and corners of each prepared as haphazardly as the placement of decorations on the tree.

"Gifts, sweetheart." Abner paused. "Would you like to open them?"

"A new cotton blouse?" Betsy asked, a mischievous lilt in her voice, the corner of her mouth rising playfully.

"Maybe a scarf. To keep your neck warm during our winter walks."

"Or a straw hat?"

"Or some mittens!" said Abner, genuinely enthused.

"Or gardening gloves."

"Or earmuffs!"

"Or a silk skirt."

"Or fur-lined boots," said Abner, less enthused, sensing the direction his wife was headed.

"Or sandals."

"Or a wool shawl."

"Or a summer dress."

"Or . . . or . . ." Abner couldn't keep up. In the battle of the seasons, his mind had surrendered.

"Or a new swimsuit!" Betsy cried. "I want to go swimming at the beach!"

Deflated, Abner said, "Very well. Open them first." He stood and tried to move toward the tree to retrieve the packages, but Betsy, still seated in the wing chair, held tightly to his hand.

"But how can I?" she said. "It's not Christmas!"

Sighing: "Christmas Eve."

"Maybe it's Easter," said Betsy, staring at an oval-shaped, white porcelain ornament with a baby, presumably Jesus, incised in its front.

"Easter?"

"There's an egg on the tree."

Sighing again: "It's Christmas Eve, sweetheart—"

"Or maybe—maybe it's All Hallows' Eve! There." Betsy pointed. Right next to the porcelain baby, an ornament of Santa's face dangled, looking ghoulish and alive in the shifting shadows cast by the restless fire. "A phantom." She looked up at her husband. "Like your face. Very scary."

Abner couldn't help but smile. Typical Betsy. Years ago, during that summer and after, when everything appeared pointless in Abner's eyes, he saw no humour in anything. Betsy, on the other hand, had gone out of her way to remedy everything with humour. It made him love her even more, if such a thing were possible. If Pip or Little Will grumbled over their vegetables at dinner, she grumbled too, calling the ones on her own plate foul but funny names, usually managing to get the children laughing—and eating! Sometimes, during those moments of extreme anger when no funny word or phrase would do the trick, she took to tossing carrots or cauliflower florets, oftentimes thumping them off Abner's forehead, across the table. He did his best to play along, acting surprised and pretending to be indignant, though his heart wasn't in it. Invariably Pip and Little Will came around, guffawing and fluttering, nibbling on their food, occasionally throwing the odd vegetable themselves.

Perhaps it was a sign, even back then—the strain of a harsh summer preying on a once strong mind, turning it fragile, causing her to do absurd, irrational things.

If Little Will ran into the house with a scraped knee, Betsy said, "Looks like we'll have to lop it off!" Then she'd vanish, returning seconds later with a hatchet. If Pip threatened to run away—as she did many times—Betsy's eyes would dart around and she'd whisper in conspiratorial fashion, "Please take me with you, sweetie? Pretty please?" And before you knew it, there was Betsy, carrying her floral-print shoulder bag, as if packed and prepared for the journey ahead.

Occasionally, when Abner dragged his feet through the door after a bad day at Wharton Wood, stinking of sweat and sawdust and carpenter's glue, she'd sniff the ripe air and tell him matter-of-factly that it was nice to know the fish were running. Later, after her husband had washed up, she'd glide around the kitchen table serving dinner in hip-waders, with a creel strapped to her waist. Abner was fairly certain she disliked fishing since she'd never gone with him, but he was never completely certain of her intentions with that hatchet, or if there was even a single thread of fabric inside her shoulder bag.

What he did know for sure was that, in each instance, before adorning herself with the props, she'd make her comments with a straight face, pausing just the right amount of time before breaking out in a big, beautiful grin.

Only now, after her "Very scary," no grin followed. Nor did she leave the room and return wearing a ghoulish mask, or, at the very least, clutching a Bible to fight off the demons possessing his countenance. Only silence followed and with it, a vacant expression.

And Abner felt a blast of summer tormenting his face . . .

"Pip!" Betsy wailed.

Abner wiped his eyes. "Oh, sweetheart."

"Little Will!"

He tried to comfort her, but it was no use. Her cries for Pip and Little Will were unrelenting.

Abner moved as quickly as he could to the telephone. Over Betsy's voice, he said, "I'm calling the doctor."

He picked up the phone, dialed, and put the receiver to his ear. His hand trembled.

Nine o'clock on Christmas Eve. The fire in the hearth all but dead, the flashing tree somehow dimmer.

For almost ten minutes, Abner sat slumped in his hickory chair. For almost ten minutes, Betsy's pleading voice fell on deaf ears. For almost ten minutes, Abner remembered that phone call. Not one *to* Dr. Glover, but the one *from* Dr. Glover, during the summer of 1957. And after—after he'd ripped the phone cord from the wall and sufficient time had passed, an hour, maybe two—when the news had spread like a wild brush fire, felling trees one by one at their door, each looking more ashen than the last, the giant redwoods and slender maples and drooping cedars with their diminutive others next to them, and next to some of them their immature saplings, unknowing and uncertain, but with them just the same, until the entire forest of Wharton had fallen upon their house.

Have you thought about the children? some asked. No, they hadn't thought. *Well, you'll have to think,* some said. Too soon to think. So a few stayed behind so Abner and Betsy *could* think, and grieve, sometimes with their backs to each other in bed, staring out into the chill black night of their room, Betsy crying, Abner angry; sometimes curled up in each other's arms, their touch foreign, yet familiar, yet very, very cold . . .

A rap at the door. The light pitter-patter of feet. Shrill voices, calling out, "Grandmama! Grandpapa!"

A girl around ten rushed into the parlour and went straight to the wing chair, followed closely by a boy of about seven.

"Pip!" cried Betsy. "Little Will!" She snatched them into her arms and gave them both crushing but glorious hugs, drowning their cheeks in a flood of warm kisses. "My, how you've grown!" she said, giddy, laughing, kissing, kissing, kissing!

"Sorry we're so late," an exasperated voice said above the giggles. Patricia slumped against the doorframe, while her husband, Mike, peered over her shoulder. "What a nightmare."

They, like their children, wore summer clothes: shorts, T-shirts, running shoes. As if they'd just come in from a fine summer's rain, a thin sheen of water coated their bare arms and legs.

And Betsy laughed, and cooed, and kissed, and cackled, trumpeting a symphony of precious life from her lucid green eyes.

Seeing all this, Abner stood and calmly left the room.

The door to the drafty house silently opened, closed. Abner, having discarded his gabardine sweater and wool pants in favour of a golf shirt, baseball cap, moccasins, and shorts, waded into the ocean of white. His thin, bright ivory legs lost themselves almost to the knees in the warmth of the rippling waves. He floated down his driveway, the hot sting of the harsh December wind wonderful in his face. Twenty paces along, he noticed a man approaching.

"Abner?" said the man, stopping and staring, his mouth agape. His hands were buried deep inside the pockets of his burly black coat. He stood stock still for only a few seconds before moving on toward the house.

Abner didn't even look at him as they passed.

At the bottom of the drive, Abner lowered the red flag and pulled down on the steeple of his brown wooden mailbox in the shape of a church. He crouched and looked inside. It was stuffed as full as a plump Christmas stocking. He removed a handful of mostly square envelopes and sifted through them, passing the envelopes from the phone and gas and electric companies. He saw one bearing a California return address, and tore it open.

Season's Greetings, the handwritten note inside the Christmas card read, *from the land of sun! Hope all is well, Gramps and Grann. Sorry I couldn't find my way there this year. This movie has us working night and day to make a February production deadline. I'll see you soon, though—and that's a promise! Weather here is unseasonably cold right now. Hope you're faring better up there . . . Love always, William.*

Abner crouched again and when he did a gust of wind tore the baseball cap from his head. It wandered helplessly across the drifts, flipping end over end over end. Abner straightened and watched it travel south down the road.

"It just breaks my heart," Betsy was saying, "to see him cry. He was always such a strong man."

"I know, it would break my heart, too," said Patricia. She was standing at the tree; having already thinned out the tinsel, she was now doing her best to reorganize the lights.

"I don't think he properly grieved when your parents passed on.

He never cried back then, but instead got angry. And then . . ."

Patricia looked back at her grandmother sitting lifeless in the wing chair. "And then?"

Betsy sighed. "And then last summer, it was as if, suddenly, something snapped. He started forgetting things, until it got to the point where he seemed to dwell only on your mother and the accident in the summer of '57 that took her life. I tried everything to combat it—explaining things; reasoning with him; reassuring him. But nothing seemed to work. Until I started pretending *I* was forgetting.

"You know, I've gotten pretty good at it, too, because, the truth is," she smiled and her voice perked up, "I'm starting to forget the odd thing myself these days!"

"Oh, like what?"

"Now if only I could remember . . . See my dilemma?"

They both laughed.

Patricia started working on the ailing gold star at the top of the tree, shifting it this way and that, trying to get it straight. Finally she said, "Why not just let him cry, get it out of his system?"

"I did at first. Some days he would just sit there, as if he were in a trance, looking very sad. That wasn't so bad. But it was on those other days, when his tears were so profound, that it just broke my heart. I couldn't bear it any longer. So one day I became so frustrated and upset myself, I—I—"

Patricia stopped what she was doing and again looked back at her grandmother. "*You* . . . ?"

"I'm ashamed of myself for this, but I pretended to forget things, thinking, see how you like it, buster!"

Betsy shifted in her chair, unable to get comfortable. Patricia, who at first smiled on her grandmother's "buster," saw this and, perhaps realizing the comment was intended to be humourless, quickly changed the subject. "That's a beautiful sweater."

At last settled in the wing chair, Betsy lightly brushed her sweater's red wool fabric. "He gave it to me in July, for my birthday."

"It's very nice."

"And you know something else, sweetie?" said Betsy, abruptly jumping back on track.

"What's that, Grandma?"

"I've come to learn that time truly is the healer of all things. I will never forget your mother. I will always love her. She was a beautiful child who blossomed into such a compassionate, lovely lady. But time has taught me to cherish her memory, embrace it, and not dwell on the sadness of her death."

In the parlour's dim light, Betsy saw only the vague outline of her granddaughter as she went back to work on the Christmas tree, but she sensed a familiar silence brewing. "You're not going to start crying on me too now, are you?" Betsy asked.

"No, Grandma, I'm not going to start crying on you."

"And you're not going to threaten to run away?"

Patricia turned to face her grandmother. "What?"

"Because I'm much too tired to start searching through my closets for that old shoulder bag of mine!"

"Oh, *Grandma* . . ."

More laughter.

Betsy continued with her story. "So I started using time to heal your grandfather. Last summer I acted like I didn't know what time of year it was, pretending to think it was winter. In the autumn I insisted it was spring. This winter I've been adamant it's summer—"

"That would explain his look of astonishment when he saw us dressed like this." Patricia pinched her T-shirt and gave it a tug.

"That would explain it."

Patricia began spreading out the tree ornaments. She took the egg-shaped baby Jesus and moved him far away from scary Santa.

"The reality is," said Betsy, "it seems to work. Whenever I see him getting all teary-eyed and I know he's drifting away, I get all huffy and puffy and excited, and that brings him back pretty quick. I think he's so terrified of losing me, it keeps him going. And it keeps him here! That's the most important thing."

"But always having to do that must put a real strain on you."

There was silence for a moment, and then out of that silence emerged Betsy's calm voice. "That is of no consequence. Your grandfather and I have been married for sixty-three years—did *you* forget that?"

Patricia chuckled. "I didn't forget that, Grandma."

"And you know, in all that time, he supported me faithfully. When your mother came along, he supported *us* faithfully, working painfully long hours at Wharton Wood just so we could get by. Then when tragedy struck, he supported you and your brother faithfully. In sixty-three years I've never heard him utter a single complaint about family or family responsibility. Sure, he complained constantly about leaking roofs and fallen eaves and faulty plumbing, but never about family. It's an admirable quality to love your family unconditionally. So, the truth is, I would pretend to forget every second of every day if necessary. That would be the least I could do for him."

Finished with the tree, Patricia moved to her grandmother and knelt by her side. She rested her head on her folded hands in her grandmother's lap. "Why didn't you tell me all this sooner?"

"And what, may I ask, would you do from way down there in Florida, other than worry?" There was no response. Betsy leaned down and kissed her granddaughter's cheek. She began stroking Patricia's flaxen hair and said, "Don't fret, darling, you have nothing to fear. As long as I'm here, this will always be your grandfather's house."

They stared dreamily at the tree, the gold star finally straight, the ornaments and lights and tinsel postcard perfect, until Mike burst into the parlour, mumbling under his breath.

"How am I supposed to call the airline and follow up on our lost luggage . . ." he grabbed a discarded copy of *The Wharton Echo* from the old leather trunk where a small supply of logs and kindling were stored ". . . if there's no dial tone on the phone?" He used the newspaper to kindle the twinkle of fire that still burned in the hearth. "How can you forget to pay your phone bill, that's what I want to know. How? *How?*"

Patricia sat up and the two women looked at each other while Mike continued mumbling. Betsy mouthed an "oops" but didn't say it, and the women giggled quietly to themselves.

At the same time, Paula—Pip to her great-grandmother—and little William—the boy's uncle being his namesake—raced into the room with the light merriment of Christmas in their feet. Having retrieved the Christmas cards from the kitchen wastebasket at the request of Betsy, they let them fall like delicate snowflakes into her lap during their rush past. Betsy started searching through them until, satisfied, she removed one and handed the remaining cards to Patricia, who in turn set them on the coffee table.

"Hey," Paula suddenly said, now scuttling about on all fours in search of goodies under the tree.

"Hey," William mimicked.

"These presents are all for Grandpapa! No fair!"

"No fair!"

Dr. Glover, who had been let in by Mike and had taken considerable time removing his coat and especially his boots on account of his prominent waistline, finally entered the parlour. "Merry Christmas!" he bellowed.

After equally jovial sentiments were returned by all (Mike mumbling his), he apologized for the unexpected visit, saying he'd just dropped by to see how things were. He lowered his voice. "But considering what I just witnessed, I'm glad I did."

With the children still buzzing around the tree and Mike still busy at the hearth, Patricia helped her grandmother up, and she moved to the parlour window with Dr. Glover. He pushed the velvet, tassel-fringed curtain aside.

There, amid the howling winds and the glacial folds of snow, Abner trotted listlessly along, like a hatless, out of shape runner in the last hundred yards of a twenty-six-mile arctic marathon.

But Betsy saw her knight in summery armour, racing south against time—or it could be north, or east, or west; she always got confused when it came to directions—greeting the seasons with a blind faith that would keep his sweetheart's spirit alive.

Dr. Glover shook his head. "I'm sorry, Betsy, but I'm going

to have to insist we get him in the rest home as soon as possible."

"Oh dear," sighed Betsy, giving Dr. Glover a sly glance, still clutching the single Christmas card tightly to her chest, "aren't the dunes of summer simply . . . *grand*."

The doctor stared at Betsy with an expression of complete disbelief. "I beg your—"

Betsy shrieked, "Help him!" as Abner collapsed and disappeared in a mountainous drift of snow.

Abner lay helplessly on his back. With the exception of his face, his body was buried in snow. He knew it was snow. Regardless of what anyone might say, regardless of what anyone might wear, nothing could change the fact that it was the snow of winter. But if his beautiful wife told him it was sand, then for his wife, it was sand.

He watched the falling snowflakes flit around him like summer moths. The sky was grey and bleak, but in his mind's eye he saw a brilliance of stars and the moon against a black summer sky.

He remembered his daughter as a child, and there she was, in the middle of a field, half hidden by tall, golden grass. He saw his grandchildren there, too, the same age as his daughter. They couldn't be any more than ten or eleven. They stood around a single pine tree in the middle of the field, decorating it with ornaments and tinsel and lights. He was standing with his arms folded, smiling, leaning against the side of his old Plymouth Road King, which was pulled off on the gravel shoulder of a road. He could feel the sting of the hot summer sun on his face.

When he called their names, the children stopped and turned. They were far off in the distance. They ran toward him, laughing, leaping through the tall grass. Just when they were about to reach him, though, they vanished, swallowed up by the gullies of time.

Abner was cold. So cold he could no longer think straight. His eyes closed, and he felt himself floating up toward the black, star-filled sky.

Fortunately Abner didn't get very far. After sounding her chilling plea, Betsy turned to Mike, the only able-bodied man around, who instantly dropped his poker in the hearth and bounded past the wing chair and sofa, his footsteps thudding loudly down the hall and smacking crisply across the kitchen's linoleum floor before the crash of the door being thrown open told her he had raced outside, T-shirt, shorts, and all. Within a minute he was back, out of breath, with Abner's limp body in his arms.

Having tried the phone in vain during the rescue, Dr. Glover hollered for Mike to waste no further time taking Abner to his second-floor bedroom. "The kitchen table, man! The table will do!" he insisted.

Now, with everyone crowding the kitchen, Betsy behind the doctor, the others behind her, a nervous silence fell. Dr. Glover stood over Abner, who had a sofa pillow tucked under his head. His eyes were closed and his bare legs and arms and face were whiter than the drift of ivory hair on his head.

Dr. Glover took Abner's wrist in his hand for a moment. Then he pressed a finger to the man's cold neck. He turned to Betsy, his expression grave.

"We'll get him a quilt," said Betsy, looking up at the doctor.

"That won't be necessary," replied Dr. Glover. He placed a hand on her frail shoulder. "I'm very sor—"

"A blanket would be nice," said Abner, peeking out from a half-opened eyelid.

"Grandpapa!" cried Paula, laughing, pushing her way past her parents to her great-grandfather's side. She curved an arm around his head and pressed her cheek to his.

"Grandpapa!" cried William, giggling, scrambling to his great-grandfather's other side. He struggled to press his cheek against Abner's but, blocked by his sister's arm, he instead resigned himself to running his fingers through the mess of thick white hair.

"Grandpa!" cried Patricia, wiping tears from her eyes.

Mike bounded from the kitchen in search of a blanket.

Dr. Glover stepped back from the table, a bit dazed, while Betsy stepped forward to stand next to her husband.

"Forgive me?" asked Abner, looking a bit dazed himself, but coherent and wide awake nonetheless.

"For what, darling?"

"For getting old."

"Don't you dare," snapped Betsy.

As quickly as he had left, Mike now came thudding back into the kitchen, this time with fabric in hand.

"Mike!" shouted Patricia, shaking her head.

"I'm sorry," he gasped. "It was all I could find." He and Patricia spread the thin, pink sheet over Abner.

"It's true. I've gone and gotten old on you," said Abner to Betsy.

"Rubbish."

"Just look at me. The middle of summer, and I'm cold."

"What does that prove?" Betsy countered. "The summer always leaves me a little cold. Why do you think I'm wearing this lovely sweater that you gave me for my birthday?"

Dr. Glover, who for a brief instant appeared to be checking his own pulse over in the corner of the kitchen, had managed to don his large black coat and boots. After mentioning something about needing to see a patient, he bellowed another "Merry Christmas!" and promptly exited the house.

Abner continued talking, even while Dr. Glover spoke, raising his voice to be heard as the door slammed behind the doctor and the kitchen window rattled. "And you also start forgetting things when you get old, sweetheart. Simple things, like checking for mail and paying bills."

"That's not true, darling."

Mike jumped in. "Yes, it is true. The phone is out of—"

Patricia clapped a hand to his mouth. "Shush," she whispered. Then she put an arm around her husband's waist and rested her head on his shoulder. This moment was for her grandparents.

"I forget things, too," Betsy admitted to her husband. "But some things are okay to forget."

"Like Christmas?" asked Abner, still cheek to cheek with Paula, his scalp still being tickled by little William. *Tickle, tickle, tickle!*

Betsy felt ashamed and dropped her gaze. She stared at the single card that remained tightly clutched in her hand. "No," she said, her voice breaking.

"Or Thanksgiving?"

Betsy said nothing.

"Or Easter?"

Again nothing.

"What about the memory of our daughter's death?"

Betsy's eyes widened in surprise. She glanced nervously at Patricia, who glanced just as nervously back.

"Should I forget that?"

Betsy nodded apprehensively. "I wish you would," she whispered.

"Why?"

"Because—"

"Because it upsets me? Oh, sweetheart." He let out a jovial laugh—far too jovial, considering the tension in the air. "How can a father who still loves his daughter not be upset by what happened, whether it occurred yesterday or thirty years past?"

"You have to let it go."

"I have, in a manner of speaking. But what I haven't let go of, and what I haven't told you, is that I remember my childhood. I may forget to check the mail—and by the way, William wrote to say it's unseasonably cold in California right now." He paused for a brief chuckle. "But for some strange reason I remember my childhood as if it were yesterday. And let me tell you, it was a wonderful childhood. I remember all the Easters and the All Hallows' Eves and the Thanksgivings; I remember tumbling around with chums in the leaves, ice skating, kite flying, and of course, all the magical Christmases. Those were best." He stopped and slowly scanned the room, as if he were a child again, seeing a Christmas tree packed with an infinite number of glorious, wonderful presents.

His eyes returned to Betsy. "What upsets me isn't our daughter's death, entirely, but her life." He glanced at his granddaughter. "And Patricia's life upsets me. And so does William's, down there in California."

Betsy gently stroked her husband's arm through the thin sheet. "Why is that, darling? Because they're so far away?"

"Yes, because their *childhoods* are so far away. I realized it last summer. It just sort of hit me all of a sudden that I miss their childhoods—our daughter's, our grandchildren's, and now these two here . . ." He brought his arms from beneath the sheet and tenderly caressed Paula's and William's cheeks.

A long moment passed in silence.

"Because with these two here," he finally said very quietly, "I'm going to miss their childhoods far more than I could ever miss mine."

"Oh, darling," said Betsy.

"Oh, *Grandpa*," said Patricia.

Abner gathered himself. "You see, all I get is a trinket of time with them. A few more Easters, maybe a couple of Thanksgivings, and if I'm lucky, a handful of Christmases, even if they take place in the middle of summer."

"We'll move!" cried Patricia, wiping more tears from her eyes.

Mike gulped. "Move?"

"No you won't," Abner told his granddaughter. "You lived here for much of your childhood, and time took that away from me just as quickly."

"Then what's the answer?" asked Patricia.

All the adults looked at each other, dumfounded. At last

Betsy spoke. "I believe the answer," she said softly, her eyes again focused on her husband, who was still lying on the kitchen table covered by a thin, pink sheet, and was still being fawned over by his loving great-grandchildren, "is for me to change into something a little more appropriate for the season." She patted her sweater and smiled. And then she gave her husband the card in her hand.

The front of the card read *Seasons' Greeting*. Abner opened it and instantly his eyes lit. "My favourite season," he said, looking up at his wife and returning her smile.

They stared at each other for a long while. Then Betsy said, "Children, why don't you help your grandpapa up off the table. Someone's liable to mistake him for a delicious ham and sit down for a Christmas feast."

"Or maybe they'll think he's a big Thanksgiving turkey!" Mike said, and Patricia elbowed him in the belly.

"What about a rabbit?" William mused, sounding more grown up than his seven years.

"A rabbit?" His sister gave him a quizzical look.

"Yeah, you know—they might think Grandpapa is the Easter bunny and eat him." The boy put his hands together, chest-high, and pretended he was a rabbit.

Grinning, Abner watched as Little Will hopped and laughed his way around the kitchen table, first passing Easter, then a week of summer vacation, then Thanksgiving, before finally hopping down the hall toward blessed Christmas in the parlour.

NINETY DEGREES

Bah, humbug, that's what I say. Well, I didn't actually say it, but that's what I was thinking when my sister walked into the room. Even though she's just three years older than me, she treats me like I'm a baby. Her pitiful excuses for hands have been tormenting me since I was five. It's not so much that her hands are really all that bad, as hands go (and believe me, I know; Mary McIntyre from seventh grade had such a set of claws on her, I can't even bear to think about them!); it's just that they don't seem able to stop tousling my hair whenever my hair and her hands are in the same room.

"Merry Christmas, Booboo!" she said, coming toward me.

Booboo? Screw off! Okay, "screw off" was a little severe because I kind of like it when she calls me Booboo, but see what I mean about thinking I'm a baby?

I was sitting in my grandfather's living room in his plain wooden chair. It's an odd thing, that chair. Not because of its four basic legs, or the perfectly flat piece of wood you sit on, or its two simple armrests, or the four spindles that rise to the backrest—I told you it's a plain chair. What's odd is its positioning: pushed up against the wall and facing away from the television at ninety degrees. And that, by its very nature, is not entirely odd; it could, after all, be screwed down to my grandfather's roof next to the chimney stack. What's truly odd is that, despite the two old couches there in the living room, and the two leather recliners, my grandfather chooses to watch TV exclusively from his chair. At ninety degrees!

Come to think of it, *I* chose to watch TV from there for over an hour, which explained why my neck was stiffer than hell. And, adding insult to that injury, my back wasn't much better, since I had to lean forward the whole time. (Some genius decided to put the Christmas tree directly in line with the TV!)

Just before Irene—that's my sister—reached me, her arm flew out. I knew what was coming. I had been thinking about this moment since the last time I saw her, almost four months ago. I was prepared.

I feinted right, then left, then a quick right/left/right. The whole time, her hand sat frozen in front of me. I didn't expect this. I feinted left again, right, farther right, then so far right I almost tipped the chair. Out of nowhere, her other hand appeared. I didn't expect this, either. Traditionally she has used a one-handed attack. She must have learned this new method during her first semester of college. I had a feeling her aspirations for a "higher education" might mess things up.

In desperation I swung hard left and the side of my skull cracked into the wall.

Irene tousled my hair. "How've you been, Booboo?"

"I'm trying to watch TV, if you don't mind," I said, shaking my head back to its senses.

"My *wit-tle Boo-boo!*" she said, regressing, as always, to baby talk. "Did *wit-tle Boo-boo* miss me?" She continued tousling my hair.

"Oh, would you get off it?" I grabbed her hand and shoved it aside. I admit it felt kind of good, the tousling, but still, I had to get her off of it. "You're interrupting my show."

She gave me some space and I leaned so far forward in the

chair this time that I had to turn my head even more than ninety degrees. Perry what's-his-name was on the tube singing "I'll Be Home for Christmas." I've watched this special every Christmas Eve for as long as I can remember, not so much because I like it, but because that's when it's always on. It seemed to have caught Irene's attention, too; in my periphery, I saw her standing motionless, staring at the TV.

And then something happened. I felt this searing pain shoot through the side of my head—the same side that knocked the wall—and my eyes started to water.

"Booboo *did* miss me!" Irene screeched, and, as I fell from the chair, she caught me by the hair.

Christmas is the same old crap every year, especially when we celebrate it at my grandfather's house. I mean, he's got these crazy decorations that belong more in a grocery store than on a tree, they really do. My earliest recollection of his tree tinsel was back around the time of first grade. I remember seeing these pasty-white, limp things hanging like spaghetti, so I started pulling some off the tree. I think I ate a dozen or so strands before my mom caught me and screamed. She really gave me hell for that one.

And then there are his measly seven tree ornaments, all long, tube-like, and a faded pinkish-red. Once, when Irene and I were in town strolling along Main Street, we passed Bennett's Butcher Shop and I swear to God, the sausages hanging in the window looked exactly like my grandfather's ornaments, they really did! That was a while ago too, and when I mentioned this crazy similarity to Irene, she said I was nuts. I never did bite into one—an ornament, that is—but I've been suspicious ever since.

Even worse, though, are his popcorn streamers. He's got a dozen or so wrapped around his tree. They are pretty pitiful, and now mostly string. I feel bad about that, I really do, on account of a couple of reasons, but mostly because my grandfather is such a good guy and all and he deserves better.

Anyhow, about the only thing remotely different so far this Christmas was that I happened to be lying on my back on an ambulance gurney, staring up at my grandfather's pukey yellowy-white living room ceiling that had all this wild swirly stuff plastered to it. Funny how I never noticed this before in all the times we visited my grandfather. It kind of reminded me of that girl I already mentioned, Mary McIntyre. A few years ago in grade seven, I had this terrible crush on her; she was super-pretty. But then one day she said some ridiculous remark about how she hated being called up front in class to write on the chalkboard because the feeling of the chalk in her hands was just too chalky. That's when, all of a sudden, just like that, I noticed her claws for hands. They'd always been there, of course, but after that I noticed them and I couldn't look at her anymore. She no longer seemed pretty.

Two ambulance guys were at either end of the gurney, peering down at me. Mom was directly to my left, Irene to my right.

The ambulance guy closest to me said, "Who applied the bandage?" I took that to mean I had a bandage wrapped around my head. Then he started running a finger through my hair, a kind of tickly finger, right through my goddamn hair!

"It's a tourniquet," answered Irene. "I didn't know what else to do. His head hit the wall one second, and the next thing I knew he was falling from Grandpa's chair."

My mom said, "You did fine, babe, just fine." She reached over me and gave Irene a comforting rub on the shoulder.

"It's extremely tight," the ambulance guy who was still tickling me said. He kept pushing his finger down between the bandage and my skull and moving it around, and it occurred to me he was more just checking the bandage than tickling me. Still, though, it tickled pretty good until finally, he stopped. "Was there quite a bit of bleeding?" he asked.

"Blood?" I mumbled, gulping.

I don't know about you, but I hate blood. There was this time back in . . . I think it was seventh grade too, around the same time as Mary McIntyre and the chalk incident, when I was out in the schoolyard with this guy in my class, Bill Abernathy. We were over by this little kind of shed thing beside the school. It wasn't one of those wooden sheds, like my dad has in our backyard, but one of those weird ones that are made out of cement with tons of small rocks and pebbles stuck to it. It's amazing, what they think up these days when it comes to making things.

Anyhow, so he was standing next to it with his pocket knife, trying to pry away some of the rocks. It was really stupid, when you think about it. Here's this guy, clenching his teeth, his face getting redder and redder, huffing and puffing, and I swear to God, there must have been at least a thousand rocks lying scattered all over the school grounds. All he had to do was look around if he wanted a rock so bad! Would have saved him a lot of trouble, the way I saw it. And naturally I *did* see it, but so he wouldn't feel so bad and stupid that he was the only one doing what he was doing, I started using my fingernails on the shed to try to pull out a rock.

Then all of a sudden he screamed and I looked over and there was blood pouring from his thumb. It really freaked me out, let me tell you, but I just stood there, trying to look cool and casual. And all the while I was thinking, *That's the very stuff that's inside me,* and the more I thought about it the more sick I felt, until finally I started pretending that I had lemonade running through my veins.

That lemonade trick worked pretty well for a while, until I started feeling really thirsty and I got this wild craving for a glass of ice-cold lemonade. I mean, the craving became so severe, I figured the sick feeling over the blood wasn't near as bad, so I went back to accepting there was blood inside me, and then I felt fine because it really was the truth. Bill had already run off with his bleeding hand, so that helped.

Funny thing about that Bill, I found out the next day that he went straight to the school office and when they asked him how it happened, he told them a horse surprised him and stepped on his thumb. He killed me with that one. I mean, I can understand him missing the thousand or so little rocks, but how do you not see a big horse coming? He just killed me.

Irene took my hand in hers, and opposite her my mom did the same with my other hand. They both looked concerned.

"No, there wasn't any blood, far as I could tell," admitted Irene to the ambulance guy. "I was just being cautious."

"You did fine, babe," Mom said.

"I could have done more."

"Now, now! I'll have none of that silly talk! If I'd been here, I'd have done the same." My mom was next door wishing old Mrs. Kimble a merry Christmas when I clunked my head. Mrs. Kimble has been like a second mother to her ever since my parents got married.

"Still, I could—"

"Hush, babe!"

"Don't worry about me," I said, my voice barely a squeak.

"Did you say something, Carlton?" Mom asked, leaning down, her ear an inch from my mouth.

"Did Carlton say something?" Irene asked, looking at Mom.

"I think Carlton said something," the ambulance guy who tickled me said, while inspecting the fingernails of his left hand.

"I said don't worry about me," I squeaked again.

"There you have it. Carlton says not to worry," Mom confirmed, springing back up. She let go of my hand and held out her open arms. "Babe, it's been almost four months!" She leaned over me, and she and Irene embraced. Their bodies formed this arch thing and for some reason it reminded me of the Triumphant Arch, I think it's called, over in France—I remembered seeing pictures of it in history class. It was weird because I had never been to France, and I didn't even speak French, but it seemed so familiar, like I'd visited the place before, and like all of a sudden I was somehow fluent in the language.

"I missed you, Mom," Irene said.

"Bonn-jour," I said. "Come a saw vatt, moan cherry." I remembered hearing that one in French class.

"Missed you too, babe," Mom said.

Nobody heard me, except maybe the ambulance guy with

the frisky fingers, who said, "Ça va bien, merci," and then he smiled.

My head was feeling heavier than an anchor, so I started turning it to see if my neck was still stiffer than hell, and just like that I started to cry. It was kind of crazy because it really didn't hurt that much. But Mom and Irene seemed so happy it just kind of got to me. That and I happened to glimpse the Christmas tree when I turned my head, and it looked so old and pathetic and it made me feel sad for my grandfather all of a sudden, because I knew he loved that tree so much. It was one of those artificial jobs and some of the branches were almost bare to the steel and with all those popcorn streamers on it that had very little popcorn left on them and were now mostly string, it just looked really bad. I mean, the thing looked awful.

"Well, we'd better get this lad to the hospital," the ambulance guy nearest me, the one with those frisky fingers, said.

They started wheeling me forward and the other ambulance guy had to duck way down to get underneath Mom and Irene's embrace.

"Tell Grandpa I'm sorry about the snow," I managed to say as I was rolling away from them. It snowed like a bugger earlier and I hated the thought of all the snow the wheels of the gurney probably dragged in with them. Even though my grandfather had really crappy carpet in the living room and peeling linoleum in the kitchen that they'd have to wheel me over to get back outside, I felt really bad. But the apology didn't much matter, or the tears, because no one seemed to notice, except maybe the two ambulance guys, who both smiled when I said it.

Just before we went through the kitchen door and out into

the cold, they tucked another blanket around me and I got the crying under control. I was glad to be away from that tree, let me tell you, but Mom and Irene and their Triumphant Arch were still visible in the distance through the hallway, and I was glad for that.

"Merry Christmas, Weenie!" I yelled. For as long as I can remember I've called Irene "Weenie." I really hate to encourage her with the baby talk, I really do, but I know she kind of likes it and for some reason I thought it was important, right then and there, that she knew everything was still okay with her and me.

The Triumphant Arch broke and I thought I heard them saying something about seeing me at the hospital, but I couldn't be sure. The two ambulance guys were busy bouncing the gurney back and forth off the doorframe when they said it.

I'll admit it was really stupid, what I did. I mean, those two ambulance guys were professionals and all, but when we got outside, I swear, the snow must have been up to their waists. And it didn't help that Irene is such a crappy driver that she parked her car at such a crazy angle, the guys had to park their ambulance way down at the bottom of Grandpa's driveway.

So they were moving this gurney through the snow. It was slow going and I started feeling really sorry for them. They were nice guys, but they weren't very big, especially the guy with the frisky fingers. Funny, though, they *seemed* bigger than they were, wearing those uniforms and all, but I could see through it. Kind of like Irene wearing the uniform of "older sister" and always calling me "wittle" and I'm about a foot taller than she is!

Anyhow, the frisky-fingers guy was kind of breathing hard,

leaning way back, pulling the gurney. The other guy was snorting and pushing from the other end. And there I was on the gurney, trying to look casual and happy, only I was feeling guiltier than hell that I banged my head in the first place and all this was happening. I mean, those guys probably had better things to do on Christmas Eve than lug around some lame-brain who couldn't keep his head on straight. So they wouldn't feel so bad about things, I figured I'd better lighten the mood a bit.

A car went sloshing by. "Merry Christmas, Dr. Glover!" I yelled and smiled, bringing out an arm from under the blankets and waving at the passing car. "Make sure there's a warm bed ready for me at the hospital!" I laughed.

The frisky-fingers guy grunted. So did the other guy.

"I think that was Dr. Glover," I said. I wasn't entirely sure if it *was* Dr. Glover. I only met the guy a couple of times, once two years before when I accidentally discharged a pellet from my pellet gun into my calf, and before that when, in pursuit of a porcupine, I fell from a tree. He did a nice job setting the cast on my broken arm and, after he tidily removed the pellet from my calf, my grandfather told me how great it was having a good old guy like him around that you could really rely on. It made sense to me when he said it, the relying on someone part, especially since I knew there weren't too many doctors around, so he was probably pretty important, besides being so damn old.

The two ambulance guys stopped for a second to catch their breath, and then the one guy—not the frisky-fingers guy—said, "That was the pizza delivery guy."

I figured he was probably right, seeing as my grandfather lives in one of those small towns where everybody seems to know everybody else. I mean, the town is so small, if you fart and it's a real stinker, everybody is going to know about it. I swear to God that's true! They even had a write-up about it once in their rinky-dink town paper, *The Wharton Echo*, and ever since I saw that, whenever I have the urge now, I race to the basement, make sure all the windows are shut tight, grab the pillow I have hidden behind the oil furnace, and sit on it before relieving myself. My grandfather is such a good guy, I wouldn't want anyone complaining to him about me. So far it's worked out okay, because I don't think anyone has.

"Oh, how'd you know that?" I said anyway, trying to humour him and keep things light.

"It said *Pizza Delivery* on the side of the car."

"Oh," I said.

They resumed slogging through the snow toward the ambulance, but the frisky-fingers guy slipped and fell backwards. He let out a groan before getting to his feet. I felt really bad for him, I mean, he was such a nice guy and all, and now his whole uniform was covered in snow.

"Can I help?" I asked.

"Stay put."

So they kept going, grunting and groaning, especially the little frisky-fingers guy, and I was thinking it would be better if *I* pulled the gurney and *he* took a rest on top.

That's when I did a really stupid thing. I sprang up and I felt this rush of blood to my head, and instantly I thought of Bill Abernathy and his bleeding thumb and lemonade and Mary McIntyre with her claws scraping against that cement rock shed and, before the two ambulance guys knew what the hell was happening, I'd gotten so dizzy I fell onto my side and right off the gurney, banging off Irene's crazily parked car, then into the snow.

"Jesus Christ!" I heard one of them scream. Or maybe they both screamed that. All I remember is hearing this loud *pop* and feeling this wild pain killing my shoulder.

After the two ambulance guys finally got me up and out of that snow, they struggled to get me back on the gurney, but my legs were flopping around like wet noodles and my left arm was flapping like the wing of a dying seagull, not to mention I was making these hideous wincing sounds on account of the pain in my right shoulder. So the bigger of the two, not the frisky-fingers guy but the other one, finally said, "The hell with it!" and threw me over his shoulder and carried me to the ambulance.

The moment he threw me, though, my leg flew out and clipped the frisky-fingers guy straight in the nose. He made this wincing sound about as hideous as mine, then went down in the snow again. I felt really bad for him, especially since the guy carrying me didn't seem to care and kept right on trudging along, which wasn't very nice, seeing as they were partners and all.

On the drive to the hospital, I rode up front and the frisky-fingers guy stayed in the back on the gurney, which I was pretty happy about because he was such a nice guy and I thought he really needed the rest.

At the hospital my head still hurt like a bugger and so did my shoulder, but I didn't let it matter and walked alongside the frisky-fingers guy, who was stretched out on the gurney while the bigger guy pushed. The frisky-fingers guy's face was covered in blood, but I forced myself not to let that matter much either, and pretended I had chocolate milk running through my veins instead of lemonade, and that worked pretty well because choco-late milk doesn't make me as thirsty and some of the blood on his face was brownish anyway, so it all made sense. I tried to pick up his spirits a bit, being that it was Christmas Eve and all.

"You're bleeding pretty bad," I said. He looked at me kind of funny. "But I've had way worse," I continued, "so I wouldn't worry too much. You'll be fine."

"Oh you have, have you?" said the bigger guy pushing the gurney.

"Sure," I said. "I'm clumsier than hell. That sort of thing happens to me all the time."

Then I tousled the frisky-fingers guy's hair with my left hand and he shoved it aside. I couldn't really blame him for doing that, though, since I always do the same when Irene gets to tousling mine. Still, I just wanted the frisky-fingers guy to know I really liked him and that he was okay with me, which made me realize Irene probably does it for the same reason, so not only is tousling not bad, it's actually kind of good.

After the two ambulance guys left me and went through the doors to Emergency, I was asked to sit down at a desk with this nurse who was wearing reindeer antlers on her head. She seemed to be in a really foul mood, which surprised me, because she was surrounded by all these nice new decorations, like glittery red garlands, and pretty wreaths, and a big tree in the corner with sparkly tinsel, shiny ornaments, and flashing lights hanging from it. I forgot to mention my grandfather has lights on his tree, but only a few of them work, and the ones that do are all a boring white since most of their coloured paint has peeled away, leaving behind only the odd flake of green or red.

Anyhow, there was even some mistletoe directly over the nurse's head that hung straight down from a piece of string attached to the ceiling.

"What seems to be the problem?" she asked in a nasty fashion. Her eyes never left the paper on her desk, and her hand held the pen just above it, poised and waiting to write.

"Mononucleus," I said, staring at the mistletoe.

She raised her eyes. "Nucleus?"

"Yeah, mono," I said, shrugging my left shoulder. "So don't you be worryin' about kissing me." I thought I'd better say something straight off just in case she had any crazy ideas. Right before the Mary McIntyre chalk incident, I used to stare at Mary's lips in class and sit there thinking about kissing them all day long, I really did, they were so pretty and pink and pouty and all. But then she said that stupid thing about the chalk and I couldn't look at her anymore and I got off her lips after that, too. Ever since then I've sort of had this fear of kissing girls, except for my mom and Irene, who sometimes sneak up on me and kiss me. But they're not really girls, so they don't count.

I admit, though, it was kind of dumb of me to say, that "So don't you be worryin' about kissing me" thing, since my shoulder was killing me even worse and I didn't have to put on a brave face any longer because the frisky-fingers guy had left. But still, the nurse's lipstick was a mess, so I figured it might be a relief for her to know she wouldn't have to kiss me, on account of the fact she'd probably kissed most everyone else tonight. I thought I was doing her a favour.

"Funny guy," she said, and sighed. "Head injury?"

"Actually, my head's feeling fine." It really was, but I think mostly because of my right shoulder. Funny how that works—I mean, I knew my head was probably still pretty bad, but because my shoulder was that much worse, I didn't notice it anymore. "It's my right shoulder that has me worried," I said.

She glanced up at my head. "Then what's with the bandage?"

"Oh, this?" I touched the bandage with my left hand on account of the fact my right arm had lost all its strength. "This is a turbine." She looked at me suspiciously until I closed my eyes, made a wacky gesture with my left hand, and said, "Praise Ali Baba."

It was a dumb thing to say, it really was, especially since she probably lacked culture, because I don't think she understood it. She immediately picked up the phone. I had a feeling she was going to call security, so I made that hideous wincing sound again, rolled my eyes back in my head for a split second, then muttered between breaths, "Please. Dr. Glover. I need to see Dr. Glover."

Dr. Glover never came. Another man did, though, a Dr. Carlisle, who was much younger than Dr. Glover, and just as nice. After I explained my problem, he had this orderly guy help me off with my clothes and on with this white kind of dress thing. It didn't bother me because the orderly guy was a professional and all, but still, it did get kind of chilly down there when he wheeled me to a part of the hospital where they took x-rays of my shoulder.

In Emergency there was a long row of cot-like beds, each one separated by a ceiling-high curtain. They kind of reminded me of stalls. As the friendly orderly guy brought me there and helped me into one, all I could think about was Bill Abernathy and that horse stepping on his thumb on account of stalls being where horses live, and so I whinnied. My heart really wasn't into it, let me tell you, but the orderly guy seemed a little down, working on Christmas Eve and all, and who could blame him. My whinny seemed to do the trick, though, because he smiled and meowed back at me and that made me smile, too. I felt pretty good until he walked away and left me alone.

I was feeling pretty bad about lots of things, right then and there—about Bill's thumb, and Mary's claws, and Irene's hands, and my grandfather's Christmas tree, because they probably weren't all that bad. I mean, they probably weren't, and I thought I was going to cry the more I thought about it until, out of this crazy blue, I heard a voice in the stall right next to me.

"Hey, is that you?" I said. I wanted to get up and push the curtain aside, but I was flat on my back and couldn't move on account of my shoulder. I heard someone walk away and then nothing. "Hey," I said, "is that you, ambulance guy?"

"Whaddaya want?"

It was the frisky-fingers guy. I'd recognize that voice anywhere!

"Hey, it's me, Carlton. How'd you make out with the nose?"

"It's broken," he said.

"Oh, I'm really sorry," I said, and I really was, what with him being such a nice guy and all.

It sounded like he needed some cheering up. "Hey, um, ambulance guy—"

"The name's Glenn."

"Oh. Hey, Gle—"

"With two n's."

"Oh. Hey, Glenn with two n's, nice to meet you," I said, now that it was official. I think you can only say you've met someone once you know his name, even if his name has two n's. "That was some pretty great French you were speaking back at my grandfather's house."

"Pardon me?"

"Your French—you know, your 'saw vatt been, mercy' kind of thing. It was really great. Think you could teach me French one day?"

"No."

"Hey, hey!" I said, turning my head quickly to face the curtain that separated Glenn and me and at the same time feeling this killer pain bite my shoulder. I grimaced. "*Ahhhhhhhhhhhh . . .*"

There was silence for a moment, and then Glenn said, "You okay?" He sounded concerned and that made me feel pretty good.

"Yeah," I said, the pain easing off just a bit. Still, I needed to cheer him up. "Hey, do you get to open one present on Christmas Eve?"

"What?"

"You know, each person opens one present on Christmas Eve. My parents let me and my sister do that."

"Carlton, I'm forty-three."

"Oh," I said, and then mumbled to myself, "I hope I haven't missed it." I was referring to the present-opening tradition while taking a faraway look at the ceiling. I've never been too keen on Christmas, let me tell you, but I admit I do like the presents. I kind of like giving them, too, especially when it's something no one expects.

I remember one time I gave Irene this present and when she ripped off the wrapping, there was this Easy-Bake oven box staring at her. I mean, her eyes almost fell from their sockets because she'd received the same thing years earlier and she was probably thinking she doesn't need two Easy-Bake ovens, not to mention she was about sixteen or so at the time. Anyhow, when she opened the box and looked inside, she started laughing and said, "Tennis, anyone?" I mean, it just killed her because she knew that I knew she hated tennis, but I was trying to get her onto the game and I thought this was the best way.

So she used that racquet a bit, hitting some tennis balls off the side of our house, but in the end she said I could have it, which was okay by me on account of I love the game and the strings on my own racquet were pretty much all broken.

Looking back now, it was probably a big mistake, pushing her like crazy the way I did to use it right away, because she probably got all frustrated hitting the ball, then missing it on the return and having to search for it in the snow. I think she lost about three or four balls that Christmas Day. Eventually I found them, of course, when the snow melted in the spring, but it was too late; she'd already turned completely off the game by then, which I still feel bad about because I really think she could have been something else, seeing as she has such quick hands and all.

"Carlton? You there?"

"Hey," I said, "I was just wondering, what's Santa bringing you for Christmas?" I kind of laughed a bit on account of his broken nose and wanting to keep things light.

Before he could run down his list, though, Dr. Carlisle walked in, followed by the grumpy nurse with the reindeer antlers and the friendly orderly guy. It was getting pretty crowded in my little stall when, a moment later, just behind them, my grandfather appeared.

He's a big guy, my grandfather—not tall big, but round big. His head is bald except for a little bit of white hair around the sides. A few years back, my mom showed me this picture of him; he might have been twenty or thirty in it. He had all this thick, dark hair and he was trim as a fiddle. I mean, I couldn't believe it. Funny how that is sometimes, people changing and all; how one day they look one way, and then the next thing you know they look different.

At first I thought my mom was playing a joke on me and maybe it was the mailman because he had this big bag slung over his shoulder in the picture, but then I noticed his eyes. Even though the picture was in black and white, I could see it was my grandfather because his eyes never changed. Funny how that is, too, how people's eyes never seem to change except for the way they see things. Anyhow, later my mom told me he used to be the town mailman for a while, and then it all made sense.

My grandfather stayed near the back of the stall on account of the fact he's a quiet guy. I could see him through an opening between the nurse and the orderly. He just stood there smiling and, the odd time, giving me these reassuring nods. It made me feel pretty good, having him around.

Dr. Carlisle stood there, too, only right over me. "First of all, Carlton," he said, "what's all this?" He smiled and tugged on the edge of the bandage around my head.

Before I had a chance to say anything, the nurse with the antlers blurted, "He told me it's a turbine!" Then she started laughing. Which started the friendly orderly guy laughing. Which started the doctor and my grandfather laughing.

I felt pretty good right then and there, I really did, because here they were, Dr. Carlisle who was so nice, the orderly who was so friendly, the nurse with the reindeer antlers who didn't seem grumpy anymore, and my grandfather who is such a good guy, all laughing like hyenas and feeling great on account of me and something I'd said earlier. I think I even heard Glenn in the next stall laughing, too. So my mind started spinning like crazy for something funnier to say, and I thought about giving them a "Praise Ali Baba," but with my shoulder hurting worse than hell, all I could do was laugh like a hyena right along with them.

Eventually, when everything quieted down, Dr. Carlisle said, "Well, Nurse Jones here will remove this *turbine* for you." Everyone smiled when he said "turbine," but this time no one laughed.

That's when I saw the pair of scissors Nurse Jones held in her hand. They were huge, those scissors, and they reminded me of my mom's garden shears. I mean, I knew Nurse Jones was a professional and all, but wearing those silly looking antlers, and with her lipstick smudged all to hell, and probably being tired from kissing everyone tonight, I kind of got a little worried about her hand slipping, especially since I was working hard at keeping my head on straight. She took a couple of steps forward.

"Can I keep it on?" I asked quickly, meaning the bandage and not my head. Everyone looked at Dr. Carlisle, who looked at me with this puzzled expression. That's when Ali Baba and praising him raced through my mind again, and so I smiled and said, "Please? For religious reasons?" I know it was kind of a stupid thing to say, but I knew Ali Baba was a religious guy and it was all I could think of.

Everyone laughed again, especially my grandfather, who was killing himself in the back behind the orderly and the nurse.

After everything quieted for the second time, and the garden shears were put away, the doctor said my shoulder was dislocated, which explained the wild pain. He'd have to sedate me through an IV and I could go home early tomorrow morning, which he knew wasn't the greatest thing, being that it would already be Christmas Day. The only other option was to take the pain, and it would probably hurt like hell while they were fixing it, but at least then I could go home almost right away.

I knew Glenn the frisky-fingers guy was probably listening to all this, so I wanted to set a good example and put on a brave face for him and his broken nose, even though I'd kind of already made up my mind. But I wanted to know something else. I looked at my grandfather. "Has Irene opened her present yet?" I asked, meaning her one Christmas Eve present.

My grandfather smiled and shook his head.

I felt pretty good about that, let me tell you, because I sure as hell didn't want to miss the Christmas Eve present-opening tradition. So I told Dr. Carlisle I wasn't worried about a little pain and I'd take it as it came and be on my way. I said it kind of loud and confident, just to be sure Glenn and his nose heard clearly. And that's when, at the exact moment I'd finished talking, a woman spoke in the stall next to me, followed closely by the sound of footsteps and a bed squeaking.

"You take care of yourself, Carlton," Glenn said in kind of a whisper from the other side of the curtain, all polite and all, on account of he was such a nice guy and probably didn't want to be rude and just barge in on my conversation with the doctor. His voice was more nasal than ever, too, but I knew it was Glenn. I'd know that voice anywhere.

"I will, Glenn," I said, "I really will. And you take care of that nose of yours." I still felt awful about his nose.

"I will."

I heard a bed squeak again.

"Oh, hey! Glenn! You never told me what you wanted for Christmas."

I glanced at the nurse, and then the doctor, and then the orderly, and then my grandfather, and they were all staring at me with little grins on their faces.

"Joyeux Noël," Glenn said through the curtain.

"Joy—er, um . . . no, ah . . ."

"Christmas, Carlton, it means merry Christmas."

"Oh. Merry Christmas to you, too, Glenn," I said, feeling sadder than hell.

"Au revoir," he said.

Then I heard footsteps and I knew he had left.

Even though I felt sadder than hell, I really was glad Glenn went when he did because a few minutes later the friendly orderly guy clamped down on my legs right there in my stall, while Nurse Jones held my left hand. Her hand was soft and gentle and looked nothing like Mary's claws or Bill's bleeding thumb, and when she leaned over a bit to pull down the top part of the white dress thing I was wearing, I saw she wasn't wearing lipstick after all and that she was actually kind of pretty, so I kind of felt sad about that, too, because I should have trusted her and let her cut the bandage off with those shears.

A second later Dr. Carlisle moved in and clamped down on my shoulder and the upper part of my arm. "If the pain becomes too much," he said, pausing to take a deep breath, "tell me and I'll stop, okay?"

"You know I will," I said, even though I had no intention of telling him if it hurt because he was such a nice guy and all and was only doing his best. Just to be safe, though, I decided right then and there I was a horse, kind of like the lemonade running through my veins trick, and it made sense, seeing as we were still in my stall and on account of horses get whipped like crazy all the time and they're so used to pain they probably don't even feel it anymore.

The moment the doctor started twisting and turning and pulling and pushing, though, I started whinnying like a stallion, let me tell you—all these crazy, high-pitched whinnies that were so loud and so high-pitched they even scared me, I swear to God, they really did! Which is why I was glad Glenn left when he did, seeing as he went through so much with his nose and falling in the snow and the fact he was pretty old and didn't get to open a present on Christmas Eve. I would have felt even worse if he'd heard me. It made me realize, too, that you never get used to the pain no matter how often you might feel it, and that made me even sadder. I mean, if I was a horse who was used to getting whipped a lot and I couldn't take it, Glenn must have gone through hell when they fixed that nose of his and all he had was himself.

Anyhow, it lasted about a minute, and when it was over Dr. Carlisle and the orderly guy left me alone with Nurse Jones, who put my arm in a sling. I kind of had this crazy urge to kiss her right then and there, let me tell you, especially with her turning out to be so nice and pretty and all, but at one point she got really close and smiled and her teeth looked so yellow, they reminded me of lemonade, which started me to thinking about Bill's bleeding thumb, which for some crazy reason started me to thinking about how much blood you'd actually have to lose before it killed you, and so I got off that urge to kiss her pretty quick and instead only smiled back and said, "Thanks."

"You're such a cutie, you know that, Carlton Cullimore?" Nurse Jones with the reindeer antlers said before leaning down and hiding those yellow teeth and kissing me on the cheek—I mean, I'm not kidding, she leaned straight down and kissed me with those luscious lips, right on my goddamn cheek!

My cheek was still tingling when she finally left and the friendly orderly guy came back and helped me on with my clothes. Then Nurse Jones returned. She handed me a small plastic bottle.

"Dr. Carlisle prescribed Tylenol with codeine for you, Carlton," she said.

I stared at the bottle in my left hand on account of my right hand was in the sling and hidden under my flannel shirt. "I'm a bandit," I said, "a one-armed one. I prefer gold."

I heard her laugh but I kept right on staring at that bottle. I didn't want to risk seeing those yellow teeth of hers again and ruining my memory of those luscious lips.

"Well, mister one-armed bandit wearing a turbine and afflicted with mononucleus," she said, and laughed some more.

I glanced up at the friendly orderly guy. He wasn't laughing, but looked kind of relieved, like he'd been thinking of kissing me and was glad he didn't.

"That Tylenol there *is* as good as gold when it comes to pain," she continued. "It's very strong and can cause hallucinations, so only use the pills when the pain is bad."

My eyes never left the bottle in my hand.

"Okay?"

I didn't say anything.

"Carlton?"

I think she thought I'd gotten all shy because of her kiss and all, but really I was feeling worse than hell right then and there on account of Dr. Carlisle having these little gems hidden away the whole time and never offering them to me, and meanwhile I'd just failed miserably at pretending I was a horse that was used to getting whipped a lot. I mean, I really couldn't be too upset with him because he was such a nice guy, but still, if he'd given me one, maybe then I'd have been the greatest, most beat-up stallion that ever lived and then I could have taken the pain. Which started me to thinking that if he'd given me a *few*, maybe then I would have been surrounded by a whole herd of horses and then I could have told Nurse Jones the truth about her yellow teeth and she could have taken the pain, being that she was a horse.

And that, for some crazy reason, started me to thinking about when I was a kid. I used to love Popeye cigarettes. Actually, I still do, but now that I'm older a lot of my friends, guys like Bill Abernathy, sometimes hide out on the other side of that cement shed thing beside our school and smoke real cigarettes, which to me is surprising, at least where Bill is concerned, seeing as he almost cut off his thumb on account of that shed, and he keeps going back to it. I mean, painful memories are hard to take, especially if you're not a horse, so you'd think he'd want to stay as far the hell away from that shed as he possibly could. I know I do—stay as far the hell away from my own painful memories as I possibly can, that is. I just can't understand that guy Bill, I really can't.

So these guys smoke real cigarettes out there by that shed. I don't, not me. Now, if it was just Bill by himself, maybe then I would on account of I wouldn't want him feeling stupid and all, kind of like the time he was going at those rocks with his pocket knife and I helped with my fingernails. As it is, though, I usually just stand around looking stupid myself, which is okay; the way I figure, it's better than standing around looking *really* stupid, chatting about the weather, while these guys are blowing smoke in my eyes and I'm taking these long, deep drags on a Popeye and blowing fake smoke back in their eyes! I mean, that would be stupider than hell, it really would. Don't get me wrong, I still love my Popeyes, but now I only smoke them at home.

Which brings me to the time when I was a kid and I bought a pack. It was just your average, nothing special pack, like the thousands I'd bought before. I put a cigarette between my lips and pretended to puff away. I always do that—pretend to smoke them first, because they taste better that way. Anyhow, for some crazy reason I put a second one between my lips. Before I knew it I had the whole pack of twenty Popeyes dangling from my lips, and there I was, puffing away like mad, clicking my heels along the sidewalk, figuring I was the coolest thing since sliced bread.

And that's when it just kind of occurred to me to shove the whole damn lot of them in my mouth. I mean, it made sense, since I knew I'd eat them eventually. So I shoved them in and started chewing away like some crazy pig and I felt pretty good, let me tell you, chomping on those things, knowing I wouldn't have to worry about remembering to eat them in the future.

People worry a lot about the future and trying to remember things. I realized, right then and there, that it's better to just get it over with fast. I mean, you feel a lot better about things when you do. Anyhow, after that I always try to get it over with right away, but I admit with the food things, like Chiclets and Gummy Bears, I don't enjoy them much on account of my jaws always get sorer than hell. Still, I feel good about it.

Once I had this vicious sore throat—I mean, it was just killing me—so I bought some Halls and ate the whole damn pack before I left the store, I really did, and I haven't had a sore throat since! I even thought about buying, say, fifteen Easy-Bake ovens a while back. My plan was to return all the ovens later, but keep the boxes. Then I'd go around and get fifteen really great presents for Irene and wrap them up inside those boxes; that way I wouldn't have to worry about figuring out what to surprise her with for the next fifteen Christmases. I felt pretty good about the idea, let me tell you, until I mentioned it and asked her if that would be okay. She just laughed, so I never did buy those ovens.

Which brings me to that bottle in my hand and why I was feeling worse than hell, besides wishing Dr. Carlisle had given it to me before I was that horse. I started thinking if I ate that whole bottle of pills, then I wouldn't have to worry about remembering to take one if the pain got bad. If I ate that whole bottle, then maybe everyone would become a horse; there'd be an entire world of horses, and no one would feel any pain—not Bill, not Mary, not Nurse Jones with the soft hands when she found out about her hideous teeth, and not my mom or dad or Irene or my grandfather when they found out I was crazier than hell, and not even Glenn with the great French and his broken nose. Which is pretty stupid when you think about it, on account of, if I could make a world without pain, why was I feeling worse than hell?

Finally, in the end, I gave up on the notion. Nurse Jones kept waving one of her soft hands in front of my face, and so instead I only nodded and thanked her again.

That's when my grandfather walked back into my stall. Just before Dr. Carlisle started on my shoulder, he'd asked my grandfather to wait outside, which I didn't think was the nicest thing on account of it being colder than hell out there, what with the snow and all, but he did as he was told, being that he is such a good guy. He came back in carrying my coat. It's a big, white, puffy thing and it makes me look kind of like the Michelin Man when I wear it, which is okay on account of the Michelin Man seems like a pretty nice guy in all those commercials. Anyhow, he helped me get my one good arm into its sleeve before zipping it up.

Then we left my stall. I kind of had the urge to whinny a goodbye, seeing as the friendly orderly guy was there, but I don't think even a meow from him could have cheered me up, so I didn't say a word.

Walking through the hospital toward the exit, we didn't speak, on account of my grandfather being such a quiet guy, and me still feeling worse than hell. I think he sensed something was wrong because, just before we reached the doors to the parking lot, he started laughing like crazy. I mean, he's a quiet guy and all, but he's got this wild, loud laugh, like there's a thousand marbles bouncing around at the back of his throat.

He grabbed my arm and stopped me. "Here, look at this, boy," he said, turning me sideways to face a mirror. "You look like a big cauliflower!" He could hardly get the words out, he was laughing so hard.

When I saw myself inside my white, puffy coat, with the white bandage still wrapped around my head and some of my curly blond hair sticking up above that bandage, it sure cheered me up, let me tell you, because not only did I look funnier than hell, I could see my grandfather behind me in the mirror, just killing himself. I hadn't really noticed it before, but he was wearing his orange winter hunting jacket and his orange toque. His face was redder than hell.

"You look like a carrot," I said.

"I'd rather be a cauliflower, boy," he said. He calls me "boy" a lot. "People love cauliflowers." He kept right on laughing. He's a pretty happy guy.

To be honest, I didn't know what he was talking about, seeing as the first time I ate a cauliflower I almost puked. Give me a barrel full of carrots, though, and I'll eat every last one of them, I really will. It's kind of funny when you think about it, with me trying to be a horse and all, since I'm pretty sure horses love carrots, too.

Anyhow, I was feeling a lot better when my grandfather finally stopped laughing. Then he kind of smiled while giving my cheek a pat. That's when I noticed the lipstick on my face, all red and bright and perfectly outlined in the shape of Nurse Jones's luscious lips! I felt pretty stupid right then and there, let me tell you, because there I'd been, meeting Nurse Jones with the reindeer antlers for the first time, and I saw her lipstick was all smudged to hell. Then she touched me with her soft hands and for some crazy reason I didn't see her lipstick anymore, and her lips looked juicier than a hamburger. And then my grandfather pointed out all this wild lipstick plastered to my face, and so it really was there on her lips all along. I mean, I felt pretty stupid, I really did.

"Oh, that," I said, turning my head slightly and staring at the red mess on my cheek in the mirror. "That's a medication cream for the pain."

He started right up laughing again, my grandfather, and so I kind of laughed, too. I didn't know what else to say. I didn't want him thinking I was a pervert or anything, especially since he and my grandmother were married for probably about seventy-five years.

We were still standing opposite the mirror near the exit doors. I looked toward Nurse Jones's desk, and there she sat, beneath her mistletoe, smiling away with those yellow teeth and the smudged lipstick and watching me the whole time. She raised one of her soft hands and waved. I forced myself to smile and wave back, even though her hand looked like one of Mary's claws waving at me.

That's when I saw my grandfather give her a wave. "Thanks

again for taking care of my grandson here," he called to Nurse Jones. I felt pretty good when he said that, because he gave my left shoulder a couple of pats and then a little squeeze as he spoke.

"My pleasure," Nurse Jones said, still beaming from across the room.

"Have yourself a wonderful Christmas, Mary," he said.

"I will. You and Carlton have yourselves a wonderful Christmas too, Bill."

I pretty near passed out right then and there, let me tell you, because here I was trying my best to keep the image of Nurse Jones's soft hands and luscious lips in my mind by not looking at those yellow teeth again, but I took a chance and ruined everything and got a good look at them and for some reason I could only see Mary McIntyre's claw waving at me. Then my grandfather said goodbye and it turned out Nurse Jones was a Mary too, so in some ways it made sense, but in some ways not. I mean, if Nurse Mary Jones had soft hands at her age, maybe she had claws when she was young, so maybe things just naturally turn around with time and maybe there was hope yet for Mary McIntyre.

And that was when it really hit me. I'd forgotten my grandfather was a Bill until Nurse Mary Jones said his name. I know it sounds crazier than hell on account of I've known my grandfather forever, but I just never think of him as a Bill. Funny how that is sometimes, how you're used to seeing someone one way all the time and then something changes and you see him in another way and you hardly recognize him. My grandfather had never looked like a Bill to me.

I remember back in grade seven, when I made the school hockey team. Mr. Mann coached it. Well, my science teacher at the time just happened to be a Mr. Mann, too. They were really good guys, both of them, so I sent them each a card at Christmas. The first day back at school in January, Mr. Mann thanked me for both cards during science class, saying one would've been more than enough. I mean, I kind of almost fell off my chair when he said that on account of I never connected Mr. Mann the science teacher to Mr. Mann the hockey coach. I always called hockey Mann "Coach Mann," not to mention he always dressed differently from science Mann, usually showing up at hockey games and practices wearing a black wool coat and these wild muffler things on his ears.

Anyhow, I pretty near passed out right then and there by the hospital exit because, after I found out Nurse Jones was a Mary, it kind of hit me all of a sudden that my grandfather was a Bill, and that started me to thinking about Bill Abernathy, and that maybe my grandfather used to be stupider than hell just like him, seeing as he's a Bill, too. I mean, if he *had* been stupider than hell when he was young, I guess time *does* turn things around and there really is hope for Bill Abernathy and Mary McIntyre and everyone else for that matter, since my grandfather is smarter than hell now.

And that was what got to me more than anything, I think— the hope. It had been one hell of a Christmas Eve so far and I'd pretty much let everyone down. I just didn't want any hope right then and there, I really didn't.

It was a miracle I didn't collapse, what with my mind spinning like crazy and all, but my hand kept fidgeting like mad with the bottle of pills in my pocket and that helped, not to mention my grandfather is a pretty strong guy and he sensed I wasn't right, so he held me by the arm and led me out into the parking lot.

It was snowing like a bugger again, with each snowflake bigger than hell, and I could feel the weight of them when they hit me. My grandfather opened the passenger door to his car and helped me in and then he got in.

"What time is it?" I asked. I felt steadier, now that I was sitting.

"Almost eleven-thirty," he said, and then he laughed a bit while he was buckling himself in. I managed to buckle my own self in. "Don't worry, boy, Irene's waitin' for you."

He thought I was worried about missing the Christmas Eve present-opening tradition. I wasn't worried about anything anymore, except maybe how my mom and dad and Irene were doing. There was something else, too, something I just had to know. "Grandpa, when you were a kid, did you ever try and cut rocks out of a shed with a pocket knife and almost cut your thumb off?"

I expected him to laugh again, but he didn't. Everyone's used to me asking pretty stupid questions, so I guess it didn't surprise him. "No, but I did pretty near cut my leg off with a chainsaw once."

"Did you bleed?"

"What's that?" He leaned over a bit in my direction.

I repeated the question. Sometimes I have to repeat myself to my grandfather on account of he's got these tiny ears.

"Shoot," he said, "I bled like a stuck pig!"

I swallowed hard and sank down in my seat.

He started the car and we left the hospital parking lot, turning right onto Frank Street. He was leaning forward now, his nose a few inches from the steering wheel. He looked nervous as hell, which made sense because he's a pretty crappy driver, like Irene. I think crappy driving runs in families. There was this one time we had to go four blocks and he ended up making about twenty right turns to get there on account of he never turns left. Lefts scare the crap out of him, they really do.

We came to the intersection of Frank and Taylor. He lived just down the road to our left.

"Come to think of it, boy," he said, swinging the steering wheel right, "*you* were sure hollerin' like a stuck pig back there." He was still trying to cheer me up.

"I was a horse." I didn't feel much like talking, but I didn't want my grandfather thinking I was a pig, seeing as pigs get slaughtered all the time.

"What's that?"

"I said I was a horse. You know, like a stallion."

"Ah, a stuck stallion."

The windshield wipers were pumping away like mad and I could barely see the road when we passed Elm Street. He needed to make a right at Elm, right at Brown, right at George, and then turn right onto Taylor again. I knew the town's cemetery was up ahead and I was getting worried, since that's where dead people are buried, but it was on the left so I felt pretty good about that.

A moment later the cemetery's gates came into view. My grandfather leaned farther forward, his nose hanging over the steering wheel. I could feel the car slowing down.

"Hey," I said, "want to go fishing?" My grandfather is wild about fishing and I didn't know what else to say. He didn't say anything. I looked to my right. "Hey, there's a rattlesnake!"

I began jiggling the pill bottle in my pocket and it sounded kind of like a snare drum, so I started whistling "Yankee Doodle Dandy" like crazy, trying to act all cool and casual. Meanwhile I was worried all to hell about lots of things right then and there, like Glenn and his broken nose, and Nurse Mary Jones with her yellow teeth, and Mary McIntyre with her claws, and Bill Abernathy who was stupider than hell, but mostly I was worried about my grandmother on account of the cemetery is where she's buried.

When I hit the second verse my grandfather joined in, seeing as he's such a good guy and a pretty great whistler, and I felt pretty good about that, let me tell you. But before I knew what was happening, with all this crazy Yankee Doodle Dandying going on and the pills rattling like mad in my pocket, the car turned left into the cemetery and everything went quiet. My heart wasn't into that whistling anymore, it really wasn't.

The town's one cemetery is small, as cemeteries go. In the city where we live there must be a dozen like it, only ours are about the size of a golf course, seeing as people seem to be dying all the time. I had a couple of distant cousins who lived near us die recently, but I hardly knew them so it worked out okay.

A year ago, when Bill Abernathy's mother died (I hardly knew her, too), I felt really bad for him. Even though he's stupider than hell, I think he knew what was going on because he didn't show up at school for almost two weeks and when he finally did, he just wasn't himself. I mean, he hardly talked anymore and he never went near that shed for the longest time. That lasted a while, until eventually he came around and started talking like crazy again and doing even stupider things, like drinking white glue and prying steel bottle caps off bottles with his teeth. He really killed me with that stuff.

Last month when his father died, everyone was shocked. I remember my parents saying that he'd seemed healthier and stronger than a horse and they found him in his bed, looking peaceful and all. It made sense, with him being stronger than a horse, because he probably didn't feel any pain. That's when Bill went away to live with his older brother and I haven't seen him since. I worry about that Bill sometimes, I really do. I hope he's okay.

Anyhow, the town's cemetery is small, with only one road that stretches around two hundred yards up this little hill straight to the back, and then does a gradual one hundred and eighty degree turn and comes back down to the street. I was almost trembling when my grandfather slowly made the turn and about halfway down brought the car to a stop. It was darker than hell out there, seeing as the town doesn't have that many street-lights, with just one by the cemetery's gates.

My grandfather turned to me inside the car. "Do you know where your dad and I went earlier?"

Before Irene finally made it here from New York, I was left alone after my mom went next door to visit Mrs. Kimble, and my dad and grandfather went out together. I didn't have a clue where, other than my dad saying they were going to run a few quick errands.

"Sure," I said.

"We visited Mrs. Meriweather. Do you know who Mrs. Meriweather is?"

"Sure," I said. He eyed me suspiciously. I was squeezing the pill bottle so hard I thought it was going to break.

"Well, your grandmother went to school with her a long, long time ago. She's a very nice lady and a very sick one. Dr. Glover doesn't think she'll make it through the night."

He sat there looking at me a long time. I think he was waiting for me to say something, so I said, "That would explain Dr. Carlisle." I was actually going to ask how the old guy was doing, meaning Dr. Glover, but I figured whoever Mrs. Meriweather was, she was probably pretty old too, and it wouldn't be the nicest thing to say on account of she wasn't doing too good, and since my grandfather is pretty old himself and obviously liked her, I didn't say it.

"Yes, that would explain Dr. Carlisle," he said with a little laugh, then, "I know you're anxious to get home, so I'll just be a minute. You can wait here if you like."

On that, my grandfather opened his door and got out. He was all hunched over like an ape. He started trudging through the deep snow. It was almost to his knees and I could see him struggling, and with the snow falling on him like crazy, his orange hat and coat were quickly turning white. I felt so sorry for him, I really did, because he is such a good guy and he didn't deserve to be alone—not now, not ever. So I left the car, feeling sadder than hell, and followed him.

He was crouched down when I finally reached him. He'd taken off his gloves and was shovelling snow with his bare hands from around this kind of dark-looking stone thing that jutted out of the snow.

"Sorry about all the snow," I said. My teeth were chattering like crazy on account of it was colder and windier than hell. It was so cold my nostrils were burning like a bugger.

My grandfather glanced back at me and seemed kind of surprised I was there. A stone cross was now visible. "You can't do nothin' about the snow, boy."

"No, I mean in your house. From the wheels of the gurney when the ambulance guys picked me up. It probably made a mess." I still felt awful about that.

I don't know if he heard me because he kept right on going at that snow like crazy.

"Sorry about sitting in your chair," I said. Nobody's allowed to sit in my grandfather's chair except my grandfather.

By now he had shovelled away enough snow that you could read *CULLIMORE* on the gravestone. My grandmother's grave. Even though she died four years ago and I'd been here a few times during the last few summers, I'd never seen her gravestone close up. I would always sneak down to the creek that runs along the front of the cemetery, where I'd catch frogs on account of they're stupider than hell, they really are. I mean, you catch one, let him go, then a minute later you're catching the same damn one! You'd think they would know enough to get the hell away. Anyhow, I'd goof around there for a while until my parents drove down to get me. They didn't seem to mind, and neither did the frogs, seeing as those frogs were stupider than hell.

My grandfather wouldn't stop and my eyes started wandering over the dark cemetery. "Sorry about the popcorn," I said. I was referring to the popcorn I'd been gradually eating off the popcorn streamers on his Christmas tree for the past few years. My teeth were chattering away worse than ever now on account of the cold and the fact that I was looking around for ghosts, I really was. I didn't want my grandfather thinking I was pretending to eat popcorn, seeing as I really felt awful about eating his, so I tried to stop, but it was no use; my teeth kept chattering away.

My grandfather stood up, stuffed his hands inside his pockets, and turned around. "Listen, boy," he said, "why are you always sorry and worryin' about somethin'?" He was breathing heavy; white smoke was pouring from his mouth like a chimney.

"I'm not." My teeth wouldn't stop chattering, my "I'm not" coming out like *I-I-I-m n-n-n-n-o-t*. I sounded like that rattlesnake I pretended to see back there by the road.

"What's on your mind, boy?"

"Nothing, really—" *n-n-n-n-othing r-r-r-r-r-e-e-eally* "—other than maybe frogs."

"Frogs?"

"Yeah, and Bill Abernathy."

"Bill who?"

"Abernathy, on account of he's stupider than hell, just like frogs."

My grandfather looked at me kind of funny. "Jesus, Carlton," he said.

He rarely called me Carlton, and I'd never heard him swear before. I wasn't sure if his "Jesus" was the result of my "hell." And I was scared worse than hell right then and there, let me tell you, because I wanted to stop, but I couldn't; no matter how hard I tried, I just couldn't stop.

"And not just Bill and frogs, but Glenn with the broken nose, and Mary McIntyre with those claws of hers, and Nurse

Mary Jones with the yellow teeth, and all of them, everyone—Mom and Dad and Irene and you and the friendly orderly guy and Dr. Carlisle and Dr. Glover and even Mrs. Meriweather and, and . . ."

I could hardly see my grandfather's face for the falling snow and a gust of freezing wind that had just rustled up a thick swirl of snow between us.

"Spit it out, Carlton," he said.

Then I saw two hands come out of that snow, hooked and misshapen like Mary's claws, and take me by the shoulders. I was trembling worse than hell, and all of a sudden I started bawling—I mean, I really did—blubbering worse than a baby and even worse than Bill Abernathy when he almost cut off his thumb.

"And Grandma," I said. I finally got the words out. I was crying hard. "She was so nice to me, and funny, and always making me those pies of hers, and we'd sit under that willow tree in your yard and she'd tell me all sorts of great stories and I'm sorry, Grandpa, I'm sorry, because no one seems to give a damn anymore and she was so nice and—and I didn't even cry at her funeral! Everyone else was crying, but I couldn't. I tried like crazy and I gave a damn, and that's the craziest part, I really did give a damn, but I couldn't, no matter how hard I tried, I just couldn't cry . . ."

I had nothing left to say, with the tears and the chattering and the blubbering coming out worse than hell and all.

"It's okay, Carlton. It's okay. You can make peace with her now."

That's when my grandfather, who was still holding me by the shoulders, released me and stepped aside and I saw the inscription on the gravestone—*CULLIMORE, MARY*—and I felt the worst pain of my life shoot from my shoulder through my entire body. Then everything went black.

"It's okay, Carlton. It's okay."

"*Grand-pa?*" I mumble.

I open my eyes and see all this pukey, yellowy-white swirly stuff plastered to a ceiling. It feels like I've been lying on my back for about ten or twenty days or something, because my back is sorer than hell. Before I have a chance to think about that, or to think about anything else, a head pops into my line of sight.

"It's me, sweetie," my mom says softly. She starts fanning my face with a newspaper and then screams over her shoulder, "Hurry, babe!"

I hear rushing footsteps and a second later Irene appears. She starts dabbing my forehead with a wet cloth. "How're you feeling, Booboo?"

"*Wee-nie?*"

A big face shoves itself right in front of mine. "Son, you have nothing to be sorry about," says my dad.

"What?" I say. I'm groggier than hell.

"You said 'I'm sorry' just before you collapsed. It's not your fault, son; we should've been holding on to you."

My dad is like a tank, he really is. He gets down low and slides his arms under my shoulders and around my chest and makes this grunting sound. For a second it reminds me of Glenn, the frisky-fingers guy, and the thought of him and his broken nose makes me sadder than hell.

Mom shrieks, "Be careful!"

"I'll be careful!" Dad snarls. He tends to get emotional, my dad.

"Where's Grandpa?" I ask. My dad has my head and back off the ground and I notice my grandfather's chair beside me.

"Oh, Carlton," Mom sighs. "He's all tuckered out. I think—"

"I'm coming!" Grandpa hollers, and I catch a glimpse of him shuffling into the room. He lets out this wild, loud laugh and it sounds sweet in my ears.

My dad takes a deep breath and lifts me, then sits me in my grandfather's chair. I put my arms on the armrests for balance and it strikes me that my right arm isn't in a sling.

"Irene," Grandpa says, now standing directly in front of me, "I believe your brother here is expecting something, seeing as it's still Christmas Eve."

"Oh, yeah!" Irene rushes away.

"What time is it?" I ask.

"Two minutes before midnight," says Dad, then he makes these crazy *oooooh* sounds, as if there could be ghosts floating around the room. He starts wiggling his eyebrows up and down like mad, smiling away and looking first at me, then at Mom, and then at my grandfather. My dad is always killing me with stuff like that, he really is.

A moment later Irene is back. She places a present in my lap. It is small, rectangular, and thin, and for an instant I feel sadder than hell again on account of there's lots of Santas in sleighs on the wrapping paper, being pulled by these reindeer, but none of them have a red nose. Don't get me wrong, Donner and Blitzkrieg and the other reindeer are all pretty good guys, but without Rudolph they'd have had one hell of a problem on their hands. I mean, here's this guy Santa who's facing this wild storm, and the only way he can make it through to all those kids is with the help of Rudolph. So Rudolph doesn't even flinch, he helps Santa, and then hardly anyone remembers him, because you never see his picture on anything anywhere. When you think about it, Rudolph probably felt pretty good about helping Santa and the other reindeer guys and all those kids, so I guess that was thanks enough for him, and none of that other stuff really mattered. So it all makes sense.

There is something else making sense to me, too, so I say, "Weenie, have you opened a present yet?"

"No, Boobs," Irene says. Sometimes when Irene is happy as hell she calls me "Boobs." I always pretend to hate it, but the truth is, I love it and I love her, I really do—I love her like crazy!

"Can you open mine?" I say it kind of cool and casual; meanwhile my insides are bursting with excitement.

"I was hoping you'd let me!" Irene screeches, and she rushes away again.

My present is in my lap. There is no tag on it. "Who's it fro—"

"Just open it, boy!" my grandfather bellows. "You've got a minute before Christmas!"

I start tearing off the wrapping paper with both hands, but my right arm is feeling deader than hell, so I stop using it and just use my left. Once the wrapping is completely off, I stare at my present in disbelief. "But . . ." I touch the side of my head with my left hand, still staring at the present in my lap. "What about—"

"You asked me to take it off!" says Mom. She sounds kind of giddy.

I raise my right arm, which is stretched out inside the sleeve of my flannel shirt. "And—"

"Same thing there. Took it off!" I start hearing these wild giggles.

"And what about my pills?"

"You said the pain was 'worse than hell,' so I gave you one," says Mom.

My dad jumps in. "Did you have to repeat it word for word?"

"Well, that's what he said."

My dad clears his throat. "I'll talk to *you* later, son." I don't think he liked the idea of me swearing.

I'm still staring at the present in my lap, a book. I turn it over in my hand. It is old and the print is faded, with these kind of stringy things sticking out of the binding near the top and bottom, but I can read the title on the spine: *Learn French the Easy Way.* I open it. There is something handwritten on the inside cover:

Carlton,

This book taught me all I know, and if you'll give it a chance, maybe it can do the same for you. It's not quite as easy as the book title makes it sound, but if you keep at it, you'll be okay. Hope the shoulder is feeling better. No hard feelings about the nose. Merry Christmas!

Your friend,

Glenn (the ambulance guy!)

"Carlton," Mom says. "Did you hear me? I said I gave you a pill for the pain."

My hands are trembling. I don't remember any of it—how I got from the cemetery to here, or asking to have the bandage and sling removed, or asking for a pill for the pain. It doesn't really matter, though, it really doesn't, because I feel nothing like a horse and I'm happier than hell. I look up and my mom and dad and grandfather have these huge smiles on their faces.

I hear the sound of paper tearing and I turn my head ninety degrees. Through my tears I see a tree so green and beautiful, it almost hurts my eyes, and then from behind that tree, Irene starts up with all this crazy laughing.

My dad leans down and whispers in my ear, "What I really want to talk to you later about, son, is—" he glances over his shoulder "—and don't tell your mother I said this—you've got to tell me all about that lipstick on your cheek."

Then Irene rushes around the tree carrying an Easy-Bake oven box. "Fore!" she says. I swear to God, that's what she says, she really does. "Fore!"

CHRISTMAS DAY

It is Christmas Day and you are in a small town. It could be any small town in Ontario, but this one happens to be called Wharton. To be exact, you are inside Floyd's Smoke Shop, and Floyd's, like any smoke shop in any small town, is located on Main Street. Main Street runs north and south and through it cut two intersections. As could be expected, considering the season, those intersections are strung with holiday lights.

You drove into town four days ago, on a Saturday, from the city where you have always lived. Instead of turning off Main and heading straight to your destination, you stopped in front of the old hardware store. It is a Home Hardware, the same store where your uncle worked for two years. During visits as a child you occasionally helped him there, taking inventory, stocking shelves, though now, at age forty, you suspect you were probably more hindrance than help. Still, the memories of those moments are strong, and they always make you smile.

You parked, and you and your family strolled from the hardware store along the sun-drenched sidewalk on the west side of Main. This town, like most towns, has one of everything; you passed the drug store, the smoke shop, the barbershop, the jewelry store, and the bakery, where the warm country goodness of fresh-baked delights assaulted your senses in the December cold. You find most stores hold special remembrances for you still, like Chester's Five & Dime where, as a child, you floated wide-eyed into its pint-sized toy section on a cloud of dreams, invariably purchasing a new harmonica each summer vacation.

Continuing on, you passed the ice cream parlour and the clothing store and the office of the town's only accountant who, it just so happens, is also the town's sole lawyer, and who, according to his sign, handles "any need from professionally prepared tax returns to professionally prepared defences of every manner of sin." You smiled and shook your head when you saw this.

All of these shops and others sit beneath a single roof in an immensely long and old two-story building, the second floor of which, you know from experience, is used for storage by some of the businesses (the hardware store, for one), while the remaining space houses small apartments (your uncle and aunt rented one for a spell).

After crossing at the intersection near the northernmost part of Main, you strolled back on the opposite side, passing the Co-op, the IGA, the butcher shop, the bank, the gas station with its single bay, the diner, the post office, the library, and many other community necessities and places of business. You recognized a new establishment, a video rental store, and shook your head again and smiled. *Progress,* you thought.

It wasn't until you had almost arrived back at your car that your oldest child, a boy of ten, pointed out a small, white placard inside the window of the sweet shop. At first you thought he was pining for a block of succulent-looking fudge, but no, it was the placard that had his attention. It read:

Come one, come all
for an intimate gathering
of neighbours and friends

at Floyd's Smoke Shop
noon – three
Christmas Day, 1985
— A day to remember —

Once you'd read it, you instantly froze. To encourage community bonding, the town has held a brief gathering each Christmas Day since before your father's birth here, some seventy-two years previous. He's often talked about them but, for some reason, you'd assumed the tradition had ended long ago; you have no recollections of attending these get-togethers yourself, when spending your holidays here in early childhood.

"That's a surprise," said you.

"What? That I like fudge?" replied your smart-aleck ten-year-old, whom you love with all your heart.

Now, having just stepped inside Floyd's Smoke Shop at 12:30 on Christmas Day, the familiar tinkle of the door's ancient silver bell only a second ceased, your brothers and their families, your spouse and your children and you all get swept into the kindred warmth of people clamouring about.

A moment later a young girl clinging to a Cabbage Patch Kids doll goes whizzing past, while a Transformer (you know this because you got your own son one for Christmas this year, a gift he opened with great delight at 6:00 this morning) follows closely behind, somehow managing to "fly" despite being wingless, in the outstretched arm of an imaginative boy. They disappear through an open doorway at the farthest corner of the shop to your right. Seconds later they come rushing back through the doorway at the farthest corner to the left, and this time it is the

Cabbage Patch Kids doll "flying" in the boy's outstretched arm, while the girl trails behind hugging the Transformer as if it were a newborn baby. With devilish little grins, your children and their cousins go racing after.

The front room at Floyd's is cool and richly scented, its air no doubt permanently imbued by decades of sweet-tipped smoking cigars and flavoured tobaccos fired in the kilns of exotic wood pipes. It is also—by all outward appearances, at least—a small shop, but there is a sense of roominess to it.

At the shop's centre are a dozen or so people crowding around an aging recliner. It is about ten paces straight ahead and facing away from you and the shop's front door at ninety degrees. It looks out of place in a smoke shop, especially considering the many wooden chairs and several small, round tables that seem to have been pushed aside to accommodate it and the gathering of people. Ensconced within the recliner's battered brown fabric, sitting upright, is an elderly woman. Her hair is pure white and straight, as neatly preened as the feathers of a dove; her face is aglow with the smile of a child. The equally elderly onlookers seem to be doting upon her. You can hear their murmuring voices, aflutter with joviality.

Off and on, it snowed heavily yesterday—never a surprise, in this town. Your father has just stepped in beside you and is stomping the snow from his galoshes. When he finally focuses on the cluster of people and the woman in the easy chair in particular, he fixes an uneasy gaze on you.

You know he is a considerate man, has always been a considerate man, and you understand the look. You smile and say, half laughing, "Go ahead, Dad," and he practically throws himself into the throng, and into a barrage of backslaps and merry Christmases.

The way you remember it, Floyd's has always been the place where the town quenched its modest thirst for vices: smoke, drink, and gambling (over the pool tables in back and over cards at the tables out front). Though your parents never forbade you from coming here, your trips inside were always brief, usually to purchase a soft drink or a bag of potato chips and, unbeknownst to them, to peek at the six pool tables in back and the men who stood over them with their plain-collared shirts and baggy pants and suspenders. They always seemed content, those men, and for some strange reason this glimpse of their peaceful existences made you love this town even more.

Fifteen feet directly to your left is the proprietor's station, where a bronze, vintage cash register abuts the wall. A man with a leathery face, lardy-looking, short black hair, and a resemblance to Floyd—or what you vaguely remember of him— stands behind the counter, wiping it down with a cloth. He appears to be in his sixties. The sleeves of his white button-down shirt are rolled up to the elbows, exposing a slick of wiry black hair that runs the length of both arms to the back of each hand.

In front of the counter are two bar stools. A tall man with a bulky waistline and narrow shoulders occupies one of the stools. He is almost completely bald, with just a thin line of white wrapped snugly around his head like a horseshoe. He wears a white oxford shirt and a blue knit tie, and he looks comfortable yet decidedly out of place, considering most others in the shop— with the exception of the man behind the counter—are wearing winter coats. You slide onto the empty bar stool next to him.

He brushes his hands free of salt from the peanuts he's been eating and turns toward you. "Merry Christmas," he says, his mouth still full of peanuts. He chews for a few seconds, then swallows, before offering a hand. "The name's Dr. Glover." His voice is slightly raspy, but carries a lilt that gives it a very pleasant, soothing tone.

As you shake his hand, you tell him your name.

"My Lord! I'll be damned! Look who it is, Floyd!" he says.

Floyd stops wiping down the counter and shakes your hand. "Well, it's *about* time."

They are all smiles, as are you. "I've been in here before," you confess to Floyd behind the counter. "Dozens of times, as a matter of fact, up until I was ten. You probably don't remember."

"When was that?" Floyd asks.

"Thirty years ago, Mr. Sullivan."

Floyd chuckles. "Stop right there! First of all, Mr. Sullivan would be my dad, Floyd Sullivan Sr. I'm afraid I'm just Junior, and simply Floyd to my friends. So please, call me Floyd."

"All right, Fred," you say confidently.

Floyd jerks forward and lets out a big guffaw that etches a deep line into each of his leathery cheeks. "Fred'll work," he says.

"Fine. Be that way. Floyd it is," you say, feigning disappointment.

After more chuckling, Floyd resumes. "And secondly, I only came back here in 1979, when my father died. To run his shop. Thirty years ago I was living in Toronto."

"I'm sorry," you say, in reference to the demise of the senior Sullivan.

You look over at Dr. Glover, who must have rotated on his

bar stool during your humorous aside with Floyd. You do the same and the two of you watch the mass of people at the shop's centre. After a few moments, and for no reason other than friendliness through small talk, you casually ask, "Why would the town hold the Christmas Day get-together here? There must be larger places."

Before Dr. Glover can answer, Floyd pipes up. "Why? I'll tell you why."

And he does. Apparently the annual get-together was held religiously in the party room of the town arena until two years ago, when some wiseacre decided to sneak onto the ice, whooping and hollering as if he was having the time of his life. Before you knew it, practically the whole party had shifted to the ice— over a hundred people, sliding around in their boots. Then someone brought out one of those yule log cakes and they started kicking it around like it was a puck. When competitive old Mrs. McAllister tried to win a face-off at centre (it seems her team was down by three goals), she slipped and broke her hip. Dr. Glover, who was playing right defence at the time, tottered toward her and almost fell himself.

"Right defence?" you say to Dr. Glover, trying desperately not to laugh.

"I know. It was stupid," replies the doctor, sneaking an embarrassed peek at you. "Our side already had seven right defencemen. We were weak on left D."

It is no use; you have to laugh and do, already feeling immensely comfortable in the company of these two strangers.

Floyd continues with the story.

Because of that incident, last year they decided to hold it at the curling rink. Big mistake. With no party room, everyone gathered around the four rink surfaces, mingling, sipping on beverages. Everything was going splendidly until some dumbbell decided to start curling, even though all the curling stones were locked up where you couldn't get at them.

You glance behind at Floyd, who is wiping down the old, pockmarked wooden counter again. "Let me guess: yule logs?"

"That would've been fine," says Floyd, "but no. Grandchildren! The dumbbell had his five-year-old grandson curl up in a ball and he curled the lad down the rink! Then *everyone* with five- and six-year-olds started taking turns curling, trying all these wild in-turns and out-turns with their grandkids, and yelling nutty things like, 'Who's got shot kid?' and 'Get that four-footer into the four-foot!' After the fifth end, one side was up eight to three. When Arnold Robertson went to retrieve his grandson—who, it should be noted," Floyd continues, speaking so slowly now it makes you believe what's coming is a comical little aside to an already comical story, "was curling beautifully at the time, and had the boy smack dab on the button—it turned out the boy's cheek was flat stuck to the ice! Took 'em ten minutes and two buckets of hot water to free him!"

Dr. Glover gives a bleak sigh. "Third degree frostbite."

"Damn," you mumble.

"Sick," says Floyd.

All the while you and Dr. Glover and Floyd had been chatting, the ancient bell had been tinkling almost nonstop with the opening and closing of the shop's front door as more people piled inside. And as they piled in, most headed straight for the crowd around the recliner, while those already there slowly broke off, forming small clusters around the shop's periphery. In your father's case, though, he's just now broken free and is going against the grain at a pretty hefty click for a man of his years. He heads toward the front door in his wool plaid coat.

Dr. Glover raises an arm and calls your father's name. Your dad waves back. Then he flips two fingers, as if to suggest he'll return in two minutes, satisfying the concerned look on your face before exiting Floyd's Smoke Shop.

"It's good to have your dad back," the doctor says.

After moving away to attend university, your father landed a job in the city after graduation. There he met your mother, got married, and raised you and your siblings. Many years retired now, six months ago he decided it was time to move back to this, the town of his birth, and three months ago he did, returning to the very house in which he'd been raised.

"Back? You knew my father before?"

Both Dr. Glover and Floyd let out an abbreviated laugh.

"Shoot," says Floyd. "Dr. Glover knew pretty well *everyone* before." He goes on to tell you that Dr. Glover has practised medicine in the town for over fifty-three years, the first twenty-five of which he was the town's only doctor.

"Funny. I don't remember you."

"Well, I remember your dad. He's a few years younger than me, mind you, and if I'm not mistaken, he was one hell of a mischievous kid."

"Really?" Your father has always been, in your eyes at least, the most responsible man you've ever known.

"Yes, really," confirms Dr. Glover, glancing at Floyd and smiling. "Like all kids."

Floyd stretches awkwardly over the counter and sticks his thick right arm between you and the doctor. On his forearm is a tattoo of a scantily clad woman who appears to have a scar across her bare belly.

"Six stitches, compliments of a barbwire fence and the doc's needle!"

"Ouch," you say.

"Ouch was right."

"And speaking of mischievous kids—those are mine there," you quickly say, pointing out your two children as they sweep past with a group of other children, most of whom are clutching a toy or two, products no doubt of a dream-fulfilled Christmas morning. Their footsteps are raucous across the thin strip flooring, which has lost its finish and is a dull, dirty grey, rickety and soft in spots, and rippled like tiny waves. The children vanish into the farthest corner of the shop, passing through the open doorway that you know leads into the back room with the pool tables.

"Good-looking kids," says Floyd.

"Beautiful," adds Dr. Glover, who then puts a hand on your shoulder. His hand doesn't even twitch, but for some reason you gain great comfort from the mere contact. "I was sorry to hear about your mother." Your mother died five years ago.

"Thank you." After a very long moment, you ask, "Do you remember my grandmother? I have no memory of her." She passed away when you were five.

"Of course."

"What about my grandfather?"

Dr. Glover suddenly looks distressed. He leans forward on

his bar stool and fixes a heavy gaze on the shop's centre. It's as if he's looking out across an endless field of ripe cotton for which he's just been given the daunting task of single-handedly picking the myriad of bright white bolls, some thick, some thin, some long, some short, some straight, some curled, and a few, of all things, brambly.

"Certainly I remember your grandfather," he says finally, his voice dissolving into a lingering silence. Still staring into that field, he slumps back against the counter.

And you remember your grandfather, too. Not surprisingly, your recollections of him were vivid just last night, celebrating Christmas Eve as you were in what was once your grandfather's house. In fact, your memories of him reside within you almost exclusively from a magical Christmas Eve in that very house thirty years ago in 1955, a Christmas celebration that would ultimately be his last. Though he actually collapsed on that night (shrugging it off seconds after as mere clumsiness), a month later he collapsed again, this time succumbing to a heart attack while awaiting his doctor in an examination room.

And instantly it occurs to you: "Were you my grandfather's doctor?"

Dr. Glover nods. His silence now makes sense. It is the silence of loss.

Despite the din of good spirits dancing lightly throughout the room, in your little corner the mood has quickly gone from cheery to funereal. This time it is you who places a hand on the doctor's shoulder for a moment before swivelling around, deciding to lighten things up.

Floyd is facing the wall, fiddling with a portable radio in a black leather case. The volume is low, its sound sibilant as he flips stations. Next to the cash register is a stack of *The Wharton Echo*, and beside that is two gunmetal display racks filled with chewing gum, assorted candy, and chocolate bars. Above these racks are some old poster ads stuck to the wall like a continuous sheet of aging wallpaper; your eyes rove over their slogans: *Hey Mabel, Black Label!*; *Move up to quality . . . move up to Schlitz!*; *Golfers on the GO . . . know Miller makes it right!* In particular, *Smirnoff Vodka . . . Driest of the dry* and *No whiskey anywhere is more deluxe than Walker's DeLuxe* tickle your fancy.

You smack a hand down on the counter. "Floyd," you holler, "it's Christmas, by God. Gimme a stiff one!"

Hoping to get a rise out of Dr. Glover, you glance at him only to see his demeanour remains deflated. Floyd doesn't budge either; his ear is glued to the radio's speaker. "Floyd?" Still no response, so you take a shot in the dark. "Fred?"

Floyd turns around.

"Pour me a stiff one!"

"Sorry," he says. "This is a smoke shop."

"Hell," you say.

Floyd points to a large red Coca-Cola chest cooler across the room. It appears to be the same chest cooler that you, as a child, could barely see over as you struggled to lift the silver steel lid, then struggled just to hold it open as you retrieved your choice of pop from its belly of ice water. "We sell pop," he says dryly.

"Oh."

You stare at the old posters some more, studying one in which Lauren Bacall and Humphrey Bogart look like the picture of happiness, Bogie at the helm of a sailboat with a cigarette between his fingers. The advertising reads: *Mrs. Humphrey Bogart says: "I love to see a man smoke a Cigarillo."* There is also an ad with John Wayne that catches your eye, touting his beloved Camels: *For more pleasure—have a Camel!*

You smile at Floyd and smack another hand down on the counter. "Well, let me ride a pack of Camels, then!" Again you glance at Dr. Glover, who appears unmoved by your attempt at levity.

"Sorry. Read the sign." Floyd points to a *No Smoking* sign on the wall.

"But this is a smoke shop," you protest.

"What of it?" Floyd scowls, leaning forward in an intimidating fashion, his muscular arms splayed out and rigid, his large hands pressed firmly down on the counter. His posture reveals dark crescents on his shirt under his arms, and the brutish stench of sweat wafts past your nostrils. "I'm the proprietor. I sell what I want." You shrink what feels like a foot on the bar stool. "We sell almost everything *except* butts," he continues. "If you need to put something in your mouth, I'd recommend potato chips."

"I'll settle for a pop," you reply.

As you slide from the bar stool, you notice Dr. Glover watching you. You ask if he'd like anything. He shakes his head. You weave through the crowd of people, stopping for a quick chat with your older brother who is all smiles and, he says, having the time of his life. He also tells you the rest of the family are having the time of their lives in the back room. You grab a pop from the Coca-Cola chest cooler (and quite easily, you are happy to note) and head back, hearing great gushes of laughter from the gathering of people around the recliner, and most notably from the old woman *in* the recliner as you pass. You again seat yourself on the bar stool.

You set your pop on the counter. "How much do I owe you?" you ask Floyd, who is hunched over, his back to you, once more seeking a suitable station on the radio.

"It's on the house," says Dr. Glover.

"But—"

"No buts. It's on the house."

"It may be *on* the house, yet someone just made me acutely aware there are no butts *in* the house." You nod toward Floyd.

"Don't be too hard on him," the doctor whispers. "It's a crazy town."

"No kidding. People curling grandchildren and playing foot hockey with yule logs. A smoke shop that doesn't sell cigarettes. A Coca-Cola cooler that doesn't have Coke." You raise your bottle of Pepsi.

"You don't know the half of it."

"I presume you know the whole of it?"

"Not the whole of it, but most of it." The doctor's copper eyes guide yours to the old advertisements on the wall. "Bogart. Wayne. Cooper," he says. "They all died of cancer related to smoking."

You now notice the ad promoting Lucky Strike cigarettes that reads, *Gary Cooper says: "It's common sense for me to prefer Luckies."*

"Floyd's heroes?" you whisper.

Dr. Glover sits silent for a moment. "No, his father was his hero. He died of cancer and the man never smoked a day in his life."

"That's terrible," you say, suddenly feeling a swelling of sadness for Floyd, who is still happily working away, now sorting what looks like receipts, completely oblivious to the conversation. The radio is finally fixed on a station, its volume barely audible.

"Sometimes that's the unfortunate cost of doing business, I'm afraid." He pauses. "When James Trammel died of lung cancer three months ago—"

"I recognize that name," you blurt.

"Recognize that name?" Dr. Glover looks at you like you've sprouted wings from your ears. "Christ. You'd have to be dead not to recognize that name around here. He was the finest builder this town ever knew. Practically single-handedly built this town."

"That's it! Before my dad moved into my grandfather's house, he needed some work done. His name was mentioned."

"Yes, well, for James, his lung cancer was the cost of doing business, too." The doctor swivels around. Given his great girth, his movement is laborious and yet surprisingly abrupt, leaving you with the impression it was done with purpose, so you do the same. "The stress of trying to please everyone and build perfect homes proved too much. He smoked a little in his own home, but a lot on the job." He lets out a heavy sigh.

"He was Floyd's good friend?"

"No, he was *my* good friend. I knew him forever. And his death was the last straw for me," he says absently, staring off into the mob of people as if searching for his good friend. "I asked Floyd to kill all tobacco products, for the sake of the town, and he happily obliged."

Dr. Glover makes what looks like an uncomfortable twist so he's able to glance over his shoulder at Floyd. "I'm very proud of him for doing it," Dr. Glover quietly confides, his body again squaring up, returning to face the crowd of jubilant townsfolk. "And you know the craziest part of all?"

"What's that?"

"Not a single person made a ruckus. And this town has some pretty heavy smokers."

Just then the ancient bell tinkles again, and in walks your father, carrying what you instantly recognize as a patchwork quilt. Your grandmother made dozens of these during her life-time, one of which kept you safe and warm on that memorable Christmas Eve back in 1955. Your mother made many as well, your own ten-year-old boy kept safe and warm beneath one of hers as last night's wonderful Christmas Eve unfolded.

The crowd at the shop's centre peels away, creating a path for your father. He stops at the recliner and begins spreading open the patchwork quilt.

"Who's that?" you whisper to Dr. Glover. "That woman in the easy chair."

He shakes his head slowly, as if he's more baffled than you by the sight of her.

You smile and give him a gentle ribbing. "I thought you knew *everyone.*"

His eyes fasten on yours. "Her name is Mrs. Meriweather. And it defies all that I know as a medical professional that she is here today."

"I beg your pardon?"

"She was dying of a broken heart—"

You burst out laughing, but immediately stop when you see that Dr. Glover is being serious. Floyd, who had been busy doing something beneath the counter, stops to peer at you before disappearing again to resume his work.

"I'm sorry," you apologize. "A broken heart, you were saying."

Dr. Glover looks unamused, but continues nonetheless. "Her husband died last year and since then she has been steadily deteriorating. Everything I prescribed failed. Last night she was delirious, getting to the point where she had almost no vitals. Three breaths per minute, her pulse at twenty beats. And yet . . ."

"She looks healthy—robust, actually," you say, and this time it is you speaking absently as you watch your father place the patchwork quilt over Mrs. Meriweather's legs. As much as you know it's merely a quilt and made solely of fabric and fine threads, you know it is more. It is the spirit of your mother and grandmother, who could not be with you today. And it is the spirit of your grandfather, who, for many years, held the fabric of your family together until that fateful day in Dr. Glover's examination room. And in all the things that it is, you know from what you learned last night that, most of all, it is an unspoken gift of love from your father and countless generations of your family.

"Yes. And just look at her hair," Dr. Glover says. "Yesterday it was grey. Today it's pure white. It's as though . . . it's as though she aged fifty years overnight!"

"Odd."

"Not odd. A Christmas miracle."

You are tempted to laugh again, but refrain, instead saying, "Come on. A Christmas miracle?"

He gives his head an incredulous shake. "I wouldn't have believed it myself, but . . ." He pauses for a long moment, his eyes finally gripping yours in a firm gaze. "Would you like to know what manifested her cure?"

Before you can answer or even nod, a boy appears next to the doctor and screeches, "Oh, hey! Dr. Glover!" He has curly blond hair and wears a burly white bomber jacket, its right sleeve empty and hanging limply by his side. His left hand holds open a tattered old book that he now consults. "Bonn-jour, moan amy."

Dr. Glover chuckles a deep, good-natured chuckle. "Well bonjour to you, Carlton my friend."

Carlton smiles like a tail-wagging puppy as the doctor introduces you to the boy. He has a funny smile, with a gap between each tooth almost as wide as each tooth itself.

"I heard about your Christmas Eve," says the doctor, who removes a pair of half-glasses from his shirt pocket and puts them on. He stands and puts his hand to the boy's forehead, then checks his pulse, then takes the boy's head lightly between his fingertips and studies it carefully. "How's the cranium feeling?"

"The crani—um—what?"

"The head, Carlton. How's the head feeling?"

"Oh, fine, Dr. Glover."

The doctor unzips Carlton's coat. You get the impression he's about to give a thorough examination right there on Christmas Day in the middle of Floyd's Smoke Shop. The next thing you expect to hear is a request for his patient to open his mouth and say "ah."

"And the shoulder?" says the doctor, who is now seemingly working the right one underneath the coat.

"Fine, Dr. Glover, it really is. I'm taking a pill a day to keep the pain away."

"Good, son. And what about porcupines and pellet guns? You keeping away from them, too?"

Carlton breaks into an infectious laugh that can best be described as hyena-like, and you can't help but laugh right along with him.

"I'd recommend, son, the next time you see a porcupine up a tree, that you grab your pellet gun and shoot the critter!"

"I will, Dr. Glover, I really will!"

The doctor settles on the bar stool again and leans toward you to whisper, "A couple years back, he shot himself in the leg, and before that, broke his arm chasing a porcupine up a tree."

You cover your mouth to conceal your smile and muffle your snort.

Carlton smacks his book-holding hand down on the counter, which you now notice has a one-dollar bill sticking out from between its pages. "Hey, bar guy! I'll take a pack of smokes!"

Carlton can't be any more than sixteen and you suspect Floyd (especially after being summoned as the "bar guy") may skip the intimidating posture and even the suggestion of potato chips over cigarettes and go straight to bopping the young customer right in the nose.

Floyd sneers. "Beg your pardon, boy?"

Carlton snickers. "Hey, that's funny! My grandpa calls me 'boy,' too!"

"Read the sign." Floyd points to the NO SMOKING sign, which you are all too familiar with, immersed as it is in the sea of old poster advertisements on the wall.

"Hey! That's funny, too! I don't want a pack of Camels. I want a pack of your finest Popeyes!" He gestures with his book toward the display rack of candy. Sure enough, on it are several packages of Popeye candy cigarettes that even you, as a teenager, indulged in occasionally.

Floyd's sneer vanishes. He sets a pack on the counter, refusing the dollar bill protruding from the book. "It's on the house," he says.

"You've got to take it," pleads Carlton. "I swear to God, you really do."

Floyd glances at the doctor.

"Doctor's orders," says Dr. Glover, smiling.

After reluctantly accepting the gift and thanking both Floyd and the doctor, Carlton offers all three of you some of his candy cigarettes, which you all graciously decline. Lacking two good hands (you noticed his right one is in a sling), he asks if you'd kindly hold his book for a moment, which you do. He then begins fumbling with the red and white package of Popeyes, only to have its entire contents of twenty candy cigarettes spill onto the counter. He manages to scoop them up. He puts his hand holding all twenty to his mouth, and for a split second you think he's going to devour them all, but when his hand withdraws he has only one between his lips.

"Here, let me help you with that," says Dr. Glover, extending his hands. His hands are large, spotted brown with age, each finger long and bony. They appear almost clawlike, and you marvel at those hands, the very hands that tended your grandfather all those years ago. You wonder what your grandfather felt when those same hands touched him, and if by touching them now, you would be closer to your grandfather in some way. But as quickly as this ridiculous thought comes to you, it vanishes from your mind.

"Hey, nice hands," says Carlton as he pours the nineteen cigarettes into Dr. Glover's cupped hands.

As Dr. Glover begins returning the candies to their package, Carlton leans against the counter and closes his eyes. He takes a long, deep, fake drag on his fake cigarette, its tip red as if lit. Then he exhales slowly, blowing a fake puff of smoke into the warming air of Floyd's Smoke Shop. He has such a satisfied look on his face, you're almost tempted to light up a Popeye yourself.

"I wonder," Carlton says in a musing tone. "What's it really like to be a horse?"

Finished with his task, Dr. Glover looks at you, and you look at him. In unison, both of you shrug and smile in bewilderment at each other.

Out of the corner of your eye, you see a woman coming straight toward you, dancing a strange jig. She is holding a newspaper in her left hand. When she gets within earshot, you hear her saying in a quiet, singsong voice, "I burned my house down. I burned my house down . . ."

Dr. Glover also seems to have heard, because he too has turned and is watching her approach.

Behind her, the ancient bell tinkles again and in shuffles a group of people—two youngsters, a middle-aged man and woman (probably their parents), and two elderly folks, all of whom have come in from the frigid December cold wearing nothing but shorts, T-shirts, and an assortment of summer footwear.

"What the hell is going on?" you whisper through the side of your mouth to Dr. Glover, unable to take your eyes off the spectacle.

Dr. Glover laughs heartily. "I told you this is a crazy town." He slides off his bar stool and opens his arms. "Mary!" he bellows, and the woman who has apparently burned her own house down falls into his embrace.

She can barely get her arms halfway around the large man. Her hair is straight and golden-blond and she has the most dazzling blue eyes you have ever seen. "Dr. Glover! My, how I've missed you!"

Carlton, who had been enjoying his fake cigarette, managing to "smoke" it down to half its original size, stands a few feet away from the hugging pair with a dumbfounded expression on his face. After Dr. Glover and the woman you now know is Mary separate, Carlton catches the woman's attention. "Grandma?" he asks.

Since Mary can't be any older than thirty, the absurdity of this comment strikes you, as well as Mary, hard in the funny bone.

"No, son," says Dr. Glover, placing a sincere hand on the boy's one good shoulder. "Your grandmother was Mary Cullimore and you lost her four years ago."

Seeming to acknowledge this, Carlton plucks the fake cigarette from between his lips like a veteran smoker, blows one last fake puff of smoke from his mouth, takes two steps forward, and kisses Mary on the lips.

"Hey! What's the big idea!" a gruff voice blurts. You immediately recognize it as Floyd's. He is grinning behind the counter. "Where's *my* kiss?"

Carlton gulps. Mary is blushing. You and Dr. Glover can't stop laughing.

Suddenly a deafening roar of applause sounds from the back room. Quickly, you, Carlton, Mary, and the doctor scurry to stand in the open doorway at the back left of the room. You see a chaotic carnival unfolding around the six pool tables you remember sneaking peeks at during childhood. Only now, at one of them, two children hold a pool cue across the table's width about a foot above its midpoint, while four other children play Ping-Pong, paddling the ball back and forth over the makeshift net. On another table, two wickets have been fastened to its green felt surface and croquet is the game of choice. Another table has a group pitching horseshoes, while a fourth table has an intense game of what looks like lawn bowling taking place. Surprisingly, at a fifth table they are actually shooting pool.

The table farthest from you seems to have caused the stir. A horde of people surrounds that table, mostly children, yours among them. Standing atop it is a young woman, perhaps twenty, with short, ginger-coloured hair that looks as if it's been blown back in a persistent wind. She grips a golf putter by the wrong end.

"Weenie!" Carlton shouts, making a twisting gesture with the book in his hand. "Other way!"

The woman looks puzzled for moment, then flips the putter around, and the crowd cheers. "Thanks, Boobs!" she calls back. "Okay, here we go. Titleist in the corner pocket."

You can't see the surface of the table for the crowd of people, but her arms make a recognizable putting stroke, and a second later the crowd roars.

"Yes!" says Carlton, pumping his fist in the air. Then somewhat shyly, looking at the three of you, he says, "Um, my sister. She's got really quick hands, she really does. I'm trying to get her onto the game."

On the way back to the bar stools, Carlton stops and starts chatting with Mrs. Meriweather in the recliner, who looks aglow and warm, her legs wrapped snug in your mother's patchwork quilt. He shows her his book, *Learn French the Easy Way*, which he says was a Christmas gift from a good friend who, it just so happens, gave it to him last night as thanks for, of all things, breaking his nose! She smiles and then asks if he's ever been to France. He responds no, but says he plans on going—once he's mastered the language, of course.

She says it's a wonderful but strange country. She winks at you before telling him bulls run wild in the streets (at which point Dr. Glover whispers to you, "Spain"), cocks fight like mad in the alleys (at which point you whisper to Dr. Glover, "Mexico"), and sometimes they feed people to the lions (at which point you and Dr. Glover look at each other and whisper, "They still do that?"). Carlton then warily asks some obscure question about France's treatment of horses, at which point you, Mary, and Dr. Glover excuse yourselves.

Now, again sitting on what is quickly becoming *your* bar stool, you listen as the doctor informs you that Mary here is none other than Mary Ellen Trammel, granddaughter of James Trammel, the finest builder this town ever knew.

"Look at this," says Mary, barely able to control her excitement. She squeezes between you and the doctor and places a yellowed copy of *The Wharton Echo* on the counter.

Dr. Glover leans in, donning his glasses, and carefully studies the front page. "Where did you get this?" he asks, dropping his hand on the newspaper to prevent Mary from turning the page.

"Grandma gave it to me as a Christmas gift. She bought it—"

"My God! The day you were born!"

Mary is in awe. "You remember?"

Dr. Glover rubs his chin, his jawline hidden beneath his substantial jowls. "June 21, 1957. How could I ever forget?"

Floyd twists around from behind the counter so he, too, can get a clear look at a piece of the town's past.

Mary goes silent. "I still feel bad about that," she says at last.

Dr. Glover places a hand on her shoulder and gives another hearty chuckle. "Mary," he says, "all was forgiven the instant I saw your beautiful face."

"Really?"

"Really."

"But it must have hurt."

"Hurt like hell, actually."

"You were brave."

"Cried like a baby."

"So did I."

"That's understandable," says Dr. Glover, smiling, "considering you *were* a baby!"

"I'm going to cry like a baby," you insist, "if someone doesn't tell me what the hell you're talking about!"

Dr. Glover explains. Apparently on that fateful day back in 1957, when he asked Carol Trammel to push during labour, the hysterical woman misunderstood and instead kicked, striking him in the face and instantly breaking his jaw. Seconds later, Mary burst into the world.

"Ouch," you say, staring at the scantily clad woman on Floyd's forearm, wondering if the cut to her belly was nearly as painful as the kick to the doctor's jaw.

"Ouch was right," replies Dr. Glover. "But on the bright side," he motions toward Mrs. Meriweather, who now has only a scattering of people around her, "I made good use of that recliner over there. Hardly sat in it a single day before I got hurt. Spent about a year recuperating in it, sucking burgers through a straw!" He laughs, as do all others in your little group.

Mary finally opens the newspaper. As she flips pages you notice a litany of handwritten notes in the columns and margins of each page. "What are all those entries?" you ask.

"Oh, that was my grandmother for you," replies Mary, continuing to turn pages. "After I was born she started recording town happenings—"

"For posterity," you say. "A permanent record for her granddaughter. Very nice."

Mary blushes. "Well, not exactly. Only the town's . . . misdeeds."

"You're kidding, right?"

"I wish I was."

Dr. Glover smiles and shakes his head. "That sneaky Claire. I should have known."

"Let me guess," you say. "Like who killed Joe's chicken, and who stole Fred's goat?"

"I never had goats!" blurts Floyd, grinning ear to ear.

"Something like that. I haven't read them all yet." She stops flipping and presses a finger to the page. "See, right there? I wrote that myself last night, when I got the news about my house in Toronto." She points to a handwritten passage in one of the columns that states Mary unintentionally burned her own house down by way of a faulty coffeemaker, just yesterday, on Christmas Eve. She is beaming. "Isn't it wonderful!"

"Congratulations," says Floyd with genuine enthusiasm.

You can't believe such a triumphant sentiment can be offered for such a traumatic occurrence but, not to be left out, you smile and add, "Way to go."

"I wish I could have been as thrilled when my house burned down." Though it's news to you, the doctor reminds Floyd (who'd heard it from his father) and Mary (who'd forgotten all about it) that his own house burned to the ground in 1959.

"Faulty waffle iron?" you ask, laughing.

"No," the doctor answers, clearly suppressing a grin. "A complete mystery. I was just fortunate to have a friend like James Trammel around." He takes Mary's hand in his and gives her a reassuring smile. "He literally began the rebuilding process the very next day."

"You know that Victorian at the top of the hill?" Floyd says, directing his question to you. "The one on the left just after you pass the town's gates?"

Your jaw drops. "That's a mansion."

Dr. Glover looks embarrassed. "I didn't want anything so grand, but that's James for you, God rest his soul."

There is solemn silence in your little corner for what seems like a long moment, no doubt in remembrance of the recently deceased James Trammel. Then the ancient bell tinkles again. In strolls another family, an elderly man leading the way. His pow-der-grey hair is so unkempt that, were it likened to a house, it would be merely the shambled, charred remains of one that burned down long ago. Behind him are three children and a middle-aged couple. Dr. Glover gets off his stool far too quickly for a man who is likely pushing eighty years, and wordlessly drifts toward the new arrivals.

Carlton is still next to Mrs. Meriweather, and has been joined by the two elderly folks wearing shorts and T-shirts. Near them, at a small table, an elderly woman with loosely curled white and grey hair chimes out Mary's name, her voice resonating much like a church bell.

"That's my grandmother," Mary says, smiling. She picks up her newspaper and folds it beneath her arm. "It was nice meeting you."

"May I?" you ask, indicating her newspaper.

Floyd, who is working again, depresses a heavy bronze key that sets the ancient cash register to clanging, no doubt ringing up all of his "on the house" sales. Appropriately enough, a little *No Sale* card pops up in the register's window.

"Oh, I don't know," Mary replies, glancing anxiously at her grandmother.

"Please? I was ten in 1955, and it was the last time I spent Christmas here as a child," you say with almost pleading sincerity.

"I understand, but—"

"And a month after that," you interrupt, "was my last child-hood experience here. Ever. It was for my grandfather's funeral."

Mary looks torn.

"Just for a few minutes. It would mean a lot to me."

"Okay, for a few minutes," she says at last, releasing the newspaper into your possession before striding over to her grandmother.

You relax on the bar stool. Immediately, the newspaper's headline grabs your attention: TWO DIE AT PIKE RIVER BRIDGE. Even tragedies, you think, occur in small towns. Certainly as a child you were oblivious to such things when visiting your grandfather. For you, this town was always a dream, and every morning that you woke in your grandfather's house, you burst from bed as if each day were a magical rebirth.

Nothing bad ever seemed to happen during your one- or two-week summer vacations here. Perhaps it was simply because you were too busy to notice, wading into creeks wearing your grandfather's floppy rubber boots in search of water striders and frogs and minnows, or racing through fields, scaring up grasshoppers from the tall grass. And perhaps other times you were simply too preoccupied by the wondrous nature of Christmas and Easter and even those autumn Thanksgivings, with their abundance of colourful family members fluttering around like falling leaves. It was your greeting of the seasons here that inevitably made all things perfect in your little world. It was the times you never saw—those in-between times—when things must have gone awry.

According to the article, a married couple took the turn near the bridge too quickly during a thunderstorm, and their car careened off the road between two pilings and through a cable guardrail, eventually overturning and plunging into the river. They were knocked unconscious, and when help finally arrived, it was too late. Dr. Glover pronounced them dead at the scene.

A hand on your shoulder startles you. It belongs to Dr. Glover. "I'd like you to meet two very special people," he says.

Standing before you is a slight boy, no older than eleven or twelve, along with the elderly man with the powder-grey, unkempt hair. Their eyes are both chocolate brown and twinkling with delight. Dr. Glover tells you the elderly man's name, and then adds, "But you can call him Old Man."

"All my friends do," the old man confesses.

The young boy looks up at the old man. "But I call him Papa."

"He does," says the old man. "Ha-ha! And I call *him* Tiger."

"He does," confirms the youngster, smiling and looking at you. "But you can call me Tommie."

"Ha-ha!"

You shake their hands. "Tommie. Old Man. Pleased to meet you."

Dr. Glover suddenly grows serious. He takes the boy by the shoulders. "Tommie, what you did last night—giving my patient an unapproved medication without my consent—was unacceptable, against the law, wholly despicable, and . . ." Tommie looks ready to burst into tears ". . . perhaps the greatest Christmas present anyone has ever given me!"

"Ha-ha-ha!" cries the old man.

Tommie can't stop smiling. The old man tousles the boy's hair with obvious pride.

Dr. Glover glances at you. "You know who this boy is?"

It sounds like a trick question, so instead of answering with the obvious, "Tommie," you remain silent.

"He's my Christmas miracle!"

You recall what the doctor mentioned earlier, about the old woman in the recliner and himself not believing what cured her. "Mrs. Meriweather?" you say.

"Mrs. Meriweather."

"Ha-ha!"

Dr. Glover leans in, as do the rest of you, huddling together in conspiratorial fashion, your heads mere inches apart. "You won't believe what Tommie administered to my patient last night."

Tommie is beaming.

"Try me," you reply, sitting as you are on a bar stool, at a counter that resembles a bar, behind which is advertised alcohol, but where nothing even remotely alcoholic is sold.

The doctor looks cautiously around the room, as if what he's about to say could compromise his integrity as a medical professional if the word got out. "A snowflake," he whispers.

"A snowflake?" you mumble under your breath, and then without thinking you pull a face that says "Good God. Holy Christ. What next?" You glance back at the apparent bartender, Floyd, who is now cleaning a glass with a towel, wishing he could produce nothing short of a Christmas miracle himself and provide a tall stiff one for your benefit.

"Ha-ha, ha-ha," cries the old man—softly.

"Dr. Glover, before I forget," whispers Tommie, "sorry about the slush."

"Nonsense. I deserved every oozing inch of it. Speaking of which, before *I* forget—" he reaches into his pocket and removes a silver pillbox "—I believe this belongs to you."

"It's not mine." The boy takes it and gives it to the old man. "My grandfather's."

"Old Man," says Dr. Glover, looking around cautiously again, "tell our friend here what you told me this morning on the phone."

Whispering every word of his story, the old man tells you that—according to him, at least—not all snowflakes are created equal. The ones that fall on Christmas Eve are special, retaining every single moment from that year's Christmas Day that each person in the entire world will experience and, eventually, will one day forget. The truth is, it's not so much that snowflakes actually retain anything, the old man clarifies, but that they possess some special magic that's put into them by—well, maybe even Santa Claus! And what that magic does is trigger those memories, bringing back the actual Christmas Day experiences so vividly—the smells, the touches, the sights and sounds and tastes—it's as if you've gone back in time and you're there living them again! And the best part of all, he says, is that snowflakes grow; the longer you keep them in your freezer, the bigger they get. And the bigger they are, the longer they last, bringing even more of that delicious Christmas Day flavour.

"It's true," says Tommie, nodding. "Papa gave me one last night that he caught on Christmas Eve, 1977. My grandma died when I was five and I would've been four in 1977. And now— now I remember her!" He looks at his grandfather and reaches what is high up for a slight boy to shag the mess of hair on the old man's head. "And now I remember Papa's hair used to be combed neat, too!"

Dr. Glover scratches a patch of white hair on the side of his own head. "You know," he whispers absently, looking at the old man, "I remember that, too."

"Ha-ha," cries the old man, ever so softly again.

You retrieve the clear glass bowl that has been sitting idly on the counter since you began your conversation with Dr. Glover. You raise it in the middle of your little huddled group, trying your best to keep an open mind, while at the same time finding it difficult not to be skeptical. "And let me guess. You eat these snowflakes like crunchy peanuts?"

Tommie is about to speak, but the doctor halts him, taking the bowl of peanuts from you and returning it to the counter. "No," he says, sounding almost too serious to be believed. "The snowflake medication is administered in a manner similar to a throat lozenge. Right, Tommie?"

"Right, Dr. Glover. The one I sucked yesterday was the size of a pea. It lasted a few minutes. And during those minutes I saw my grandma, felt her sweep me off my feet, heard her voice the same way I'm hearing your voice now."

"Oh, really. What did she say?" you ask.

Tommie's eyes are ablaze with excitement. "It's not so much *what* she said, exactly. It was more . . ." Tommie's gaze drops to the strip wood floor for a moment. "It was more a sense of great love that I felt from her."

And instantly you are struck with a sense of familiarity, and, most of all, belief! You realized this yourself, just last night—that true gestures of love are far more important than any spoken "I love you." People get it. They just know.

The old man flashes the pillbox before your eyes. You notice a *55* written on the label affixed to its silver top. "Caught this one Christmas Eve, 1955," he says.

Your mind is adrift. Christmas Eve, 1955! Your grandfather's

last Christmas Eve and the last Christmas your entire family—
the aunts and uncles and cousins—assembled to celebrate the
festive holiday.

Dr. Glover chimes in with something about the snowflake
bringing back the memory of Mrs. Meriweather's late husband
by letting her relive a long-past Christmas Day when he was
present, and that was the miraculous cure for her, but you're
hardly listening.

Strangely enough, you remember that Christmas Eve in '55
vividly, yet you don't have the slightest recollections of the following Christmas Day. Only because you are here now, you
know for certain you were there then, and you want desperately
to feel it again from your grandfather, that love you believe, deep
in your heart, he felt for you. Though he is thirty years passed, a
mere ghost in your mind, you sense he is just inches away, so
close to you now you can almost feel him.

You reach out and lightly take hold of the pillbox that the
old man still grips. "May I . . . taste it?" you ask quietly.

"I'm sorry," replies the old man, opening the empty pillbox.
"Tiger gave this one to Mrs. Meriweather last night."

"Do you have another one?"

"About twenty."

Your eyes widen.

"Fourteen we caught yesterday, seven of which we managed
to snag in a flurry just minutes before midnight." The old man
winks at his grandson. "And six others from the past couple of
Christmas Eves."

You feel yourself noticeably sink, but you smile nonetheless.
"Well, that was sure a great story," you say. "I don't think I'll look

at a snowflake the same way again." You give a feeble laugh.

"Ha-ha!"

Tommie tugs on his grandfather's coat sleeve. "Can we go say hi to her now?"

And the two of them say goodbye and head off in the direction of Mrs. Meriweather. Dr. Glover watches Tommie and the old man go.

You feel somewhat deflated but certainly not crushed, today bringing with it no expectations of anything beyond what it is, a wonderful Christmas Day with your family. Quickly forgetting the disappointment of not remembering more of your grandfather, you swivel around and pick up the newspaper.

As you read, you find the handwritten notations far more interesting than the articles themselves. And most *are*, as you half-jokingly suggested, stolen chickens and goats—minor indiscretions—until you come to one that almost knocks you from your bar stool. "Dr. Glover?" you say. "Dr. Glover?"

He is distracted, studying the elderly woman wearing baby blue shorts and a baggy T-shirt who is now slowly approaching the two of you. Her hair is white and flat on top, with silver-grey curls on the sides.

You nudge him in the waist, and finally gain his attention. "You're not going to believe this."

This time it is Dr. Glover who says, "Try me."

"Would you like to know who burned your house down on June 28, 1959?"

"Pardon me?"

You repeat the question.

The doctor puts a hand to his forehead . . . and then smiles!

"No," he says with a raspy chuckle, shaking his head, "I'd rather not know."

"Speaking of which," you say, now studying briefly the woman approaching before skimming the shop, noting there are as many grandmothers as grandfathers present, "how many turkeys do you suppose are unattended this very minute?"

"Your point is?"

"Faulty ovens. Angry turkeys. Houses could burn!"

The doctor laughs, as do you, until the petite, elderly woman arrives.

"Merry Christmas, Betsy," says Dr. Glover, kissing her rosy cheek. He introduces you to the woman.

"Nice Christmas duds," you observe, still jubilant from the success of your humorous aside seconds earlier. You realize the instant you make your comment that it was thoughtless and somewhat callous. Clearly anyone who comes in from the dead of winter dressed for a heat wave has issues and, perhaps mentally at least, is not all there. Not surprisingly, the doctor quickly grabs your arm and gives his head a demure shake, as if to say, "Don't mention the Christmas duds."

"Christmas? Rubbish! It's a beautiful summer day!" she says.

You roll your eyes and turn your head away, but respectfully say nothing.

She continues: "Dr. Glover, can you reconsider what you said yesterday about putting Abner in the rest home?"

Dr. Glover looks the woman over from top to bottom. "Actually, Betsy, I was thinking it would be best if both you and—"

"Oh my," she suddenly gasps, her eyes focused on the newspaper. "Oh my, oh my, oh my."

"What is it?" Dr. Glover puts on his glasses again and studies the front page. "Oh my," he mumbles.

Betsy is crying quietly. "I miss her so much," she says.

At the doctor's request, Floyd hands him, of all things, a cocktail napkin. Dr. Glover uses it to dab away Betsy's tears. He calls over his shoulder, and immediately a woman who looks to be in her mid-thirties comes to Betsy's aid and escorts her away.

"That lady there?" He points to the woman escorting Betsy away. "She's been an orphan since she was a very young girl."

"I beg your pardon?" you say, watching the younger woman's red shorts and slender legs disappear into the thinning crowd.

"That's Betsy's granddaughter." He motions toward the newspaper's headline: *Two Die At Pike River Bridge.* "It was her parents who died."

"My God," you say, feeling a surge of sympathy for Betsy that surprises you, and a wave of guilt for being somewhat cruel to her, though no cruelty was intended.

"Yes, time has taken its toll on them. I think they are both slowly losing their minds, if they haven't lost them already."

"Betsy and her granddaughter?"

"No." Dr. Glover gestures toward the elderly man in shorts and T-shirt standing next to Mrs. Meriweather. "Betsy and her husband, Abner."

Although you wouldn't know Betsy and Abner from the king and queen of England, this news is sadly numbing; you feel it in your limbs.

"I stopped by their place last night," continues the doctor, "only to find Abner out for a Christmas Eve jog."

You take this as a positive and your mood brightens. "He likes to exercise?"

"Yes, apparently, and dressed much like he is today."

You shake your head. "Oh my."

Both you and Dr. Glover stare down at the newspaper for a long moment. "That's so terrible," you say of the headline.

"It is. I pronounce two people dead one day, and the very next day I bring new life into the world."

"Mary Trammel?"

"Mary Trammel." He draws a long, deep breath and flashes an awkward smile. "We lost the battle two to one back then, but just look at this place now. It's brimming with life!"

You look at the place. "Brimming with loss would be more accurate," you reply, finding it difficult to be optimistic, considering most here, including you, have lost cherished loved ones, and some quite tragically.

"Ah, I see I'm sitting beside a skeptic."

"Not a skeptic. A realist."

"Well, I'd say brimming with love would be most accurate," says Dr. Glover, who immediately becomes distracted again, staring off into space.

You are equally anxious to shift toward a more positive, nostalgic light, and so you resume reading the newspaper. The crowd has dispersed throughout the shop, sitting at tables, huddled in small groups here and there. Occasionally you hear a roar of applause or cheers from the back room, but even those are few and far between and much more reserved than earlier. Carlton still stands next to Mrs. Meriweather, along with the old man and his grandson, Tommie Mullen, as well as poor old Abner Wright.

And suddenly you hear your grandfather's footsteps, thunderous in your ears. Distanced by thirty years, but banging at you the same way they did on Christmas Eve in 1955, just before he collapsed outside your bedroom door. Ringing. Strident. Blood-curdling. Tearing at your living fibres!

You hear a voice—Floyd's. "Are you all right?"

You take a moment to gather yourself. "Fine," you say.

The cash register clangs again. You turn and stare at Dr. Glover. He hears your thoughts, he must, because he turns and looks at you with fearful eyes. You sit silently staring at each other for a long while, until finally you speak.

"Why?" you ask.

"Excuse me?"

You point to a handwritten notation in the newspaper. "You killed my grandfather." Dr. Glover's face instantly blanches and you know what you read is true. "How could you?"

"Can I explain?"

Your body is engulfed by a searing grief, while at the same time you feel a surge of the most profound, fiery anger. "Explain? *Explain?*"

"I'm sorry," he says, placing a hand on your shoulder.

You jerk back. "Don't touch me!"

You don't want to think about it, but you can't help yourself. All those years lost—perhaps he could have had one, or two, maybe even five more. The possibility of so many other memories of your grandfather that could have been, that almost were, floods your mind.

Dr. Glover hesitates, and then talks softly, and you let him. You have to. You are crying. "He'd had a long history of acute indigestion, and complicating that was a heart condition in the last year of his life. When he came to see me in January of '56 complaining of chest pains, his vitals were good. So I assumed—"

"A badly digested bit of beef?" you say bitterly, unable to hide your anger.

"I should have had him lie down immediately and gotten him to the hospital on an ambulance gurney. He needed a great deal of bedrest." Dr. Glover's face appears grave as he looks down and studies the palms of his empty hands, as if searching for an answer that isn't there.

"You misdiagnosed him?"

Dr. Glover looks at you. "I misdiagnosed him."

You slam your fists into your legs and buckle forward on the bar stool. "It's—not—fair," you growl through clenched teeth. "You were his doctor. He trusted you."

Dr. Glover is silent.

"Is that the way it works around here?" you finally ask, wiping away tears that are instantly replaced by others.

"I don't know what you mean."

"You community doctors get comfortable and simply go through the motions."

"The motions? Listen, your grandfather was my good friend—"

"Exactly! He comes to you complaining of chest pains and you probably chat for an hour about the weather and this person and that person, telling a few jokes in between, and then at the end you say, 'Aw, heck, probably indigestion!' My grandfather didn't need a good friend, he needed a good doctor!"

"Everything okay here?" asks Floyd, who has assumed his

intimidating pose at the counter again and is glaring at you.

"Fine," says Dr. Glover. "Please, Floyd, can you give us a moment?"

"Sure," he says. "Why not." His gaze lingers on you as he slowly drifts back, eventually hunching over the radio again.

Though Floyd's interruption startled you, it by no means severed the cord of indignation that continues to tug away at your insides. "You made a big mistake."

"I'm human."

"You probably made other mistakes."

Dr. Glover doesn't say anything. You look out across the shop, at what you had earlier thought was a field of ripe cotton. Only now you see it as a sparse crop, a crop that could have been much richer, much fuller, a bumper crop. "Where does that leave them?" you ask the doctor. Again he says nothing. "I should stand up and tell everyone what you did. Scream it out at the top of my lungs."

"Please, I cared for these people," he says, his eyes dry and looking like two pennies at the bottom of a deep, abandoned well. "And I *care* about these people." A hand reaches out, then stops abruptly, as if at last accepting his touch is no longer wanted.

"You should have your licence revoked. You're not fit to practise."

He shifts restlessly on his bar stool. "I—I plan on retiring next year."

Just then the ancient bell tinkles again. You see a hand high up holding the shop's front door open, and beneath it a young boy of about seven races in. He heads straight for you, veering at the last second to leap into Dr. Glover's lap. "Grandpa!" he screams with delight.

Dr. Glover swallows him in a loving embrace. "Theo!" he screams with equal delight.

And you realize this grandchild could be any grandchild. And Dr. Glover could be any grandfather. And the love they share is the same love you shared with *your* grandfather.

A loud bellow rips at your eardrums. Your heart skips two beats and you find yourself cowering when Floyd springs up, standing over you like a ten-foot tall beast on the counter. "Hey! Everybody! Listen!" he hollers.

The shop goes deathly silent. He has the radio perched on his shoulder and he turns the volume way up. Shooting through the speakers is no soothing Christmas carol, but an electrically charged acoustic guitar and a snappy snare drum playing what sounds like the intro to an up-tempo song.

When John Cougar Mellencamp's raspy voice starts in with the lyrics, all the elderly folks in the shop sing along:

"Well, I was born in a small town,
And I live in a small town,
Probably die in a small town,
Oh, those small communities . . ."

Everyone is standing—including Mrs. Meriweather—clapping their hands, waving them like small town banners in a breeze, smiling, laughing, making funny faces, winking, giggling, some turning in circles, and a few playfully poking others in the belly.

"All my friends are so small town,
My parents live in the same small town,
My job is so small town,
Provides little opportunity . . ."

Dr. Glover's grandson is giggling too, still in the doctor's arms, only now elevated three feet above the floor as he and his grandfather do what could best be described as a brisk, herky-jerky waltz.

"But I've seen it all in a small town,
Had myself a ball in a small town . . ."

You notice Carlton, who apparently doesn't know the words, struggling with the worst moonwalk you've ever seen, giving you the impression not that he is moving forward while actually moving backward, but rather that he is moving sideways—and in fact he is moving sideways!

One elderly lady with blinding white hair, perhaps recalling her days of youth, attempts a pirouette. Her technique is good but, lacking the strength, she bangs into a chair and knocks it over, laughing the whole time. Mary Trammel is embroiled in a giggling fit with her grandmother as they tango across the floor. Tommie Mullen has been whisked up onto his grandfather's shoulders to be strutted around like a conquering hero.

"No, I cannot forget where it is that I come from,
I cannot forget the people who love me,
Yeah, I can be myself here in this small town,
And people let me be just what I want to be . . ."

The voices of the elderly folks are off-key, but there is an undeniable spirit and energy to them. It is the energy you your-self remember from not so long ago. It is that distinct, oft sought-after yet never forgotten energy . . . of youth! And you, yes you, sing along on Christmas Day.

"Well, I was born in a small town,
And I can breathe in a small town,
Gonna die in this small town,
And that's probably where they'll bury me."

Though the last line's message—as a subject for discussion—is unpleasant by the conventions of most in society, in such an upbeat song it comes across as a triumph. And perhaps that's what it really is, a triumphant testament of love and loyalty, to be born and raised and to live and die in a small town, to shirk the possibility of fame and fortune for the sake of beloved friends and family. Perhaps those are the ones who have it right. The ones like your grandfather.

The song finishes and a resounding cheer shakes you to the core and brings you back to where you were with Dr. Glover. Floyd, who had been making rather merry up there on the counter during the entire song, jumps down, while the doctor finds his way back to the bar stool. Dr. Glover looks you in the eye and seems to sense where you still are inside your mind.

"Could you give me a minute?" he says to the middle-aged man next to him.

"Okay, Dad," the man replies. He takes Theo's hand. "We're going up. See you in a bit?"

"Sure thing, son."

It just occurs to you that the young boy and his father burst into the shop without coats, and you have to ask as you watch the two leave, "Up?"

Dr. Glover points straight up. "I live upstairs." He sees your confusion and adds, "In the apartment above Floyd's Smoke Shop."

"This is *your* house?"

"Yes," he says, the pleasant tone of his voice soothing to your ears. "This is my house."

"Wha—"

"What about the mansion on the hill? When my wife died years back, that house was just too much for me." He glances up at the shop's dusty ceiling, as if missing his son and grandson already and trying to glimpse them in his apartment. "No, one bedroom, one bathroom, one couch. That's all I need."

You sit staring silently at your hands, your anger now replaced by a profound sense of emptiness. Your grandfather is gone. Forever. There is nothing you can do about it. What Dr. Glover did cannot be changed, and no one can do anything about it. Now or ever.

"And one recliner," you say, managing a slight smile that carries with it not humour but forgiveness.

"And one recliner." Several moments later, Dr. Glover says, "I am truly sorry about your grandfather."

You nod. It's all you can do. He places a hand on your shoulder and you let him.

"He was a remarkable man, and it was quite miraculous how he hung on."

Hung on? What did he mean, hung on? Your mother told you he died in his doctor's examination room. You can only stare.

"She never told you?"

"Told me what?"

"He collapsed in my examination room as he was leaving for home. We rushed him to the hospital and he hung on for two hours. I sat with him the whole time, holding his hand. And do you know what he told me?"

"He was conscious?"

"For a short while. I think he knew the end was near. He said—" Dr. Glover stops and moves closer to you. "He said he was going to miss his grandchildren most of all."

You can't speak. All you can do is cry in Dr. Glover's arms, hoping for a split second your children don't see you, then realizing in the next instant that this is something they need to see, and these are the things they need to know about. Love. And life. And loss.

You take a few minutes to regain your composure. Dr. Glover watches you closely the whole time, his hand comforting on your shoulder.

As an elderly man with surprisingly black hair walks near, apparently on his way toward the front door of the shop, Dr. Glover reaches out and grabs him by the arm. He asks the man if he knew your grandfather.

"Certainly," replies the dark-haired man in a rough but confident voice, "and very well, in fact."

When Dr. Glover invites him to tell you a story or two about your grandfather, the man looks befuddled for a moment. Then he smiles and shrugs. "Sorry," he says, "I don't remember any."

Following right behind the man is a woman with slate-grey hair, and when Dr. Glover asks the same of her, she relays a vague, somewhat confusing tale of your grandfather before she, too, carries on.

"I'll be damned if I'm going to accept that," says Dr. Glover, watching the woman exit the shop. His finger momentarily prods around inside the bowl on the counter. "Open your mouth," he demands.

You manage a faint smile. "Sorry. Saving myself for the turkey."

"Doctor's orders!"

You reluctantly comply and he places a peanut on your tongue. "Now don't chew. Suck. Like a throat lozenge," he says with a wink.

He raises his arms. "People!" No one is listening. They're clamouring and clucking about like wild chickens.

"Hey! Pipe down!" hollers Floyd with a snarl, and the doctor has everyone's attention.

Dr. Glover tells them your name. Then he asks who here remembers your grandfather and has some stories to share. His words are inviting and blow like a warm gust of wind.

And out of what only minutes earlier seemed a field of ripe cotton, a wondrous Christmas Day snowfall now appears, a blizzard of the most beautiful snowflakes, laughing and chortling and smiling, blown in your direction by a glorious December breeze, some long, some short, some thick, some thin, but all the purest white, with vibrant Mrs. Meriweather swirling at the head of the onrushing storm.

Blissful eternity passes in what is only thirty minutes. You hear dozens of stories about your grandfather, most funny, a few sad, some showing his genuine compassion for people. All bring tears of joy to your eyes. Ironically, most are from those in-between times, those times you weren't—or wouldn't have been—here to witness anyhow, so in many ways, by being here *now*, you've gained even more of his *then*. You could have hoped for nothing more.

When an unseen gust of wind finally scatters the snowflakes

throughout the shop, Abner Wright, in his tie-dye T-shirt, neon green shorts, and moccasins, is left standing alone in front of you. His hair is ivory white, neatly trimmed, and parted to one side.

"Hello," you say, smiling.

"Hello," says Abner.

You wait for a moment, but when he makes no further comments, you ask, "You have a story about my grandfather?"

"I do. Dozens of them."

Again you wait for a moment, and again he makes no further comments. So you say, "Can I hear some?"

Abner thoughtfully scratches a cheek and glances at his wristwatch. "I'm a little pressed for time," he says.

"How about one, then?"

"Okay, one."

He tells you that your grandfather was an avid fisherman—something you already knew. One morning they went trout fishing together on the outskirts of town. They stood facing each other, fishing from opposite sides of the stream at its deepest, widest part. Behind Abner was the access road that brought them in; behind your grandfather, a farmer's field full of cows.

"So he hooked one," he says.

"A nice Holstein?" you interrupt, trying your best not to smile. When Abner gives you a look that is either a glare or confusion, or a combination of both—you can't be sure—you quickly correct yourself and say, "I meant, a nice rainbow trout?"

"Shucks, no. A monster brown! When I saw him pull it up on shore, I knew it must have been at least fifteen pounds!"

You are smiling. You now expect to hear he caught a dozen more like it, that his fishing skills put Abner's to shame.

"So he backed up farther and farther away from the stream as he reeled the line in," Abner continues. "At some point the beast threw the hook. Fortunately your grandfather had it well clear of the stream by that time. He dropped his rod and managed to corral the flopping monster. When he held out the brown from nose to tail for me to take a gander at from across the stream, he was beaming. I wasn't smiling, though. I was worried. Just then he *heard* what I was *seeing*. So he turned to face the bull—a bull that may have been the monster of all bulls, I might add, and standing no more than five feet from him!" Abner pauses. "Are you with me so far?"

You are so "with him," all you can do is nod like an excited ten-year-old.

"Okay. Well, I imagine your grandfather's heart was in his throat, but if it was, it sure didn't appear that way. He kept his eyes on that bull as he calmly took the trout by the gill, then bent to pick up his rod with his free hand. Then he said, 'Blackie, I think I'll be going now.'"

You are on the edge of your bar stool, anxious beyond belief to hear how this story ends.

"And slowly he started backing away, and all the while 'Blackie' was snorting and rutting out large clumps of turf with his angry hoof. When your grandfather had backed about ten feet away, 'Blackie' charged! Your grandfather let out this high-pitched 'Ahhhhhh,' turned, and ran like hell on wheels, rod in one hand, big brown tucked under his arm. When he hit the water, it was up to his knees, and he fell down three times, dropping the brown and his rod during all the chaos. 'You son of a bitch,' he said, shaking a dripping fist at 'Blackie' from across the stream.

"Once he'd come to his senses, the two of us walked downstream in search of his rod. About fifty yards along, washed up on shore, there it was . . . the damn monster brown! Must have gotten scared senseless by good old 'Blackie'! Never did find your grandfather's precious rod. The very next day we went down on Main Street and he bought himself another one in the hardware store where your uncle was working, cussing that 'Blackie' the whole time."

You are swelling with joy.

His story finished, Abner glances anxiously around the shop, and abruptly says, "I noticed you talking to a man here for a while."

You glance around, too. It suddenly occurs to you that Dr. Glover has disappeared, probably now upstairs with his son and grandson. "Yes," you say. "A very kind man."

"I sure would like to meet him and say hello."

"Meet him? But you already know him. He told me he stopped by your place last night."

Abner stares blankly at you.

"Dr. Glover? He's practised here for over fifty years?"

Abner's expression quickly becomes cross. "What are you talking about? Dr. Glover died in the fire that destroyed his house over twenty-five years ago."

You can't believe your ears, and then you remember what Dr. Glover told you about Abner and his wife and his belief that they are slowly losing their minds.

"He's a ghost. Like your grandfather; like all of them," he adds, sweeping out an arm that is as thin as it is ghostly pale, encompassing the entire room with the gesture.

Despite what Dr. Glover said about the Wrights, and despite the seeming clarity with which Abner told his story about your grandfather, you can't help but roll your eyes and turn away briefly. "Cuckoo," you whisper.

"Beg pardon?"

"Nothing," you say, and pause. "Then how do you explain Mrs. Meriweather getting saved last night?"

"She didn't get saved because Dr. Glover wasn't there to save her."

"But Dr. Glover *didn't* save her. It was that kid over there. Tommie Mullen. He saved her."

"Oh, um . . ." Abner looks nervously around.

"And what about *that* kid? Over *there?*" You point to Carlton, who is clearly much younger than twenty-five and is now sitting at a table reading his book. "Dr. Glover fixed his broken arm and pulled a bullet from his leg. He practically saved *him.*"

Abner rubs his bony chin, a study in perplexed concentration.

"And what about Mary's newspaper?" Though it holds no relevance to this conversation, you throw it in to further befuddle the old guy. You reach around, only to find the newspaper has vanished from the counter. "Okay, forget the newspaper. But who are you, anyhow? Clarence the angel?"

"Beg pardon?"

"Ever see the movie *It's a Wonderful Life?*"

"Yes! My grandson produced it!"

"Your grandson?" Despite Floyd's claims about the sobriety of his smoke shop, just to be sure you lean forward, attempting to get a whiff of Abner's breath. "How old is your grandson?" you ask when that turns up nothing.

"Thirty-three."

"A-ha! That movie was made in 1946! You're telling me he produced it before he was born?"

"Could happen," replies Abner defensively.

Not intending to be rude, but unable to resist the temptation, you twist and whisper over your shoulder, "Floyd, would a snifter of cider be possible?"

There is no response. Floyd is gone. You turn back and discover pretty much everyone has vanished. Abner has scurried away during your brief aside to the nonexistent Floyd and is now standing behind Mrs. Meriweather, who is recumbent in the recliner at the shop's centre. Abner is smiling and looking directly at you. Beside him is the old man, and beside the old man is Carlton, who is smoking another Popeye while reading his book. Next to Carlton is Mary who, somewhat to your relief, is holding her newspaper.

You listen for sounds from the back room. Nothing.

You head toward the little group, and as you do you watch Carlton set his book in Mrs. Meriweather's lap. Then he takes what appears to be another deep, satisfying fake drag on his Popeye. Before he blows out a puff of fake smoke, he smiles and winks at you. Then he exhales and what looks like a single snowflake flutters from his mouth. You blink in disbelief.

Like you, the old man is watching closely, and immediately he opens his pillbox, snatches the snowflake out of midair, and just as quickly snaps the pillbox shut. Then Mary snatches the pillbox from the old man's hands and begins writing feverishly in her newspaper. All three are happy. Mary is laughing, her golden-blond hair glowing like the sun. The old man is giddy, his hair looking as powdery and grey as the surface of the moon. And in the middle, Carlton is smiling, his blond hair somewhere between the sun and the moon. Silence fills the room.

When you reach them, Abner Wright tosses you what looks like a Christmas card from the opposite side of the recliner. It flutters like a snowflake for a moment before falling through your fingers to the floor. You bend down and from there the peculiar spelling of an age-old message on the front of the card grabs your attention: *Seasons' Greeting*.

You open the card and inside there are no words. There is only a picture. A pretty picture, really, of a small, quaint Victorian home. The house's gabled roof is dripping with snow and smoke pours from its chimney. In a window there is the distinct glow from a hearth, and you can see a group of young children gathered around a Christmas tree. In front of the house, snow is piled high, but a path has been cleared. Standing on that path is an elderly man wearing a large, black coat and grey pants and black boots. His hands are bare and he holds a shovel upright, the shovel's handle supporting his relaxed arms. He looks content, staring off into the distance. He has a bald crown and a thin fringe of white hair on the side his head. His facial features are not completely clear. He could be Dr. Glover. Or he could be your grandfather, or anyone's grandfather, for that matter.

You rise and now all have vanished—Mary, Abner, the old man, Carlton—all gone, with the exception of Mrs. Meriweather, who is lying back in the recliner. "What the . . ." you mutter.

In her lap you see Carlton's book, *Learn French the Easy Way*, and beside that is Mary's ancient copy of *The Wharton Echo*.

These things rest comfortably on your mother's patchwork quilt, and beneath this is Mrs. Meriweather, whose eyes are closed. She looks peaceful, too peaceful for you to be afraid for her, or for your children, or for anyone you love with all your heart.

You take your mother's patchwork quilt in your hands and pull it snug to Mrs. Meriweather's chin. Then you place the card Abner just gave you in her lap. "Merry Christmas," you whisper, your words fading into the warm, sweet air.

It is Christmas Day and you expect nothing in return.

But then, miraculously, she gives you something. A word? A touch? No. The smile of a child.

It is many years later now and though you feel much older, your hair having turned a pure and ancient white, strangely enough, you remember everything. You remember your father, who is long passed, with great affection, and you remember that Christmas in 1985 as if it were yesterday. It was a magical time, and if there was one thing it taught you, it was that life consists of only the past and present. It's all any of us really have.

The future—or that mysterious thing people refer to as the future—only exists, like all of us, in passing. When it finally arrives it is present, and in the blink of an eye it is past, long gone, forever relegated to the reliquaries of our minds.

And it is in these reliquaries that we seek our fortunes; in the memories of our father and our father's father, our mother and grandmothers and aunts and uncles and brothers and sisters and children and all those we love.

And if in these reliquaries our fortunes subsist, and the past is simply an infinite, forever number of former presents, then it stands to reason the present is simply a spectacular gift, like a wondrous Christmas gift beneath a tree, wrapped and packaged, a present that all should cherish.

You are staring at the Christmas tree twinkling before you when your grandson of six comes bounding into the room and leaps into your lap. You give him the hug of a million Christmas presents wished, and a million Christmas presents granted.

You glance down, your grin almost as big as your grand-child's. And it's happening again, you reflect, another past, another wonderful present, another Christmas at Grandfather's house . . .

Acknowledgements

As the saying goes, the whole is greater than the sum of its parts. Nothing truer could be said of the combined stories within this book, or the work that led to this book's creation.

I am deeply grateful to Marg Gilks, who believed in this book from the start, and for being both editor extraordinaire and a real trouper. When the going got tough, it was Marg who got going.

To Susan Meisner, the best damn publicist, and one of the best damn people to ever walk the face of this planet: I am eternally indebted to her for her calm, levelheaded guidance, and, as true friends always do, for telling me what I needed to hear, which oftentimes wasn't what I wanted to hear. Susan, I can't thank you enough.

And a big thanks to Sarah Cooper—literary agent to the stars—and Peter Gentile—filmmaker and maker of stars—for encouraging me in small doses, but often.

For his counsel, I also want to acknowledge Dr. Vinny Puri, specialist, and a special friend for almost thirty years. Thanks, Vin.

To those friends and family members who are too numerous to name here, and whose enthusiasm and encouragement drove me toward "loftier" literary pursuits, thanks from the bottom of my heart.

And lastly, to my wife, Maria, and my two boys, Matthew and Mitchell, who inspire me beyond words, and who make life's impossibilities seem possible.